Magiks
and
The Crown of Guilledon

Enchanted Chronicle LLC

Text copyright © 2021 by
Janet Loup Maupin Gajigianis

Illustrations by Nick Harris, Arthur Bowling and Loup Gajigianis

Cover design by Euan Monaghan

All rights reserved.

Published by Enchanted Chronicle LLC.

The logo and lantern decoration are registered
trademarks of Enchanted Chronicle LLC.

All rights reserved. No part of this publication may be duplicated, manufactured, distributed, transmitted, used, or reproduced in any manner whatsoever, including but not limited to information storage, photocopying, recording, or other electronic or mechanical methods without the prior written permission of the publisher, except for the use of brief quotations in critical articles and reviews permitted by copyright law. Inquiries for permission requests outside of those terms should be addressed to the publisher.

Typography

Centaur, Chiller Std, Algerian, DK Halewyn, P22 Muschamp

ISBN 978-1-7372361-2-2

21 22 23 10 9 8 7 6 5 4 3 2 1

First Edition

Magiks
and
The Crown of Guilledon

BY
Loup Gajigianis

Illustrations by Arthur Bowling,
Nick Harris, and Loup Gajigianis

Enchanted Chronicle LLC

For Sonny,
The most wonderful person I've ever met.
May all your dreams come true.

Everything I achieve is due to Him.

Yea, though I walk through the valley of the shadow of death, I will fear no evil: for thou art with me; thy rod and thy staff they comfort me. (Psalm, 23:4)

Thank you . . .
Anna Bowles, Fiona McLauren, and Kaitlyn Johnson for your insights and edits, Nick Harris and Arthur Bowling for your extraordinary illustrations and Euan Monaghan for your exceptional designs.

CONTENTS

A Shadow in the Dark 1

Saint Frances Institute for ~~Heirs and Orphans~~ Loonies 4

The Festival of Gondolas 32

Unexpected Visitors Are Rarely Welcome 71

The search for Sir Isaac Newton and the Blue Moon 102

Meanwhile, In A Place Not So Far Behind... 132

Ghost Tavern 145

Creepy Shadows 173

A Secret Meeting . . . Shish! 184

The Fairy Ferry 220

Shadow Walkers Chase 246

Brume Gate 249

The Monsters and the Airships 260

The Troll Guard 289

The Thief 298

The Hijacking 328

The Vanquisher . . . No? . . . Well, We'll See. 346

Nick Harris

CHAPTER ONE
A Shadow in the Dark

A dark shadow floated above the grassy mound, searching. It had come from far, far away to find the girl with the crown. The girl was useless. Human. Disposable. But the crown was special. It carried great and powerful magic. Some had begun to believe it was only a legend. Now an *ordinary* human girl was wearing it. The very thought was foolish.

Pausing in front of a sign, the shadow searched for the path that led to the orphanage. The path to an ancient crown, whose magic would change the course of its life forever.

An old man dozed on a bench beneath the sign as if it were his habit to sleep in such a strange place, but something about the chill that passed from the shadow stirred him from his slumber.

"Huh, who's there?" He rubbed his aged eyes, and said in his tired voice, "I knows yor there an' you bes' show yourself."

A Shadow in the Dark

The shadow considered the man. Fear wasn't something it had felt in a very long time. It moved freely throughout the world without dread or reservation, without pause or doubt, and this man was ordinary. A frail, disgusting thing it is to be ordinary. It could pass by without the man ever knowing.

"I says to show yorself." The man wobbled his cane into the dark harmlessly.

The shadow had no problem killing, for it had killed many times before. Tingling with anticipation, it twitched towards the man's throat.

"Face me lik' a man . . . don' hide lik' a coward." Spit bubbled from the old man's mouth.

From the darkness, the shadow grew, blocking the faint glow from the moon. Looming over the man, one shadowy limb transformed into a gleaming, black knife. Pleasure brought the tip of the blade to the man's throat and pressed against the soft flesh. A smile spread across the shadow, where a face should have been, as its victim gasped for air.

But what was the point really? The shadow was here for another, the girl with the crown. It glanced again at the sign and released the pitiful man. The blade faded back into a shapeless shadow. "Not tonight," it whispered like the breeze.

The old man shuddered as blood trickled to his

collar. Meanwhile, the shadow floated past — up the path to St. Frances, where it most certainly would kill soon.

CHAPTER TWO
Saint Frances Institute for ~~Heirs and Orphans~~ Loonies

St. Frances Institute for Heirs and Orphans is a home for boys and girls that come from all walks of life — raising both privileged children and orphans together. It is positioned at the top of a grassy hill, somewhere in the great expanse of the United States, in a tiny village called Hasty — whose closest neighbor is the town of Fetching. The inhabitants of Hasty had, at one time, petitioned for their village to be forthwith called a town, but as it was, there simply were not enough dwellers. They settled with a village then, for at the very least, their village was not a hamlet, as it did possess a church. A hamlet, they all agreed, would be a very awful thing.

Several weeks had passed since the attack on the old man. Quite a spectacle he made when he hobbled into Mr. Frinkley's store and announced that a ghost had nearly *done him in*. The inhabitants of Hasty were quite uncertain of the peculiar events that may or may not have occurred just a short walk down the path — so they continued on as normally as before.

Saint Frances Institute for ~~Heirs and Orphans~~ Loonies

The heritor and governess of St. Frances Institute was quite another matter. Ms. Augustine Frances III — a plump, overly particular, and traditionally mannered woman — was quite interested in the rumblings of the old man. She had grown up in the institute with the orphans and heirs and had come to know that peculiarities were not altogether unbelievable. So, she questioned the old man herself . . . and hadn't slept peacefully since.

♛ ♛ ♛

As the dim light shone through the dusty paneled windows, Devon Connor, a penniless orphan, fumbled with the repair of a busted watch she had recovered from the garbage. She had proven to be quite handy with this or that when the occasion arose. And repairing this watch was just another trick to be mastered. Perhaps, if she had parents, she would already own a watch and wouldn't be up, in the early morning, trying to fix this one.

What might they have been like? Her parents? Of course, she had asked Ms. Frances, but each time the stern, hard-nosed woman avoided Devon's questions. Sometimes, she pretended not to hear Devon at all.

Once, Devon snuck into Ms. Frances's office and

Saint Frances Institute for ~~Heirs and Orphans~~ Loonies

spent the afternoon looking through her files. While she learned quite a lot about her roommates, the only thing inside her own file was an old black-and-white photo of herself — looking exactly the same as she did now. Strange — that she didn't remember taking it ... but either way, it didn't tell her a thing about her parents.

Perhaps they were ocean-explorers and spent many years out at sea — or treasure hunters on an expedition. Maybe even, they planned to come back for her — *if* they weren't dead. That's what Devon liked to imagine — they were still alive and on an adventure in a faraway place. Sure, she was a bit old for fantasies, but a tad bit of hope gave her peace, even if it was just for a short time.

Her parents could be anywhere in the world. And her light honey-colored skin and dark hair suggested a heritage from many places — which only encouraged her imagination. Her thick eyebrows and striking brown eyes were perhaps of some Mediterranean descent. A bit of Hispanic was prominent in the bright summer when she tanned as dark as toffee, and according to Mr. Frinkley, the slight arch on her nose — that was certainly Greek.

While Devon tinkered with the watch, she pushed her long hair (dark like the cattails in the setting sun)

Saint Frances Institute for ~~Heirs and Orphans~~ Loonies

from her face, and drifted into a daydream, as she sometimes did, where her parents were stuck in one of those countries far away. Surely, they had meant to come back for her.

After a moment, Devon stopped herself. . . . No. They were gone, and in an institution with eighty-seven children, she was anything but lonely. Now that she was twelve, she only had a few years left at St. Frances Institute for Heirs and Orphans. She just had to wait out her remaining time here and stay out of trouble (not that it had been easy so far). . . . Once she turned old enough, she could go anywhere she wanted — maybe even become an explorer herself.

Devon adjusted the simple, gold headband that she always wore and squinted over the mechanics of the watch. Just a little further — a tiny twist of metal and —

CRACK.

Devon jumped, dropping the watch and all its pieces. They rolled across the floor into cracks and crannies. She scrambled to her feet and scanned the quiet dormitory for the source of the splintering sound. Her roommate stirred, stretched, and sank back into her pillow — still fast asleep.

Devon relaxed. It wasn't like her to get caught off guard. But this morning, she was so engrossed in her broken watch, she hadn't even realized the time passing. Soon, orphans and heirs would wake up all over the mansion.

"Ahhhhhhhhhh," a voice screamed shrilly.

Devon whirled around. This time, her roommates stirred.

"What happened?" asked one of the younger girls, too drowsy to open her eyes.

"I don't know," Devon whispered back, already tiptoeing across the dark room. The scream had come from the other side of the door. . . .

"Agh. It's only Devon," grouched an older girl, who was in her last year at St. Frances. She flopped back on her pillow and pulled the blanket over her head. "Go back to sleep."

Devon didn't bother with a retort. *Usually, it was her.* It was true, she caused her fair share of trouble. She'd own to that. But there was a point to everything she did. Even if it wasn't immediately obvious.

Devon peeked around the door as a group of children in frilly nightgowns and matching pajamas ran to Sophia (a nine-year-old orphan, crouched in the corner of the hall). She sat in a panic-stricken daze, surrounded by broken glass.

"Sophia, what happened? What's wrong?" Himba, a dark-skinned heir from a wealthy family in Namibia,

Saint Frances Institute for ~~Heirs and Orphans~~ Loonies

rushed over. He wrapped his arm around her and tried to soothe her.

Devon let out a sigh of relief. If someone reported the broken vase to Ms. Frances, it wouldn't be him. "Be careful of the glass," Devon warned, already scanning the long carpet for the source of mischief. Her gut instinct told her it wasn't Sophia. Sophia never caused trouble. Of course, it could have been an accident, but that didn't explain the guttural scream.

Sniff. Sniff. Sophia sucked in a bubbly sob, holding back her tears.

Claudia, an heiress with pretty brown skin and curly hair rushed over. "I heard the crash — what happened?"

"We don't know. See if she's cut." Devon crept down the length of the manor, but other than a few curious heads that peeked from their rooms, the hall was empty. The scene around Sophia, however, was getting crowded. If they weren't quiet, Ms. Frances would hear them, and to her, order and etiquette were everything. There were strict rules about noise . . . and more rules about rules. Each one harshly enforced.

"She won't say anything," Claudia said, when Devon returned.

"Sophia, are you all right?" Himba asked again.

"I t-think s-so." Sophia sighed in a tremulous voice. "S-something w-was . . . th-here."

Satisfied there was no immediate danger, Devon checked Sophia herself. It was likely, with all the broken glass, she was hurt. But, a loud voice down the hall stopped her.

"OKAY! CLEAR OUT!" the voice ordered.

Devon gritted her teeth and slipped back to her room. That was a voice she would recognize anywhere, even if she were blind.

The cluster of children dispersed, mumbling and grumbling, but none of them argued with Vanessa. Vanessa ruled here. Not only because she took pleasure in tyrannizing the others, but because she was given the official title of monitor by Ms. Frances herself — a promotion she earned out of favoritism.

It took every bit of effort for Devon to stay put (behind the door of her dormitory). It wouldn't help Sophia by getting involved. Especially, when Vanessa was in one of her moods.

"What did you *do*, Sophia?" Vanessa snapped.

"She said someone was in the hall," answered Theodore, a fickle and easily miffed boy, in pinstripe pajamas, who had not fled like the others.

"Was I asking you, Theodore?" Vanessa demanded ungraciously. She swiped a strand of curly hair from her face. "I said Sophia, didn't I? Your name is Theodore."

Theodore shrunk back, hurt. His cheeks flushed. "S-sorry."

Devon grasped the door tightly, her knuckles turning white, and resisted the urge to burst into the hall. Vanessa hadn't done anything really terrible, yet ... and fortunately, she hadn't noticed Devon behind the door. *You'll only make it worse,* Devon told herself.

"Sophia! Are you saying someone broke in?" Vanessa stuck her hands on her hips. "Well, where did they go?"

Quivering, Sophia pointed her finger towards the window ... a shadow lurked beneath it.

"T-there."

Unperturbed by the gloomy shadow, Vanessa strode over to the window and tugged hard. "It's locked!" She rounded on Sophia. "Are you playing a trick?"

"N-no," Sophia stuttered. Her eyes flickered to the shadow —

"Augh!" Vanessa slapped Sophia hard across the face. Pain flittered across Sophia's eyes, and tears leaked down her rounded cheeks.

Devon started around the door, heat flushing through her chest. There was no way she'd stand by and ignore that. A jerk on Devon's shirt wrenched her back into the room.

"Don't!" whispered Leni Dupré. She was Devon's closest friend, and had it been anyone else, Devon would have shaken them off and strode right into the hall. Leni was one of the few people Devon respected in this wretched mansion. Together, the pair of them had gotten in, and out, of their fair share of trouble.

"Sophia is just a kid," exclaimed Devon, "I can't stand here and do nothing!"

"I know . . . but think," whispered Leni. "A broken vase. Sophia hurt. Vanessa will jump at the chance to blame it on *you*. She hates you, and somehow, she'll get away with it. If you go out there, you'll only make it worse —"

Breathing hard, Devon let her head rest against the flat plane of the door. Leni was right. Vanessa loved getting other children in trouble, and any trouble that couldn't be accounted for, Vanessa blamed on Devon, even when she was innocent (though, those times were rare).

"All right." Devon pulled her shirt free. But she *would* make Vanessa pay for this later. That was a promise.

Vanessa's voice carried through the hall. "You —" she rounded on Theodore and Claudia. "Clean this

Saint Frances Institute for ~~Heirs and Orphans~~ Loonies

up! I have *important* things to do," she barked and stomped off.

When the clack of her footsteps faded, Devon peeked around the corner. The rest of the dormitory had awoken from their beds and crept up behind Leni. They broke into hushed whispers of gossip. Devon slipped around the door and headed for Sophia.

"What happened?" Devon asked her softly.

"I'll tell you what happened," griped Theodore. "That dunce knocked over the vase and then made up a story so she wouldn't get in trouble. Now *I* have to clean it up!"

Sophia's eyes glistened, and Devon shifted awkwardly. Tears always made her uncomfortable. "T-there was someone . . . by the door," Sophia whimpered between sobs. "It h-heard me . . . and . . ."

"Um . . . which door?" Devon peered down the hall. There was only one door by the window. "You mean *my* door?"

"Yeah." Streaks of tears ran down her face.

Devon's breath caught in her throat. "Someone was outside *my* room!"

"You're a liar!" Theodore barked. He tossed the last piece of glass into the trash and stalked off.

Claudia shrugged apologetically and hurried after him.

Saint Frances Institute for ~~Heirs and Orphans~~ Loonies

"Don't worry about them." Devon scratched the back of her head and walked over to the window to inspect it. Like Vanessa said, it was locked — and more, a thick layer of dust remained undisturbed. Beneath it, paint had dried along the edges, sealing it in place. It hadn't been opened in ages. "Are you sure it wasn't one of the other kids? They might have tried to play a prank."

"No," said Sophia, more bravely. "It was . . . sneaking."

"You keep saying *it*, not he or she."

Sophia shivered. . . . She glanced around the hall for anyone that might be eavesdropping. "It was a shadow."

Devon raised her eyebrows. This wasn't a prank. Sophia was nuts. . . . Or, maybe she had a nightmare.

Devon frowned at the recently swept floor. Something else didn't make sense. "What happened to the vase?"

Sophia held up her hands, eyes wide. "I didn't do it. I swear!"

"Then . . . how did it break?" A coolness shivered down Devon's arms. Something was telling her she didn't want to know.

"The shadow threw it before it went through the window." Then, with the same startled look as before, Sophia hurried down the hall, and for the rest of the day, no one could find her.

♛ ♛ ♛

~ The trick to any successful mischievousness is not just for it to be thoroughly thought out — but to have backup contingencies, and for your backup contingencies to be better plans than the original one ~

It wasn't until late in the afternoon, when the day slowed to a boring drag, that Devon's plan for retribution fell into place. Deep in her bones, she knew getting caught was practically guaranteed. Nobody escaped Ms. Frances's watchful eye *and* her devoted hall monitors. Then again . . . maybe this was one of those times Devon got away with one of her schemes. But either way, slapping sweet Sophia in the face couldn't be ignored.

It wasn't hard to come up with a plan. Vanessa's disadvantage in following a strict schedule was that she could be found at a particular place at any specific

Saint Frances Institute for ~~Heirs and Orphans~~ Loonies

time. And it was well known by the children of St. Frances that once-a-week Vanessa snuck away and came back with a parcel of forbidden commodities: Chewing gum, fizzy drinks, and other forbidden items she used as bribes and kickbacks, keeping her popular in the institution — despite all the nasty things she did to people. Today was the day of that delivery, but today, Vanessa wasn't going to keep that parcel.

Devon tucked the heavy gold watch she borrowed from her roommate's drawer back into her pocket. It likely cost more than all the things Devon ever owned, tenfold. Still, she was *only borrowing it*. If she had fixed her own stupid watch, she wouldn't have lifted this one.

According to the ticking of the pearl hands, Vanessa should be turning down the hall any moment. The plan was simple. Simple because Devon had discovered that complicated schemes created, well . . . complications.

All she had to do was follow Vanessa to the secret place she received her *unauthorized* packages, cause a distraction, and steal it. Once Devon had the package, Vanessa couldn't report it missing, because she wasn't supposed to be getting the parcels in the first place.

Of course, it would be best to steal the package before Vanessa got it. Then, Vanessa wouldn't know who had it. And originally, that was Devon's plan — but there were a number of complications that made it impossible: Firstly, Devon didn't know where the secret meeting place was. Secondly, (even if she did manage to find the secret meeting place where the parcel was delivered and get there before Vanessa) Devon had no way of knowing if Vanessa had a safeguard to ensure no one else received her packages. Maybe there was a codeword or an attack dog. And finally, the postman was likely expecting Vanessa and would refuse to hand the parcel off to anyone else. This was why the plan had to happen *after* Vanessa had possession of it. Which made this the dumbest — riskiest thing — Devon had done in a quite a while.

Not to be disappointed, Vanessa's cruel voice carried easily through the manor as she barked at Theodore, who unfortunately, got caught in her path. "Why are you in the hall, Theodore? That's twice today you disobeyed explicit instructions! First mine and now Ms. Frances."

Theodore's mumbles barely carried down the hall. "B-but you're out of class too —"

"Stop! . . . If you cross me Theodore, Ms. Frances will hear about it. You know that, right?" Theodore mumbled unintelligibly, and Vanessa cut him off. "Get back to class."

Saint Frances Institute for ~~Heirs and Orphans~~ Loonies

Devon slipped further back into the nook and held her breath. The voices died off, and Vanessa's footsteps grew louder. She strode past Devon, oblivious to her hiding spot.

A grin curled in Devon's lips, and she tiptoed down the hall after Vanessa, making sure to tread lightly on the thick Persian carpet. As Vanessa was one of Ms. Frances's favorite children, it was vital her plan went smoothly.

Devon checked the flashy watch again. Nearly everyone was detained in St. Frances's daily Etiquette Instruction for another fourteen and a half minutes (leaving this part of the manor empty), so Devon followed Vanessa leisurely. But once the Persian carpet ended and the hall narrowed, the floor creaked and the threat of getting caught became precariously easy.

The stairs down to the kitchen groaned underneath the lightest weight. The halls (devoid of windows, hangings, and doors) offered no place to hide should Vanessa glance back. As Devon crept after Vanessa (deeper into the mansion), her breath quickened, cool air bit at her skin, and her heart thumped heavily in her chest. Still, she didn't turn back.

"HIMBA!" Vanessa snapped — startling Devon and making her heart race faster.

Devon had been watching Vanessa so closely that

she hadn't thought to look ahead. Now, Himba would plainly see her sneaking behind. *Stupid.*

"Himba, what are you doing?" Vanessa demanded.

Devon put her finger to her lips and slowly backed up.

"Um —" Himba's posture turned rigid. Wide-eyed, he glanced from Vanessa to the ceiling (so not to give Devon away). Silently, she thanked him. "I was . . . um . . . sent on an errand," stammered Himba.

"What errand?" demanded Vanessa. "As hall monitor, *all errands* go through me —"

Knock. Knock. A tap on the window through the kitchen, interrupted them. The postman squinted into the dark room. "Hello?"

"Don't go anywhere." Vanessa jabbed her finger in Himba's chest and started for the backdoor.

A heavy feeling sank to the pit of Devon's stomach. Her plan was quickly falling apart. Any second, Vanessa would get the parcel and come back, and Devon couldn't cause a distraction with Himba as a witness. This was supposed to be a stealthy snatch and run. Besides, it wouldn't be right to get Himba in trouble. Stealing was bad enough. Something Devon didn't usually approve of. And no one else was supposed to be involved.

Devon's feet remained frozen to the spot, unsure of what to do. Of course, Vanessa would get away with her outbursts, lies, bullying, and terrible temper. Who knew when Devon would get another chance at this. Next week? Never? ... As Vanessa crossed the kitchen, headed past the pantry, Devon hesitated, and then rushed forward and shoved her inside.

"Whaa ... ?" Vanessa stumbled onto the floor of the pantry, knocking into a tall shelf crammed with beans and cornmeal. Devon slammed the door shut and bolted it.

"DEVON!" Vanessa screamed. There was a muffled crash, followed by a dozen smaller ones. "IT'S DARK IN HERE!" Vanessa pummeled the door with her fists.

Heart hammering, Devon swung back around to Himba. "She slapped Sophia ... ," Devon spouted, breathing heavily.

"I heard." Himba bit down on his jaw disapprovingly.

"Sophia is just a kid." Devon blocked the door, so Himba couldn't open it. "She didn't do anything."

"Sophia deserved it!" shouted Vanessa. "She's a liar! Now let me OUT!"

"NO!" Devon shouted back through the door. "Just think of this ... as ... reflection! You're awful to people! It's not right!" Devon whispered to Himba, "I'll let her out ... eventually."

Still rooted to the spot, Himba puckered. "Okay,"

Saint Frances Institute for ~~Heirs and Orphans~~ Loonies

he agreed and then glancing around nervously, took off down the hall, leaving Devon in the kitchen with the mess she'd made.

A knock rattled on the window. . . . *"Hello?"* the postman called. He rapped again, impatiently.

Devon leaned around the corner and spied, while the postman tried to peer through the glass. Her mind raced. If someone didn't open the door, he'd leave — taking the parcel with him. She couldn't let that happen. Without that package, she didn't have any leverage over Vanessa. Which meant, as soon as she let Vanessa out of the pantry, Vanessa would go running to Ms. Frances. Trouble didn't begin to describe what she'd face. "Coming!" Devon called.

There wasn't time to come up with an excuse for why Vanessa wasn't here. How she was going to convince the postman to give up the parcel was beyond her, but there was only one way to find out. "I'M COMING," Devon called louder.

"NO! Don't you DARE!" Vanessa's muted voice yelled through the door. "Let me out! LET ME OUT!"

The postman's eyes widened with surprise as Devon unlocked the kitchen door and reached for the package. "Where's Vanessa?" he asked, tightening his grasp on the box.

Saint Frances Institute for ~~Heirs and Orphans~~ Loonies

"She couldn't make it. She'll be here next week." Devon pulled the parcel free, kicked the door shut, and strode right out of the kitchen before anyone could stop her.

♛ ♛ ♛

At suppertime, Devon sat with the other stiffly uniformed children. In hushed whispers, they took their assigned places and waited. Several of them shot Devon gracious smiles. Vanessa's parcel of forbidden commodities had proven to be even more delightful than Devon had imagined. Everything in that box was banned at St. Frances. *Tisk. Tisk.* If only Ms. Frances knew what her prized hall monitor was up to — bribing other children with contraband. But this week, all the fizzy drinks, candies, and toys had gone to the children Vanessa terrorized the most. It didn't make stealing okay, but in Vanessa's case, Devon wouldn't lose too much sleep.

Theodore waved, and a few chairs down, Claudia passed the serving plate of steak to Devon — so she could choose first, from the juicy pieces of meat.

Devon straightened, smugly. *So this is what Vanessa felt like when she handed out her parcel of treats.*

"Why is everyone looking at you?" Leni sat

delicately in her chair and eyed Devon beneath her white-blonde hair.

Devon glanced back at her beautiful friend. At St. Frances, the first thing you knew about someone was where they came from (not that it was fair). You were an heir or an orphan. And there was a stiff divide between the two. Leni Dupré was not only an heiress, but one of the wealthiest children in Hasty. Still, she was Devon's closest friend. That she didn't care where Devon was from, made her worth more than any other villager in Hasty.

Devon's smile faltered. A tinge of guilt panged in her chest. She hadn't included Leni in her plans. Hopefully, she wouldn't be angry. They did everything together. And the last time Devon got kitchen duty for a month, Leni was right there beside her. But this time was different. Vanessa knew exactly who stole her parcel of treats. By not including Leni, no matter what happened, Leni would be innocent. "I, uh . . . I passed out some . . . stuff earlier. Here, I saved you these." Devon dumped a handful of Leni's favorite ginger chocolates in her lap.

Leni's face lit up. "Where did you get these?"

"*Well.* . . ." Devon played with the ends of her messy ponytail, unsure how to start. "I um . . . got them from Vanessa."

Saint Frances Institute for ~~Heirs and Orphans~~ Loonies

"Vanessa?" Leni's head shot up; her forehead puckered.

"Yeah." Devon avoided Leni's penetrating scrutiny.

Leni raised an eyebrow, but deciding not to ask, she tore off a shiny wrapper and popped the candy on her tongue. "Yum. It's good."

Devon laughed and swept the wrapper out of sight. "Just hide them, okay?"

"I won't show a soul," Leni pretended to zip her lips, and Devon chuckled. Of course, Leni could keep a secret.

Quite contrarily, the boy assigned to the seat across from them couldn't be trusted with a butter knife. Though most of the girls thought Michael Finn was pretty to look at, with his dark hair and sharp features, he also happened to be the monitor of the boy's side of St. Frances Institute. He was one of Ms. Frances's most valued insiders and was nearly as bad as Vanessa, though not so cruel.

Leni blushed as Michael sat down. To Leni, Michael was perfect, and by the way he stole looks back, Devon suspected that Michael felt the same way about Leni.

"Where is Vanessa?" Ms. Frances's pert voice carried easily across the room. She draped her fur cape over the chair and waited expectantly. No one blinked an eye at her imported beads and overstated fashions anymore. Having no children of her own, nor a husband, she spent hours vainly decorating herself with powders and perms, and she spent the fortune left to her on silks and shoes — never thinking anything of it.

When no one answered, Ms. Frances repeated herself in forced politeness, "Could someone tell me, where Vanessa is . . . ?"

A sudden realization struck Devon and she resisted the urge to slide further down in her seat. A whisper spread across the room. No one, it seemed, had any idea where Vanessa was.

"Michael . . . ." Ms. Frances pointed to the door. "Go find her."

"Yes, Ma'am." Michael stood up, scraping his chair across the floor, and motioned for two others to follow.

A hushed chatter arose as they left, and Leni leaned in towards Devon's ear. "Vanessa is never late. Something must have happened."

Avoiding Ms. Frances's scowl, Devon ducked behind Leni. She had made a *terrible* mistake. She never went back for Vanessa. At first, she just delayed, letting Vanessa wallow, but then, caught up in the fun of passing out the forbidden treats, Devon forgot

Saint Frances Institute for ~~Heirs and Orphans~~ Loonies

about Vanessa entirely. Still . . . , someone should have found her by now. She had a trove of followers. One of them should have noticed she was missing . . . unless . . . they *did* notice, and nobody cared. . . . That seemed more likely.

"You look guilty," Leni accused. "Did you do something?"

Devon slipped further down in her chair. "Maybe. . . ." She was certainly in trouble, now. After being trapped half the day, Vanessa would be furious —

Ms. Frances's eyes fell on Devon, resting there for a moment. *You're always breaking rules*, Ms. Frances had said once. *Gallivanting all over the manor like you own it.*

As Ms. Frances continued to glare, Devon's face flushed, and heat spread across her cheeks.

"Devon," Leni asked apprehensively, "what did you do?"

"You didn't see the way she slapped Sophia —"

"Oh no. . . . Devon, where is Vanessa?"

"She's fine," Devon promised. "Just not here." Panicking, Devon rushed on. "I didn't forget her on purpose . . . Fine. I'm a *little* sorry — a little! But I shouldn't be . . . because it's Vanessa!"

Leni sighed patiently. "Vanessa is horrible — we both know that. But now, whatever you've done is going to get *you* in trouble. Not Vanessa." Leni forced a reproachful frown across her face, but even in her attempt to scold, it was hard to be intimidated. Leni was just too small. Devon on the other hand was taller, sturdier, and quite strong for a girl that was supposed to be twelve.

BAM. . . . BAM. . . . BAM.

Devon jumped in her seat as each door in the halls below *slammed.* Vanessa was free.

Devon pushed back the rising dread. "Maybe I'll just have to stand in the hall, like that boy who flooded the foyer with milk."

Leni's eyebrows drew together. "Did you pour milk on her?"

"No . . . ! I didn't pour milk on her. What good would that do?"

Leni shrugged.

"Ms. Frances looks angry — Quick, tell me what you think she'll do?"

"That depends on what you did," Leni pointed out. "Maybe you'll get grounded again."

Devon let her shoulders relax.

"Or . . . *maybe* . . . Ms. Frances will make you eat meals in your room again — like when you let those chickens in her office. Remember that brown stew?"

A sick, queasy feeling turned in Devon's stomach. "They were roosters," she muttered. Then, Devon lurched forward, grabbed a handful of sweet rolls from the table, and stuffed them in her pockets. The last time she had to live on that disgusting, boiled fat for a week she was sick, miserable, and starving — from refusing to eat it.

Once Devon's pockets were full of rolls, she began cramming potatoes and pastries in the waistband of her pants. When there were no more places to stuff food, she grabbed a slice of steak and started chewing frantically.

Himba's mouth fell open with a mix of surprise and disgust.

"What did you do!" demanded Leni.

"I . . . uh . . . ."

The door crashed open, and a wild-eyed Vanessa stormed in, camouflaged in white powder. Dried beans fell out of the creases of her clothes, leaving a trail that led back to the kitchen. Her tangled hair, matted with a greasy paste, stuck up behind her like a raving, maniacal villain.

A grim-faced Michael toed in on her heels — keeping a short distance between himself and the crazy-eyed girl in front of him.

"SHEEEEE . . ." Vanessa threw her arm at Devon dramatically, "LOCKED ME IN THE . . . THE . . . ," Vanessa stuttered, searching for the name . . . ,"CRAWLSPACE! WHERE YOU KEEP THE FOOD."

Several children snickered.

"QUITE!" Ms. Frances flared, her nostrils bulging.

Just as the room settled, a red-faced boy snorted, bringing on more snickering. The room was suddenly filled with children fighting back their sniggers and chortles, and unable to contain it any longer, Claudia burst into squawking laughter.

"That's enough!" Ms. Frances banged her hand on the table, startling the room into silence. Her thick, fur cape slid to the floor. "Where *exactly* did she lock you, Vanessa?"

"I don't know what it's called!" Vanessa stomped her foot impatiently. "It's for servants!" She bristled indignantly.

Silent giggles spilled out again.

"Technically . . . it's a pantry," Devon explained, her hands full of blueberry pastries.

Leni let her face sink behind her hands and hid there.

"She had food and water," reasoned Devon. "And there's a hole where mice get through . . . for air."

"AAAAARRRGH!" Vanessa launched at Devon.

Just as Devon braced herself for a fight . . . Michael got a hold of Vanessa and dragged her back.

"ENOUGH!" shouted Ms. Frances.

The room fell silent. Vanessa crossed her arms and stuck out her chin, indignantly.

Saint Frances Institute for ~~Heirs and Orphans~~ Loonies

Satisfied, Ms. Frances yanked her cape off the floor and huffed. "It's a good thing you were never adopted," she quipped at Devon, cruelly. "You do absolutely nothing you're told. I can't imagine any parent having to put up with you. I wish I could send you to another institution myself, but . . . under the circumstances . . . it appears I'm stuck with you. Just, go to your room." Ms. Frances whipped her arm towards the door with a snap. "Michael, make sure she gets there."

"Yes, Ma'am." Michael let go of Vanessa, marched over to Devon's chair, and grabbed Devon by the arm. "Come on," he snarled.

Grudgingly, Devon lumbered to the door. Ms. Frances's words hurt, even though by now, they shouldn't. Still, she refused to follow rules when they were stupid or unfair. Maybe she shouldn't have taken the parcel, but Vanessa Pegwell got away with everything, and it was about time somebody did something.

As Devon trudged forward in a walk of shame, she swiped one more slice of steak from the table and stuffed it in her back pocket. Michael shoved her forward, and Devon glared back at him. The only thing she'd let herself regret was, if she had been quicker, she might have got a slice a mushroom pie too.

Just as they reached the door, Ms. Frances quipped,

Saint Frances Institute for ~~Heirs and Orphans~~ Loonies

"Tomorrow you're not to leave your room! I'll have stew brought up to you."

Devon whipped around. "But . . . tomorrow is the Festival of Gondolas!" she exclaimed. The Festival of Gondolas only came every ten years. *Everyone* in Hasty was going — even the babies.

"You *can't* let her go!" cried Vanessa.

Ms. Frances sneered and patted her fur cape, relishing the chance to deny Devon something she wanted.

Leni jumped up from her chair. "But . . . St. Frances will be honored at the festival! Someone might notice Devon is missing. It will make all of us look bad!"

Ms. Frances's sneer turned to a pained face. If word got out that naughty children attended St. Frances, it could hurt their reputation. A bad reputation meant that the wealthier families would find another school to board their children. That meant less silks and furs for her. "Fine. You'll go. But after that . . . , you'll take your meals in your room . . . for a month!"

Devon cringed, feeling the weight of the potatoes and dinner rolls in her pockets. She planted her feet, digging them into the carpet. But Michael shoved her forward, and she stumbled through the door, with Vanessa's complaints trailing after them. Nobody noticed the *shadow* lurking above.

CHAPTER THREE
The Festival of Gondolas

The following day passed by in a blur. Girls rushed from room to room borrowing brushes and creams and trading shoes and ribbons. All rubbish, as far as Devon was concerned, and by six o'clock, St. Frances was a madhouse with no place left to hide. Ms. Frances stalked up and down the halls shouting at girls to behave, quiet down, and stop running around like barn animals.

By the time the sun had set, Ms. Frances had completely lost her voice. It was a struggle to say anything above a whisper, so she made scratchy sounds and pointed when she wanted something. By the time the moon had risen, she was so frazzled, the pins in her hair had come out, giving her a slightly deranged look. Duke, her assistant, insisted she let him drive the children, so she could rest.

Somewhere deep in the mansion, Devon and Leni got ready for the biggest night in years.

Leni stood in the mirror putting the finishing touches on her already perfect face. A light blue

The Festival of Gondolas

dress with sparkles flowed to her knees in a puffy sort of way. On any other girl, it would have looked silly, but it suited Leni just fine. Meanwhile, Devon had overturned the entire room trying to find the pair to her old, black, dress shoe. She had hoped she would never have to wear the wretched things again, but Ms. Frances had insisted everyone wear their Sunday clothes for the festival. Since she was already in trouble, Devon put on her best dress and didn't say one word about having to wear dress shoes.

Leni stood back admiringly, and then turned to Devon. "You look good."

"Thanks," Devon said grudgingly. Her dress was a hand-me-down — passed on from an older girl that had already left St. Frances. Still, since she had to dress up, it was nice to hear she didn't look awful.

"Devon?" Leni asked, in that curious way that preceded a lengthier question.

"Hmm?" Devon grunted and ducked under her bed to look for her other shoe. Being that she was an orphan, there was little more than dust.

"What do you want to be when you grow up?" Leni asked.

Devon crawled out from under the bed and glanced up at her friend. Leni was beautiful, smart, and charming with a whole world of possibilities before her. Devon, on the other hand, had a hard time with everything. She didn't have family, or money, and it was hard to imagine her future when she couldn't even be herself. "I don't know."

"Well, what are you good at?" Leni put down a makeup brush that Devon had no clue how to use. The first thing that came to mind was fighting. Devon usually won those, even when her opponents were bigger. But according to Ms. Frances (and the Hasty police station) that was a *bad* thing. *Even* when she was just standing up for someone else . . . or wasn't the one who started the fight in the first place.

"Sewing? Drawing? Maybe you can be a chef . . . or a businesswoman?" Leni suggested. "Oooh!" she squealed. "What about calligraphy? Don't you just love the beautiful way those letters swirl?"

Devon made a face. There was nothing wrong with those things. Good for all the people that could do them. Really. But just thinking about doing them herself . . . bored her to death. "Have you seen my handwriting?" Devon walked over to her dresser and dug through the drawers. "It's chicken scratch."

"Good point," Leni agreed.

Finding nothing in her drawers, Devon switched to her closet.

"Well, there has to be something you're good at —"

Devon hid her face while she burrowed in her closet. There were plenty of things she was good at. They just weren't helpful things. Not in the way Leni was asking. Devon was instinctive, confident, and naturally athletic. Instead of gossiping about clothes or boys, she was usually playing with them. Basketball. Soccer. Even football. Whatever game of pick-up was going on, she was in the mix of it (as long as Ms. Frances wasn't around). But there were other things she was good at too. She was gutsy, perceptive, quick-witted, and creative (if you considered the inventive pranks she played). But none of those things would help her with a job when she grew up. "I . . . um . . . I don't know." Despite the things she was good at, she was still just a lost kid with no money, no parents, and no future. Devon pulled herself out of the closet. "I just want to be someone. You know."

"Be someone . . . ?"

"Like . . . someone important." Devon avoided Leni's gaze. "I don't want to be a nobody my whole life."

"You're not a nobody!" gasped Leni. "No one is a nobody. I know it doesn't feel like that sometimes, but there's something you're meant to do. Everyone has a gift inside them that makes them special — something they can do that other people can't. You just have to figure out what that is."

"Yeah." Feeling a bit better, Devon shut the closet. "Did you find your shoe?"

"Not yet." Devon ducked under one of her roommates' beds, scooted a box of sweaters aside, and finding nothing, checked under the next bed. As she searched, the room darkened, and a gloom hung from the ceiling.

"Can you turn the light back on?" Leni looked up from the mirror.

Devon slid out from under the last bunk. "I didn't turn it off." At this point, she was ready to go without dress shoes.

"I know it was on." Leni strode over to the lamp and flipped the switch. The light turned off, and the room got darker.

"Huh. That's weird. . . ." Leni flipped the switch again, turning the light on, and looked up. Hanging from the ceiling — a shadow clouded the room, giving off a dull, gloomy glow. She snapped the cover on her shiny make-up container, dropped it in a dainty purse on her shoulder, and edged closer to the door. "Are you ready?" Her voice shook.

"Still no shoe." Devon ducked under her roommate's desk.

Just then, the door burst open and an irritated Vanessa stormed in, breathing heavily.

Devon groaned inwardly. *What now?*

"Where is my necklace?" Vanessa demanded. "It was on top of my dresser, and now it's gone!"

"Leni, did you hear a knock?" Devon turned her back to Vanessa and continued her search, ignoring the intrusion.

"I don't think so. . . ." Leni turned back to her mirror, mimicking Devon's game. "Hmm . . . Nope. No knock."

"Huh. Well, the door is open." Devon glanced up, straight past Vanessa. "Do you see anyone?"

"Ugh!" Vanessa stomped her foot impatiently. Her cheeks swelled, reddening with rage.

"Nope. Don't see a thing," chimed Leni.

"Leni, you're just jealous your parents abandoned you and mine didn't. My parents miss me and send me gifts, but yours don't," Vanessa spat viciously. "I bet they don't even want you."

Devon's jaw ticked. That was low . . . even for Vanessa. Tears built up in Leni's eyes, threatening to spill over.

Vanessa took a step closer. "You're a nobody. . . . What does it feel like, to have rich parents that don't want you —?"

Devon dropped the pile of clothes she was digging through and moved next to Leni. She'd give Leni a chance to stand up for herself — not that she liked it much. Just one more second. If Leni needed help, she'd step in. There was no way she would let Vanessa hurt Leni.

"Nothing to say . . . ?" Vanessa spat. "I didn't think so —"

Leni hit the play button on their roommate's music box, and it blasted mid-song, drowning out Vanessa. That was brave, considering Vanessa's temper. On cue, Vanessa screamed and ran at Leni. . . . Just as Vanessa leaped, Devon tackled her and slammed her on the carpet.

"Ouch! Et off!" Vanessa screamed into the carpet and dug her hand deep into Devon's hair. "Gerrrroffff!" She screamed again, as she pulled Devon down with her. Surely, the whole house could hear them, and fighting was strictly forbidden. Devon tried to pull free. She needed to end this now, or she'd face more punishment than a grounding and terrible stew. Pushing Vanessa's elbow to the floor, Devon twisted it behind her back —

Vanessa let go of Devon's hair . . . then she hollered, "AAAGGGHHHHHHH!"

That was when Ms. Frances found them. The precise moment Devon had Vanessa pinned to the carpet screaming. Ms. Frances bounded into the room, panting like she'd run up a hundred flights of stairs. "Can't . . . you . . . behave yourself?" she rasped, swatting Devon like a fly.

Now that her hair was free, Devon jumped up nimbly and faced Ms. Frances with defiant red streaks across her face. Leni hit the mute button.

"I wish I could say I was surprised," Ms. Frances squeaked, hoarsely. "But I'm not!"

"It's not her fault," interjected Leni. "Vanessa —"

"She stole my necklace!" Vanessa accused, cutting Leni off harshly.

Ms. Frances turned on Devon, her face bulging. "No festival!" her voice cracked. "Now give Vanessa whatever you've taken and —"

"That's not fair!" chimed Leni.

"Vanessa . . . !" Claudia ran in, bubbling with excitement, and completely unaware of what she was interrupting. "Look!" She held up a silver necklace with a dangling amethyst. "I found it!" She stuck out her chest, proudly. "It fell behind your dresser."

Sophia ran in next. "Ms. Frances, Duke needs you in the foyer. He said to hurry!"

Ms. Frances clutched her head between her hands and squeezed.

As if that weren't enough excitement, in came Sarah, a tiny toddler that feared just about everything. She waddled in and bumped into Sophia — shaking all over. "Ms. F'ances. Ms. F'ances," she tugged on Ms. Frances's frilly night shawl, "Tubby brout anotha mouse to da kitchen an' Cook is makin' a big mess. She is trying to squish it."

Ms. Frances's face puffed rosy red, ready to explode. She hated mice. And she thought Tubby, their fat, old cat, quite useless. "That cat is supposed to catch mice inside and kill them. Not catch mice outside, bring them in . . . and *let them go!*"

"Pfft." Ms. Frances patted her hair down and composed herself. "Sophia, inform Duke that I'm on my way. Take Sarah with you. And Sarah, stop sniveling. It's not ladylike."

Sarah sniffled and straightened up.

"Yes ma'am." Sophia grabbed Sarah by the hand and headed for the door.

"Leni . . . , go help Cook with the mouse. Devon, you might as well change." Ms. Frances strode off — the tap of her dress heels clicked down the hall.

Vanessa snatched her necklace and elbowed Claudia ungratefully. Devon hit the play button — blasting the music again.

That was when it happened.

Vanessa grabbed the metal clock off the writing desk and flung it at the back of Devon's head. It should have hit her. That's what Devon told herself over and over the rest of the night. It should have cut open the back of her head and knocked her clean out. Instead, it smashed against the wall in a dozen pieces. *But how?* Devon had been looking the other way, the music was deafening, and a vengeful Vanessa moved fast. Nobody saw the well-aimed, metal clock flying through the air, but Devon felt it. If that was possible.

She felt the air stir as Vanessa reached for the clock. She heard the prongs of metal scrape against the wood as it was yanked from the table. She felt the vibrations of the rattling mechanics knock against the inside of the clock. She heard it all: the music, every beat of the drum, every cord of the guitar. . . . And yet somehow, she knew the clock was hurling towards her, so clearly that she felt it.

At the last second, Devon moved with imperceptible speed. The metal clock blew by her head, taking a few strands of hair with it. It smashed against the wall and shattered. . . .Then the door was empty, and Vanessa was gone.

Leni turned off the music. "Are you okay?" She grabbed Devon by the arm — pulling her from a trance — and checked to see it she was cut. "Thank the saints Vanessa has a crappy aim." Leni crossed herself. "She could've taken your head off."

Devon's forehead creased. Hadn't Leni seen her move out of the way? She had sensed that clock. Not just heard it. And Leni was acting like Vanessa missed. . . . Devon rubbed the creases from her forehead. *Maybe Leni was right, and she was imagining it. . . . But then, why did she feel like she had done this before? Why did she have the strangest feeling that . . . sensing that clock, hurtling through the air, was . . . natural?*

"You should go to Ms. Frances about this," insisted Leni. "Drat! I have to deal with the mouse. I hate mice. *Of course* Ms. Frances didn't make Vanessa do it."

Devon forced herself to move. "I'll get the mouse. It's getting late. Help me find my shoe."

"But . . . are you still going then?" Leni brightened.

"Of course. Vanessa will think she's gotten one up on me if I don't." And though she wanted to stay out of trouble, she wasn't going to let Vanessa push her around either.

Devon shuffled around the room, overturning it at a quicker speed. The shadow was gone, and the room was bright again. *Strange* — but there was no time to be unsettled by table lamps and shadows. She shrugged and continued looking. "Hurry. Help me find my shoe so we can go."

They searched together in silence and finding the shoe in a chest of blankets, hurried downstairs. Devon peeked around the corner. "Go scout for Ms. Frances. I'll get the mouse." When the coast was clear, Devon hurried for the kitchen.

Cook, the Institute's chef, paced the kitchen irritably, putting things away as she went. Of course, Cook wasn't really the woman's name, but that's what everyone called her, though no one could say why, other than she was the cook.

The kitchen was a disaster. A tornado of fury had swept through the cabinets, leaving cupboard doors open and the contents strewn across the countertops. Pans, roasters, and dishes littered the floor — some in pieces.

"Cook, I've come to get a mouse for you," Devon called. She had always liked Cook. She put aside a plate of breakfast when Devon slept in, with little more than a roll of her eyes.

Cook shuffled around the corner with an armful of pots. She jabbed her thumb at a dead mouse on the floor. "I've got it now. Dead as dead can be. Not that Ms. Frances helped none — came right by here, while I was chasing the darned thing, and went right on by. Ruined a perfectly good pot too." Cook waved a silver pot stained with blood.

Digging a piece of cardboard out of the trash, Devon scooped up the mouse from the floor. It was too bad she hadn't gotten here sooner. The mouse might have lived.

Cook dumped the pots in the sink and turned on the water. While the basin filled, she gathered more pans. "Thank you, Devon. I can always count on you. Can't count a lick on half the people here, but I can count on you."

"Remember that while I'm grounded . . . send me up some *good* leftovers."

Cook scoffed. "So long as next time you lock Vanessa up somewhere else. Not in my pantry! She made a terrible mess in my sugar. And the flour had to be thrown out."

"Deal," Devon promised as she kicked open the screen door and hurried outside with the mouse. Without a spade, Devon dug a hole with her fingers. She buried the mouse hastily, before heading back inside.

In the foyer, Leni was stalling Duke, the butler. "She's here! She's here." Leni pointed to Devon. "I told you she was coming."

Duke's bushy eyebrows crinkled over his light brown skin, and the lines in his stern expression deepened. He didn't like when the children made him late. And when he didn't approve of someone stepping a toe over the line, he planted a disapproving look across his face. The steely looks he gave the children had left permanent creases across his temple — though he wasn't harsh or cruel in the least. He was quite the opposite actually. And while Ms. Frances owned the Institute, Duke was the reason it ran smoothly. "Let's go then." He shuffled them towards the bus.

"What did you do to your nails?" Leni scolded. "They're covered in dirt."

Devon tried not to think of the dead mouse. "Forget it. Just tell me the plan."

"No plan." Leni clapped her hands together. "We're all clear. Ms. Frances locked herself in her room to get ready. She must have forgotten to say something to Duke, because he didn't know anything about you not going."

Devon frowned. "What about Vanessa?"

"Special privileges," Leni rolled her eyes. "She already left on the first bus."

♛ ♛ ♛

By the time they arrived at the festival, nearly the whole inhabitance of Hasty had already converged beneath the clusters of hot-air balloons. Duke couldn't get past the lines of cars parked alongside the road. "You'll have to walk from here," he said regretfully. They all tumbled out —laughing and talking — too excited to care. "If anyone wants to leave early . . . ," Duke called after them, "I'll be here." But the children barely heard him and went on with hardly a look back. Just as Devon thought she was in the clear, Duke called after her. "Devon. Hang on a minute."

The color drained from Leni's face. "Do you think he knows?"

"I don't know. Go on, just in case. I'll catch up." Devon climbed back on the bus and faced Duke. He had refused to change out of his pressed blazer, grey vest, and striped trousers, even for the festival. "What's up, Duke?"

"I heard about earlier." His forehead creased into one of his disapproving looks. "I shouldn't have brought you — but I suspect Vanessa had a hand in some of that trouble."

"She did," Devon bit.

Duke's face softened beneath his white beard. "Ms. Frances isn't too fair when it comes to her favorites. Don't let it get you down."

Devon smiled, a little relieved to have him for an ally. "Thanks, Duke."

"See that you don't get into any mischief while you're here." Duke leaned back in the driver seat. "For my sake."

The Festival of Gondolas

"I won't. I promise." Devon skipped off the bus and hurried to catch up with the others. As she ran her blood pumped with excitement. The Festival of Gondolas was here, and she couldn't wait. The cool air nipped at her cheeks, and the rising moon cast a faint glow onto the path. An old man slid out of the shadows, leaning heavily against his cane.

Devon stumbled back. "Where did you come from?"

"Be careful —" The old man shook his cane, with wild eyes. "There are shadows here tonight." The moonlight illuminated a thin scar across his neck.

"I know you. . . ." Devon backed up, putting more space between them. "You're the man that wandered into Mr. Frinkley's store . . . you said a shadow tried to kill you." All of Hasty had been talking about it. And since then, stories had spread of his insanity.

"Keep your eyes open." He wobbled his cane at the moon. "It could come for you too!" He swung his cane down with a *whoosh* — then poked it at Devon. "It ain't human —" His eye bulged, and he leaned in —

"Okay." Devon darted around him. "I'll watch out." When she was past him, she broke into a sprint and ran the rest of the way. By the time she reached the festival (packed with every mom, dad, and child in Hasty) Devon had forgotten all about the kooky, old man and his shadows.

Long strings of tiny, white lights gave a faint glow. Giant balloons blocked out the sky — all of them bright colors and shaped like flying piñatas.

"This is amazing," Leni exclaimed.

Whissssh. Fiery blue heat blasted from a nearby burner lighting up a colossal, silver dragon.

"Agh." Leni jumped back with a girlish squeal.

"Ha-ha," laughed a boy from inside the basket-shaped gondola. He let go of the burner and the fire died out. All around them, dozens of pilots pulled their burners at once. Each balloon glowed, fiery bright — flickering like Christmas lights. Then one by one the pilots released their burners, and the sky faded dark again. Cheers echoed across the field.

As the crowd settled, a soft breeze carried the smell of delicious foods. Devon's stomach rumbled. It was known that the village bakers brought only their best cakes to the festival, but unfortunately, they cost quite a bit of money. Devon sighed. What did it matter if she didn't eat tonight? At least she was here, enjoying the festival. She breathed in deep, savoring the moment of freedom. Nothing could mess up tonight.

A strong breeze blew against Devon and Leni, and a low-hanging shadow slid above them. Leni shivered. "I . . . w-wish I . . . b-brought a j-jacket."

"We'll go stand by one of the burners," suggested Devon.

"Y-yeah." Leni steered for the nearest balloon and nearly walked straight into Niko Throntropt —

"Just missed," teased the teenage boy, dressed in clothes too expensive for Hasty. Niko Throntropt got attention wherever he went. Not a surprise for a wealthy, businessman's kid, who lived in one of the largest houses in Hasty. Nobody had ever met his parents. He just showed up a few months ago. Since then, his dark hair and almond eyes were the talk of the village.

"It's Devon, right?" Niko flashed pearly white teeth. "And Leni?"

"U-umm . . . ," garbled Leni, unable to put her thoughts together.

Devon shot Leni an exasperated look — she was gaping like a fool. "Yeah."

Aware of his affect, Niko grinned bigger. "Would it be all right if my friend and I joined you?" He shifted, smothering a flush before it came. "I've actually been wanting to meet you for a while." He stole a glance at Devon. "We could check out the festival together . . . ," he coughed and added, "as a group."

Devon opened her mouth, a firm *no* forming on her lips.

"Sure!" Leni perked up.

Devon elbowed her. "I'm not supposed to be here, remember?" All she wanted was to enjoy the festival — without Ms. Frances discovering she was here. Hanging out with one of the most talked about kids in Hasty was not the best way to do that. "Someone will see us."

Niko's eyes twinkled. "Did you sneak out?"

"It will be fine, " Leni muttered, her eyes on Niko.

Niko jumped on the first *yes,* he could get. "Cool. He's headed over now." He waved to Michael Finn — the very monitor that had escorted Devon to her room.

Michael walked up grinning, like he just won another swim trophy. "I see you made it out," he scoffed at Devon.

Devon's eyes flashed. "Look here —"

"I won't say anything." Michael threw up his hands, and his eyes darted to Leni. "Just this once."

Leni turned beet red and mumbled something unintelligible. Her voice cracked . . . and she coughed.

"Are you okay?" Michael leaned over Leni, inspecting her. "Are you choking?"

"No," Leni croaked.

"Do you need a drink?" he asked smoothly. He motioned for a baker's stand, with pitchers of lemonade. "Not that I would mind much if you blacked out and needed CPR." He grinned. "I'm fully certified you know."

"I'd . . . like that," Leni managed, blushing.

Michael grinned bigger. "Yeah?"

"I mean the drink, not the CPR. . . . Not that I wouldn't like the CPR though," Leni said in a rush. "I would . . . probably . . . I mean definitely . . . I would like that too. That would be good, you know, if I needed it . . . air and stuff. I like air."

Devon clapped her hand over her forehead and hid behind it.

"Er . . . ," Niko muttered, awkwardly.

"I'm going to check out the hot-air balloons," Devon grumbled between her fingers. The last thing she wanted to do was hang around Leni and Michael as a third wheel. *Yuck. Leni really should rethink her taste in boys.* Devon jabbed a finger at Michael. "Don't tell anyone I'm here. . . . And give Leni your jacket. She's cold."

Michael shrugged out of his jacket. "I never saw you," he gritted, with more warning than kindness — which was fine with Devon. She didn't want to owe *him* any favors.

"Want some company?" Niko started after her.

"No!" Devon barked and sauntered off before he could come up with a reason to tag along. It was easy to disappear in the crowd. The fiery balloons hypnotized the villagers, leaving openings between the clusters of people to weave through. She stopped behind a crowd that oohed and aahed for a robot-shaped balloon, with fire blasting from its feet.

Among them, a man with dark skin and stylish clothes caught her attention. Short dreads spiked forward over his head, with a design etched into the sides of a tapered fade that swirled up his hair like magic. A high-collared, flowing coat, with patterns of gold stitching, just touched his ankles. Beneath it, he wore a black silk, dashiki shirt, trimmed in tribal print. His cuffed pants stopped just above a modernized sort of loafer. And the strangest thing about him was the tall walking stick — which he obviously didn't need — carved out of black wood. It twisted up, nearly the height of his head, with an amber stone on top. Something about the stylishly blended fashion between old and new was intriguing, but his disinterest in the exuberant display of festivities topped off her curiosity.

Unaware of Devon's notice, he slowly faded, becoming more and more translucent, until he was gone completely. The empty space filled, and people carried on as if he had never been there in the first place.

"He vanished." Devon's mouth fell open, and she whirled around, searching for the strange man. An impatient voice carried over the cheers of the crowd.

"Excuse me. . . ." A younger girl, somewhere between eight or nine years old, with a ribbon in her fiery-red hair, pushed her way through the crowd. "Pardon me." She stopped in the exact spot the man had just been.

A swirl of wind rose up. It gained speed. A cyclone formed, twirling faster, and it took the shape of the stylish man. With a subtle wave of his hand, his staff shrank to a thin, wooden stick. He placed it in the air, much like placing it in a cupboard, and it disappeared.

Devon blinked. *How did he do that?* Wide-eyed, she glanced around, but the crowd was fully engrossed in the festivities. No one had noticed. Devon rubbed her eyes, but the peculiar man and red-haired girl continued on, as if nothing remarkable had happened at all. Unable to contain her curiosity, Devon pushed closer and watched intently.

"We're running out of time," the redhead said in a thick, Irish accent.

"She still wears the crown," the stylish man replied. He pulled his flowing coat around him. "She knows nothing. As long as she knows nothing . . . she's safe."

The young girl's eyes darkened. "How can you be sure that's the *real* Crown of Guilledon?"

"I can feel it's magic," he said simply.

The girl folded her arms across her chest. "If only she knew what it was — she'd throw it in the ocean and solve all our problems."

The man's nostrils flared. "We can't be certain of that . . . which is why we cannot act rashly. We do not know who, or *what*, she is. The shadow walker's involvement makes it eminent there are no mistakes."

Devon leaned closer. *What were they talking about? Magic? Shadow walkers? A Crown of Guille-don?* It wasn't really her business. Normally she wouldn't spy on strangers . . . but somehow, that man had *disappeared* into thin air . . . and then reappeared again. It was like . . . magic.

Overcome with curiosity, Devon crept closer —

until she was nearly beside them — and ducked behind a crowd of kids that were talking and laughing blissfully. As long as they didn't move, she wouldn't be spotted —

"Where is she anyway?" The redhead girl turned her freckled face to the clusters of people, sweeping right past where Devon was hiding.

"Ah. It appears she has slipped away." The stylish man pointed to where Devon had just been, now an empty spot in the crowd. "Perhaps I lost her when I evanished."

"Evanished?" The girl cocked her head.

"The shadow walker was close . . . ," he explained. "So I disappeared."

"I know what *evanished* means. You went somewhere else!"

"No . . . I was nowhere . . . I evanished. I ceased to be — here, or anywhere."

The redhead threw up her freckled arms. "So . . . you lost her?"

"It appears so. . . . No matter. We'll find her again. . . . Did you find out anything that will help us?"

"No. There's no record of a Devon Connor anywhere. Not in our world or theirs."

Devon's head snapped up. They had said *her* name.

And there were no other Devon Connors in Hasty. Not that she knew of anyway.

"*Hey!*" yawped a loud, teenage voice. The lanky, mechanic's son started forward. Devon waved her hands back and forth.

"*No. No. No,*" she mouthed noiselessly.

To her horror, the gangly boy strode right up to where Devon was hiding and bent over laughing. "Whatcha doing down there, huh?"

"Shhh . . . ," she shushed frantically. *What was his name? Parker? Paul? Peter? Something with a P —*

"Oh! . . . *Sorry,*" he said — not quietly enough. "Who ya' hiding from huh?" P-boy leaned in, with big, nosy, bug-eyes, blocking her view.

Devon leaned around him and locked eyes with the angry-faced redhead. *She was caught!* Dread cringed through her chest and her next breath burned. She stood up abruptly and elbowed P-boy as she passed. "I wish you!"

"OW! Whacha do that for . . . ?" he called after her, but she didn't stop.

Fear had jolted her forward, making her movements rigid. Whatever was going on, it wasn't something she wanted to get mixed up in. That man had vanished, and it gave her chills. Worse, the girl had said Devon Connor — *her name.*

The Festival of Gondolas

Devon squeezed through the crowds of people, zipped around a giant pinata, and weaved past the butcher's caddy. She sped forward blindly and didn't stop until she reached the downtown market, and only because her shoe caught on the cobble.

"Darn it." Devon picked at the torn sole. Breathing heavily, she limped on. No one was around this part of Hasty. The shop owners had closed, locking up early, so they could enjoy the festival with everyone else. Dark windows gave the street an abandoned feeling. So instead of feeling better, an eerie tingle bugged her —

Devon glanced back, down the empty street . . . and nearly fell over. The stylish man floated towards her, his coat billowing behind him (without a breeze).

Devon crouched, ready to spring into a run.

He flickered and disappeared.

Devon's breath seized, and she whipped around the empty street. *It had to be a trick! Yes. That was it.* Somehow, all of this could easily be explained. She just needed to work up the courage she normally had, march straight up to him, and ask how he was doing it — except, he was gone.

Devon peered down the dark line of shops, the deserted street only adding to her uneasiness. It would be safer to head back. A flicker caught her eye, and the stylish man reappeared, barely a couple feet away.

"AHH!" Devon leapt back and fell hard in front of the dressmaker's shop.

The man tucked his coat behind him and leaned over, a serious expression plastered across his face. "You almost slipped away."

"What do you want?" Devon sputtered.

"Only to h—"

Pebbles tumbled down the side of the dressmaker's shop — clicking against the brick wall, pranging against the dressmaker's window, and bouncing off Devon. Slowly, she looked up.

A head of fiery red hair crawled toward them. She slithered down the wall, upside-down, hair swaying with the wind.

"AHHHHHHHHHHHH." Devon screamed, kicked off the sidewalk, and bolted down the street as fast as she could, with a broken shoe. There was no explaining it away. That man could fly — and vanish! And the girl (if that was a girl) could crawl down the side of a wall. She stuck to it like a lizard. The thought sent a cold shiver prickling down her skin. Her legs pumped faster. Just as the festival came into view, someone reached from the shadows and grabbed her around the middle.

"Ahhhhhhhh!" Devon screamed again. That was three times in one day, and she never screamed. Frustrated, Devon balled her hands into fists and whirled around with bared teeth. She was a fighter, not a sissy.

"Woah . . . It's me!" Niko jumped back, holding his palms up wide. "Someone's following you."

Recognizing his dark hair and concerned eyes, Devon grabbed his shoulders. "There's a man back there! He can disappear and pop right back," she exclaimed wildly. Her pulse pounded in her ears. "And there's a girl. . . . She crawled down the side of a building. She sticks to it!"

Niko raised his eyebrows, doubtfully.

"I'm telling the truth!" Devon shook him. "You have to believe me. Everything that old man said in Mr. Frinkley's shop is true!" Her eyes widened. *Poor Sophia was telling the truth too.* Which meant, there was something going on in Hasty, and she was willing to bet that redhaired girl and bizarre man were behind it.

"Okay. . . !" Niko held up his hands, surrendering.

"You don't believe me —"

"I believe . . . something scared you, and whatever it was, we'll go around it. I know a path around the festival. We'll find your friend and you can go home," he promised. "She's probably still with Michael."

Devon exhaled. "All right."

Niko nodded towards the lining of the trees. "This way." He took off and Devon hurried after him, as fast as her torn shoe would allow. They didn't slow until they reached the thin lining of the woods. The cool breeze bit at her skin, numbing her hands.

"Do you know what they wanted?" Niko asked lightly and slowed to a walk.

"No. I didn't hang around to find out." Goosebumps shivered down her arms — but she wasn't sure if it was the cold . . . or something else.

"I've been wanting to ask . . . ," Niko said, as he pushed through the foliage, holding back the branches for her, "where are you from?"

Devon's first thought was Hasty, but truthfully, she didn't know. "I'm an orphan."

"Ah." He shot her a look of pity. "So you don't know *where* you're from — ?"

Devon's face went pink. She didn't like talking about this. Mostly because it *was* a mystery to her. Didn't he realize that she had all the same questions. "I'm thirteen. I'm an orphan. I don't know anything more than that. I don't know my parents and I don't know if I'm from Hasty or not."

Niko turned to face her.

She was sure the next question would be, *why didn't*

you ask where you came from? . . . But she had asked — countless times. And Ms. Frances's answers always resulted in a sour look and a complaint. Never anything helpful.

Niko pointed to the gold band on her head. "Where did you get that?"

Stumped, Devon fumbled with the thin, gold headband. Her fingers brushed over the green stone in the center. Most people hardly paid it any attention. Sometimes, she even forgot it was there.

"I got it at a market a few years ago." She could still remember the woman's matted, black hair with gold coins braided into it, her shabby clothes with purses tied to her belt, and the long cloak that swept across the ground. But it was her crystal, blue eyes that startled her the most: clever, like they knew secrets she didn't. The more Devon tried to remember beyond that . . . the fuzzier the memory became.

A gleam in Niko's glance shone in the darkness, and he leaned in to examine the gemstone. Devon knew, even in the dark woods, the colors swirled together like an emerald star in the night sky. The stone always looked like that.

Niko shook his head, confirming a secret thought. "I believe it's been slightly longer than that." A bit of malice flared unsettlingly, and he reached for it.

"What are you doing . . . ?" Devon took a quick step back. Her torn shoe caught on a root and broke the rest of the way. "Great." She pulled it off and stood barefoot. "I know you don't believe me, but we need to find Leni and get out of here!"

Niko's almond eyes glinted lethally. "I believe you —"

The leaves rustled around them, and the wind blew hard against the branches. A dark, unnatural shadow crept around Niko. It rose up, surrounding him, and he disappeared in the midst of it. The shadow twisted into frightening things — creatures with no names.

Devon yanked off the other shoe and carelessly dropped them on the ground. Her stomach twisted with an eerie feeling that told her to run. It seeped into her gut until she felt sick.

The mutating, unnatural shadow sank back to the ground. It reshaped, growing bones, muscles, flesh, and lastly . . . terrible, piercing eyes. Niko Throntropt stood in front of her. A malicious smile crept across his face. "What do you think?"

Devon repressed the urge to look back the way she came. She needed to run — but this time, she knew she'd never make it.

"Why are you so quiet? . . . Aren't you impressed? . . . Are you afraid?" Niko sneered.

No words came out, just a stutter, "A-ah."

"Come now, this is no fun," Niko taunted. "Tell me what you're thinking. I don't usually let ordinary people see my true magic."

"T-the-the old man . . . said a shadow attacked him," stuttered Devon. . . . "Sophia said a shadow . . . broke the lamp."

Niko grinned, impressed. "Those were both me."

"What are you . . . ?"

Niko faded away, becoming the shadows. His voice spoke from the empty woods. "I'm the most powerful presence on earth. I thrive in darkness, unconfined by the weaknesses of mundane, ordinary humans. I am a shadow walker."

Two gleaming eyes appeared from the emptiness. Then a knife.

Devon felt the dispersion of air as the knife came down. Her senses heightened, and she felt everything: each blade of grass blowing in the breeze, every breath of wind, even the tiny animals that scurried within the woods. At the last moment, Devon threw up her arm, to protect herself. Her soft flesh hardened.

CLANG.

The knife broke into shadows. . . . And the forest was empty.

Devon fought a rising panic as she held up a long,

steel blade, where her arm had once been. Her pulse quickened. She let her finger trail over the metal.

"You're not human . . . !" Niko reappeared, the shadow billowing around him. Controlling the darkness, he pulled it closer into himself, and it vanished, leaving just a boy in the woods. He stood, completely ordinary, and handsome again. "What happened? He gave her a grim look. *"How did you do that?"*

"I don't know," she panted, taking a step back.

Her skin tingled and her arm ached. The silvery steel melted, glimpsing bone, and her flesh grew back. Devon wiggled her fingers (perfectly normal again) and stared back at Niko in terrified awe. *Had her arm really just turned into a sword?*

"You shouldn't have been able to shift with that on!" Niko accused.

"You attacked me." Devon's eyes narrowed, cautious and angry. "You tried to hurt me!"

The ground crunched under her, as she shifted her weight. *Think. Think,* she scolded herself. They were still a good distance from the festival. She had to distract him . . . and then run.

"You don't understand!" Niko gnashed his teeth together and spat through them. "Even if you're not human — a spell was cast on that crown!" He jabbed a thin finger at the band on her head. "That's the *curse* of the Crown of Guilledon — magic becomes ordinary!" Niko paced irritably, without taking his eyes from her. "You must somehow be overpowering it." His eyes dawned. "Which means the council is right. The Shadow Reign can use the crown to invade Thysia! . . . If the curse can be beaten, we can wield it's magic and get past the wall!" He whirled and slashed his blade again, harder.

"What are you — ?" Devon shielded her head from the attack. CLANG. The force clashed against her arm, again. The blade hit stone and broke — wisps of shadows puffed like rain clouds.

Niko glared, his mouth agape. From her elbow to her wrist, her skin had turned to a greenish stone. "Nephrite," he spat. His face fell into a disgusted sneer as he realized something else. "You're a shapeshifter!"

"Shapeshifter?" Devon backed away, her arm tingled, turning normal again. It didn't matter what he was raving about . . . she needed to run . . . she needed a distraction. "What do you want?"

"I want the Crown of Guilledon!" Niko held out his hand. "Give it to me."

"No." None of this made sense. Her headband was just a headband — not a crown, but once she handed it over, there would be no reason to let her live.

"You must be strong to overcome the curse," Niko sneered, jealously. "Which means I can't let you live —"

"Tell me what's going on!" Devon yelled. Her mind raced with all the odd things that had been happening in Hasty: The creepy shadows in the institute, the bizarre man and inexplicable way he disappeared.... Not to mention, her arm had just turned into stone. And, all the while she wanted answers, her mind screamed at her to run.

"I suppose you have a right to know." Niko leaned casually against a tree, close enough that he was within reach. "Death can wait a few more minutes ... but it will come tonight."

Devon shifted her weight, leaning away. Any second ... she would run —

"Some time ago you stumbled across a ... colleague ... of mine. At least, that's what you can call him, for we are of the same kind. In his travels, he stopped at a tavern and in ignorance, boasted that a human girl wore the *Crown of Guilledon*. Of course, that was unbelievable," he sneered. "A human girl with the legendary Crown of Guilledon. Preposterous. But the traveler assured everyone it was true, and that was his most grievous mistake. For that very night, a true supporter of the Shadow Reign overheard and slit his throat."

"What does any of this have to do with me?" She

took another step back, using her voice to cover the crumpling leaves.

"You're the human girl. You wear the Crown of Guilledon. Except, you aren't human, are you? Perhaps, if you were a shadow walker, I might spare you." His lip snarled over his teeth. "But you're a *shapeshifter* — the most traitorous falsifier one can be. I'll give you the chance to run. Since that's obviously what you want." He grinned wickedly at his game. "Like I didn't notice . . . ha . . . go on now. . . . Hurry." Niko's flesh rotted against the tree, fading away until only a shadow remained. A deadly blade glinted in the moonlight — his favorite way to kill.

The forest flew past as Devon pounded against the dirt. Stones, leaves, and pinecones prickled the bottom of her bare feet, but she didn't slow. Instead she ran faster — searching for the path back to the festival.

"Devon," Niko's voice carried through the trees. "You're running the wrong way."

Devon skidded to a stop. *He's right,* she decided, and she bolted the other way, just as Niko sliced off a thick branch and launched it like a javelin. It cut through the forest, whistling. Devon felt the dispersion of air as the branch ripped through the trees. She slipped to the side, and it whooshed past, catching her stomach. A sharp pain shot through her.

The Festival of Gondolas

Devon stumbled, clutching the warm blood seeping through her shirt. A chilly wind was her only warning before she was shoved hard from behind, and rammed face first into the grassy lawn at the edge of the festival. In the distance, crowds of people cheered and celebrated around the colossal balloons. She had made it — but no one would hear her scream.

"You can't outrun me, Skin Thief," Niko spat.

Devon sucked in air — trying to get the wind back that was knocked from her lungs.

Niko yanked her up.

"Devon?" a soft voice called.

Niko disappeared, leaving Devon alone on the edge of the field. She didn't have to see the blonde hair and slight frame to know who the voice belonged to. She'd know it anywhere. Devon forced a steady breath, trying to stay calm, but she wanted to scream — scream for Leni to run.

"Are you okay?" Leni's voice wavered.

"Yeah," Devon turned slightly, hiding her bloody shirt. Leni had never seen her like this — terrified and panting, with scraped knees and blood soaking through her clothes. "J-just get back to the festival. I'm f-fine."

A wicked smile appeared behind Leni.

"LENI!"

Devon reached out — a horn impaled Leni from the shadow behind her (all the way through her stomach). Leni's eyes widened. Her mouth fell open. And she slumped against the horn — surprise petrified across her face.

The horn vanished, and Leni fell to the ground.

"NO!" Devon grabbed Leni by the shoulders, holding her upright. "No. Please be okay. *Please.*"

The sky darkened above them. Magnificent black wings beat against the wind, blocking out the moon. Niko reappeared from the shadows, but before he could flee, a blinding, bronze light flashed and struck Niko through the chest, like lightning.

"AAAGHHH!"

The shadow around Niko exploded, leaving him sprawled across the grass, unconscious. Soft, padded feet raced toward them, and a massively muscled cougar leaped between Devon and Niko, growling, low and guttural.

Devon pulled Leni close. Tears ran down her face. "Please get up."

The bronze light landed beside Devon. "Run," said a voice, from inside the light.

Devon squeezed Leni tightly. "I can't leave her —"

Niko moaned and stirred . . . and the cougar let out a rampant chorus of vicious growls.

The silhouette of a man formed within the bronze luminescence. He waved his staff and a soft glow illuminated from Leni. The wound in her stomach began to heal. "You can do nothing more," said the light. "The magic will heal her." The silhouette pointed at Niko. "He's only after you. If you leave, he'll have no reason to harm your friend."

Devon nodded, open mouthed. *He was right.* Niko wanted to kill her, not Leni. Leni just got in the way. Still, she couldn't leave just her. "I can't —"

"If you stay, you're condemning your friend to die. Is that what you want?" The light spoke harshly. "The shadow wants you. Run. Hurry. He's waking up. . . . We'll hold him off."

"B-but —"

The cougar whipped around — spitting and snarling and snapping at Devon to run.

Devon stumbled up — Niko burst into an angry cloud of shadows. The bronze light and the cougar attacked at once. With one last look at the life returning to Leni, Devon ran, and she didn't stop until she was back among the crowds of people.

CHAPTER FOUR
Unexpected Visitors Are Rarely Welcome

It was much easier finding Duke than Devon had expected. He hung by the mini-bus, already tired of the festival — or perhaps, he had anticipated being needed, like an over-protective parent and lingered nearby just in case. The bus itself was a funny sight. Somehow, Duke wedged it in a space so small, he must have driven onto the sidewalk to do it.

"Everything all right there, Devon?" he frowned at her bare feet, then the dried blood stuck to her knees.

"Yeah," she managed, for his benefit. It wasn't like this was the first time she'd come back slathered in dirt and blood. He should be used to it by now. She'd gotten in enough fights that she didn't need to come up with excuses anymore.

"I see." He frowned deeper. "Are Vanessa and Claudia all right? He gazed longingly at the crowds of people, wanting to go see for himself.

"I'm sure they're having a blast."

"So everyone is all right?" The pitch in his voice rose anxiously.

"Yeah." Devon's face heated, and she blinked hard, eyes burning at the lie. *Leni had to be okay. She had to.*

Duke relaxed a little. "You look like you wanna go home."

"Yeah." Devon walked around the mini-bus and tugged on the handle. When it didn't open, she waited silently for him to unlock it.

"What about your shoes?" Duke walked around the bus and paused with his hand on the handle. "Do you want me to get them for you? I don't care who has them . . . ," he said sternly, showing he meant it.

Devon shook her head. Niko wasn't a neighborhood bully. *If only he knew . . .* but she couldn't begin to explain what happened to him or anyone else. Who would believe her if she started raving about shadows and magic crowns? No one. The people in Hasty would cast her out just like they had the old man. "I think I'll leave them where they are." She tugged the door handle again, letting it snap back loudly.

"You sure — ?" His eyes darted towards the crowd.

"Yes, Duke." The thought of him facing that killer made her hands shake. She didn't want him or anyone else near that monster. She had to get far away from Niko so no one else would be in danger. "I'm sure. I want to go home." She needed a moment to think — to plan. And to do that, she needed to get away from here.

Duke opened the door, and Devon stumbled in, sore and tired. She fastened her seatbelt — then locked the door — but it didn't make her feel any safer.

As they drove back to St. Frances, fiery balloons lit up the sky from her window. People celebrated, laughed, and delighted in the festivities. They were fools — oblivious to the terrible danger amongst them. But, somewhere in the midst of it all, a blinding bronze light and a fierce, wild cougar protected them. Hopefully, Leni was all right, and silently, Devon prayed.

Duke pulled into the long driveway and sped up the hill to St. Frances. With everyone at the festival, the Institute was bleak and lonely. Duke unlocked the door to the fancy foyer where Ms. Frances liked to welcome important guests. Now, all the lights were out — leaving the halls dark and cool.

Duke hovered in the doorway. "I can't stay," he said, eager to return to the other children.

"It's fine." She shrugged stiffly, but not because being left alone bothered her like Duke thought. The fear on Leni's face, as blood soaked through her shirt,

Unexpected Visitors Are Rarely Welcome

burned into Devon's head, and she shook it, trying to erase the vivid images. "It's getting late." Devon patted Duke's shoulder. "You should bring everyone back . . . quickly." There was no time to waste. Niko had been living in Hasty for months. He had been spying on her . . . he had been in the Institute!

"Right." Duke interrupted her thoughts. "I'll be back shortly." He stalked out, but just before the door shut, he stuck his head back inside. "Try to stay out of trouble," he added, and locked the door, leaving her in the dark foyer, alone.

Soon he would realize Leni was missing. *Would she be alive when he found her? Did leaving save her life? . . .* And how long would it be before Niko crept into the halls of the Institute? For now she might be safe, but not for long. . . . This was the first place Niko would come looking. Devon shivered and ran to her room, turning on every light along the way.

She swung open her dormitory and slammed the door shut, throwing her weight against it, as she bolted the lock. Chest heaving, Devon scanned the dark room, full of empty beds, lonely dressers, and dark shadows. . . .

Tiptoeing further into the room, Devon flipped on the light. When nothing happened, she scurried across the wood floor and turned the radio on low,

Unexpected Visitors Are Rarely Welcome

hoping the noise would help her relax — instead, she paced.

Would the police question her? . . . Would the glowing light heal Leni? . . . And who would believe her if she told stories about a murderous shadow and a man that could fly? Ms. Frances would lock her away in an insane asylum. "Ugh." That monster had come for her! . . . Leni wasn't supposed to get hurt!

Devon continued to pace . . . but the more she worried and wondered about the mysterious events of the evening, the fuzzier the memories became. Already the details were slipping away. *Why was I attacked? . . . What did Niko want? . . . Who was the shadow? . . .* Devon stopped pacing and pressed her fingers to her temple, grasping onto the memories. *What is wrong with me? . . . Is Leni alive? . . .* A fuzzy image of Leni bleeding flashed, and all the memories flooded back again. Leni was hurt.

Devon threw a lamp across the room, shattering it. She had always watched over Leni and all the weaker kids at the Institute. Not because she was particularly good or kind, but because she was the only one with enough guts to stand up to Ms. Frances and the bullies at the Institute. Now when Leni had needed her most, she was helpless.

Devon swiped the contents of her desk, splattering them across the room — but it wasn't enough. She kicked the metal trash can, again and again, until it crumpled. Breathing hard, she blinked at the mess. Soon Duke would return with the first round of kids.... She tilted her head toward the walls, listening for sounds within the institute.

Hearing nothing, she picked up the litter of things on the floor and tried to make sense of the night — repeating it over and over, so the memories wouldn't be swept away. All of this, somehow, could be explained. It had to be. Too many strange things were happening: A floating man, a kid that stuck to walls, a wild cougar in Hasty. Then the light. The unexplainable, brilliant light that struck Niko through the chest, stunning him. And why were the memories fading away?

Tap. Tap. Tap ... came a noise from outside, startling Devon from her thoughts. She held her breath —

Nothing happened.

Pulling her courage together, Devon tiptoed to the window. She reached for the glass ... and the noise came again.

Tap. Tap. Tap.

Yanking the heavy drapes aside, Devon stared at her reflection. Feeling childish, Devon dropped the drapes ... and headed back across the room. Catching her foot on something strewn across the carpet, she tripped, swore, and grabbed the blasted thing. It would feel good to throw it. She lifted it over her head . . . and stopped. Stunned, Devon held up her torn, black shoe. On the floor was the match. Someone, *something*, had brought her shoes back from the festival. Whatever it was had been in her room —

Slowly, Devon turned her head. The room was still empty. She treaded on her toes to the closet and paused in front of the door — not wanting to open it. She took a deep breath, gathered her nerves, and swung it open.

Nothing.

Devon checked under the beds . . . and behind the tables. Still, nothing.

TAP. TAP. TAP . . . came the noise from the window — urgent now.

Goosebumps shivered down her arm. *I'm not opening it,* she told herself. *I need to get out of here — go somewhere safe — somewhere Niko won't find me.* It was time to run. In three strides, she crossed the room, unbolted the door, wrenched it open, and nearly walked straight into the fiery redhead. It took every bit of strength to swallow her scream. Slamming the door, Devon fumbled with the bolt, hands shaking. Once it was locked, she backed away from the door.

"What do you want?" she called in a wavering voice.

The radio turned off behind her.

Devon's throat clamped shut, and she whipped around. In the middle of the room, stood the freckled redhead — perfectly still, like a doll.

"I told Kamau you wouldn't open the window." The girl smiled smugly and called over her shoulder, "That's right Kamau! I beat you inside! Some warlock you are."

"How did you get in here?" Devon's voice shook.

The redhead rolled her eyes and strode to the window, straight for the source of the tapping. It took half a second too long for Devon to realize what she was about to do. Devon dove for the fiery redhead, but instead of tackling the wispy girl, found herself flying backward. She crashed into her roommate's bunk with a horrible CRACK and toppled under the pieces. Dazed, Devon looked up as the room spun.

The redhead unlocked the window, and a large hawk soared in. Midair, it transformed into the stylish man. His flowing coat swished behind him, from the funnel of magic, and as it dissipated his eyes fell on the crumpled bed, tightening disapprovingly. "You always break something, Bree."

Bree shrugged, unapologetically.

Kamau pulled Devon up with an incredible amount of strength. Bewildered, she eyed him, as the room spun around her. "Here." He handed her a handkerchief. "I apologize for the way this evening —"

Thump. Thump. Thump — someone banged on the door.

"What the devil is going on in there?" Ms. Frances yapped in a raised voice. She jiggled the handle. "What is all that racket? I hardly get through the front door before I feel the house quaking!"

There was a fumbling of keys ... Ms. Frances unlocked the room ... and she stomped inside, still in her frilly dress from the festival. "Why in tarnation is the bed broken? W-what happened to the room?" She stopped at the sight of the uninvited strangers and shook her finger at them. "There aren't to be any visitors inside the institution without my express permission!"

For a fleeting moment, Devon was caught between relief and horror at Ms. Frances's abrupt arrival, but the hope Ms. Frances might be of use, was short-lived. She rounded on Devon, livid, and eager to blame the whole mess on her. "YOU ARE THE MOST WICKED CHILD!"

Devon started for the door, but Kamau was quicker. He pulled out a twist of wood from the air. It grew at both ends, intertwining like thorny vines ... and transformed into a staff. A glowing sphere lit the room with brilliant, bronze sparkles.

Unexpected Visitors Are Rarely Welcome

"Everything is fine, Augustine," Kamau said smoothly.

A dazed expression spread across Ms. Frances's face. "Everything is fine," she repeated in a stupor.

"Perhaps you should go to bed." Kamau's staff radiated.

Ms. Frances yawned . . . and passed Devon at the door. "Perhaps I should go to bed."

"Ms. Frances?" Devon grabbed her, in disbelief. "What's happening to you?"

"Enough dear, these magiks mean you no harm."

Dear? . . . Magiks? . . . What was she talking about! "Ms. Frances!" Devon shook her. "Leni might be dead! . . . Do you understand me?"

Ms. Frances jerked free, with unnatural strength, and swept from the room without another word. The door swooshed shut behind her, magically, and Devon faced the intruders.

"Your friend is not dead," Kamau said calmly.

"How do you know? . . . Why should I believe anything you say?"

"Because I healed her," Kamau said matter-of-factly. Kamau raised his staff. He glowed a brilliant bronze, becoming the light, and the light deepened, sparkling around the room.

"You," exclaimed Devon, "you saved me!" She whirled to Bree. "That means you're the —"

Bree roared — a terrifying, blood-curdling roar. The sound echoed around the room, bouncing off the dressers and wardrobes and faded to a rumbling growl. "Cougar," Bree finished, pleased with herself.

The light faded and Kamau reshaped. "Yes. That was us. Under my spell, your friend's wound recovered. But unfortunately, we were not able to capture the shadow walker."

"Where is Leni?" Devon kept close by the door. The first sign of trickery and she'd bolt.

"I transported her to our hospital. The Magik Emergency Rescue was able to take over from there." A glowing orb discharged from the tip of Kamau's staff and floated to the middle of the room. Inside, a vision of Leni sleeping peacefully showed strange doctors caring for her: one, barely two feet tall with pointed ears, took readings of her vitals . . . another, with glittery translucent wings, made sure she was comfortable.

Devon sagged against the wall, relieved. "Thank you —"

"She'll be back in the morning," Kamau said kindly. "She won't remember a thing — only a blissful night at the festival — as will everyone else. Now . . . there is an important matter we must discuss," Kamau pressed, urgently.

"I guess if you wanted to kill me, you would have done it already." Devon stepped away from the door.

Kamau shrugged. "Bree and I aren't killers."

Bree stuck her hands on her hips. "Of course not! . . . You could have made this a lot easier by not running . . . or trying to tackle me."

Kamau waved his staff gently. "Bree . . . you should have patience."

"I have patience," insisted Bree, "Just not an endless amount."

Devon crossed the room and picked up the lamp. Some of the things she might not be able to repair, and she was sorry for that. She straightened the trashcan and examined the dent — it was probably permanent. "Tell me what's going on while I get my things. . . . Then I'll be going."

"Going?" asked Kamau.

"It's not safe here anymore," Devon said blankly. Leaving St. Frances didn't upset her. Actually, it was the opposite. She felt relief — suddenly hopeful of all the world could offer. Tonight had been proof of how short life could be. And while she didn't have the slightest idea where she'd go — she would figure out on the way.

"Perhaps I can be of assistance." Kamau waved his staff. Rubble soared from the floor, rebuilding itself into a sturdy bunk. Blankets and sheets tucked themselves in neatly. The contents of the desk soared back to their original places, the shattered pieces of lamp glued back together, and the trashcan popped back into its smooth, rounded shape. A duster polished the room — quick as a wink — and disappeared with a tiny pop.

"Um . . . thanks." Devon gaped. There wasn't a single thing out of place, nor a speck of dust in sight. "That was definitely faster."

Bree snorted, and Kamau shot her a look. "What? I thought she was making a joke."

"It's the least I can do," Kamau said to Devon. "And if I may be so bold . . . I believe you leaving is wise. I was going to suggest it myself." Kamau's staff shrank back to a wand. He placed it in the air. It flickered and disappeared. "My name is Kamau. I am a warlock of Gulu. This is Bree, a shapeshifter of Gulladuff. As you've seen, we're not human. We are magiks."

"You're a wizard?" Devon asked, incredulous.

"He's a warlock," Bree grumbled with a scowl. "Wizards that pass the *Impossible Examination of Wizard Cunning and Talent* become warlocks. Didn't you see his staff? Kamau hasn't been a wizard for seventy-two years."

"Ninety-seven." Kamau cleared his throat humbly.

Devon leaned around Kamau. "Where is your cloak?"

Kamau chuckled and plucked his wand from the air again. Gently, he flicked the wand, and his high-collared coat transformed into a sweeping cloak of the same black fabric with delicately stitched, gold swirls. "Better?"

Devon blushed. "It was fine before —" she mumbled, embarrassed. "It's just, I thought wizards . . . I mean warlocks . . . wore cloaks."

"Of course we do — when we want — but perhaps we should get to the matter at hand. Like I mentioned, there is something we must discuss." Kamau cleared his throat, putting the wand back again. "The shadow walker that attacked you is part of the Shadow Reign. He would have murdered you, your friend, and anyone that stood in his way." His grave look met Devon's, impressing the danger of what transpired.

"What is the Shadow Reign?" Devon asked, stiffening.

"The Shadow Reign is led by a council of shadow walkers. They work against our government for control of our magical world. They don't think the way the government runs is fair, and while that may be true, an overthrow would not be better." Kamau's gaze pierced, grimly. "The Shadow Reign wants to start over with shadow walkers as the leaders of our magical world."

"And what does that have to do with me?"

Kamau slowly gazed up at the top of Devon's head. "One of our spies informed us that Niko Throntropt, a Shadow Reign assassin, was tracking a *human girl* wearing the Crown of Guilledon."

Bree scoffed. "Of course, it was hard to believe . . . a *human* with the Crown of Guilledon."

Devon shuddered at the thought of an *assassin* tracking her. "I thought it was just a headband."

Kamau shot a curious look at Bree and then he pointed to the side of Devon's head. "Have you noticed —"

"That the blood stopped," Bree cut in. "Obviously . . . or I'd have something to say about you explaining this to an ordinary kid."

"I'm not a kid," Devon said.

Bree scoffed again. "Ordinary was the offense."

Ignoring Bree's taunt, Devon touched the dried blood. She hadn't the slightest idea how she was healing so fast. The pain had already faded . . . but human or not, they were underestimating her. "What does this crown do?"

"The Crown of Guilledon allows any magical creature to borrow the magical abilities of another at his or her whim," said Kamau. "It was designed for changers. A shapeshifter for instance could turn into a shadow, like a shadow walker. There are limitations of course, but it is one of the most powerful . . . and dangerous . . . magical objects ever created. It's been lost for centuries. I'm not sure how you got it, or what exactly the Shadow Reign planned to do with it, as it only gives power to the one who wears it . . . and that is assuming the curse placed on it could be overcome, which may not even be possible."

"It's possible," Devon said numbly. The room fell silent, and Devon's heart pounded in her chest. "I've done it." Kamau's eyes widened, and Bree took in a sharp breath. The uneasiness in their expressions didn't make Devon feel better. "That's not all. . . ." Bree and Kamau exchanged apprehensive looks. "Niko said the Shadow Reign is going to use the crown to invade a place called The-si-a."

"Thysia," Kamau corrected.

"Are you certain that's what Niko said?" demanded Bree.

"Yes . . . why?"

"It's the last, entirely fortified city for magiks in the world." Kamau's expression turned hard. "All types of magiks live together in peace — mostly." He stared down at the crown, no longer captivated by it. "We can't let them get it —"

Feeling like she was missing something, Devon asked, "What exactly is a magik?"

"A magik is an anthropomorphic being that possesses magical abilities," Kamau explained half-heartedly, distracted by the dreadful news Devon delivered.

"He means . . . it's a human-like being that possesses magic," Bree explained simply, also crestfallen from Niko's terrible plans. "And Thysia is the last place in the world where every species of magik is welcome and lives together peacefully.

"Exactly." Kamau's eyes misted, and he gazed up at the ceiling, deep in thought. "Bree is a shapeshifter, and I am a warlock, but we're both magiks. And we both have a home in Thysia."

"What about Niko . . . ," asked Devon, "he turns into a ghost . . . so is he a magik?"

"He is a magik but not a ghost," Kamau clarified. "A ghost is the dead manifesting as the living. Niko Throntropt is very much alive. Therefore, he cannot be a ghost — he is a shadow walker, and a shadow walker, like a shapeshifter, takes on the forms of others — both animate and inanimate."

"So, if shapeshifters and shadow walkers both . . . morph . . . or shift," Devon concluded, "what's the difference?"

Still troubled, Kamau could only offer a half-hearted response. "An intelligent question. You've deduced that shapeshifters and shadow walkers are spectacularly alike — you have an intelligent mind."

Bree snorted.

"Ahem." Kamau carried on. "Thousands of years ago there was only one type of metamorphosing magik, known as changers. But as war between empires endured, further dividing the nations and their cultures, changers evolved, eventually leading to the division of them entirely, into shapeshifters and shadow walkers."

Pleased by the complement, Devon asked, "So, if they were once the same thing, how are they different now?"

"Unlike a shapeshifter, a shadow walker cannot take the full embodiment of another object or creature," explained Kamau. "It can only take a partial form, *and* it can only take on the essence of it. Half a sword, the roar of a lion, the talons of an eagle, the belly of a bear. But not the entire being of any of those things. A shadow walker will always remain a shadow of the form it takes. It is both a limiting and immeasurable power. Immeasurable because a shadow walker maintains a constant flow between a tangible and intangible manifestation. A shadow walker is exceptionally difficult to defeat while in its full shadow form. Almost impossible really."

"And shapeshifters?" pressed Devon.

"While shadow walkers are light and fluid — shapeshifters are incredibly dense," said Bree. "It allows us to take the full embodiment of anything we wish, within reason. An entire bear. A working lamp. A tiny spider. A wild cougar." Bree smirked, slightly. "As long as you're strong enough, you can become whatever you wish."

"So with the crown's magic, I could be both?" Devon concluded.

Kamau looked at her doubtfully. "In theory . . . but it would take an exceptionally talented changer —"

Devon opened her mouth, but nothing came out. Her world suddenly felt so small. "Niko said the crown could help the Shadow Reign get past a wall. How will that help invade Thysia?"

"That is what troubles me now. I don't know. The full potential of that crown is untested. But the wall that guards Thysia is its strongest defense."

"Well, what are we going to do?"

"Ha," squawked Bree. "She thinks she is a part of this. She thinks she can stop the Shadow Reign."

"I'm afraid she is as much a part of this as us. The question now . . . is what sort of magik are you?" Kamau frowned, deliberating. "It's certain you aren't a human."

Devon ran her fingers over the healed cuts. According to Niko, she was a shapeshifter. That would explain how her arm morphed — how she sensed the clock Vanessa had hurled at her head — and how she dodged the branch Niko launched at her — mostly. Jolted, Devon checked her stomach. The skin had already scabbed over. *How was this possible?* "Niko called me a Skin Thief."

A feral growl escaped Bree, and she began to transform — human to cougar. Hair sprouted from her face, her eyes turned yellow, and fangs grew from her gums. "Dirty slang for a shapeshifter," she snarled.

"Calm." The word radiated from Kamau, expounding across the room.

Bree turned back to normal, but by her expression, she was on the verge of rage.

"So, Niko believes you to be a shapeshifter," surmised Kamau. "That explains why he tried to kill you, instead of just taking the crown."

"I guess," Devon grumbled. How else could she explain the strange things happening to her?

"But," Kamau interjected, "we cannot go off his word alone. A changer isn't confirmed until his or her first transformation is witnessed by another magik. Niko, an exiled murderer, who isn't here to attest to what he witnessed, doesn't count."

"This can be easily solved," quipped Bree. "Try shifting now."

Stumped, Devon stared back, speechless. Did Bree really expect her to just morph into something without ever having learned how?

Bree picked up a large book. "Turn into this."

"Perhaps something simpler," Kamau suggested.

Bree huffed and dropped the book. "All right. Turn into whatever you want."

Devon closed her eyes and tried to think of something to turn into, but all she could think of was Bree and Kamau watching her —

"Why are you closing your eyes?" Bree's voice cracked. "You're not focusing."

"I am." Devon's eyes popped open. "Nothing is happening."

"No. You're not." Bree scooped up the book and tossed it high enough that it nearly touched the ceiling. In the second it took for it to stop ascending, Bree turned into an exact copy of the book. Right as it fell, picking up speed, Bree turned back again . . . and caught it.

"In moments of danger, when our senses are heightened, changers have the ability to sense their surroundings. We *feel* the proximities and densities of everything around us. . . . When I take the shape of another object. I *feel* it. I become it. I know it as if it were a part of me. To do that . . . you have to focus."

Kamau looked on Devon kindly. "It will come, in time. . . . Whatever you are, the Shadow Reign knows you have the Crown of Guilledon, and *any creature*, in possession of it, is in danger."

Devon reached for the thin band of gold. The crown, which she had mistaken for a headband, had nearly cost her life . . . and Leni's too. "We should get rid of it."

"Wait! Bree grabbed her hand, stopping her. "It's too late. Niko won't stop until he has it. And even if we get rid of it, he'll still come after you."

"Bree is right." Kamau's face turned sullen. "You're the one they know has it. They'll send an army of shadow walkers after you. You should leave Hasty — get as far away from here as possible — but you have to take the crown with you. Getting rid of it, won't stop the shadow walker from coming for you first, and if he finds you without it, he'll kill you out of spite."

"But what if Niko gets it? . . . It's safer with you."

"The magic from that crown is too tempting for a warlock. And much too dangerous."

"And I'm not touching it," Bree put her hands on her hips. "I don't want my mind messed with, thanks."

"What do you mean by that?"

"It's cursed duh — it erases memories!" Bree exclaimed, and Kamau shot her a warning look.

Devon tromped over to her desk. "Looks like I don't have much choice." She yanked open the drawer. Her mind was made up about leaving anyways. *She didn't belong here.* She pulled out her knapsack — torn from when Michael had once tried to drag her to Ms. Frances's office. It felt like a lifetime ago.

Kamau's eyes fell on her shabby bag, but he was polite enough not to remark on it. "May I ask," he said kindly, "where you plan to go?"

"The closest town is Fetching . . . from there . . . I'll see where it takes me." Devon gnawed her lip. She would never be able to walk through Hasty again without looking over her shoulder.

"If I may . . . I have a friend that may be able to help," Kamau offered. "He has a deeper knowledge of historic, magical artifacts than myself . . . and connections that I don't."

Devon stopped in front of her dresser. This was what he had wanted the whole time — for her to take the crown to someone who knew more about it. . . . She eyed herself in the mirror while she considered what to do. It was a better plan than wandering around Fetching. Maybe this friend would be able to answer some of her own questions. "Where do I find him?"

"New York City," Kamau said with relief. "Find the Blue Moon and ask to speak to Sir Isaac Newton. He'll know what to do."

"Go to New York . . . find the Blue Moon . . . and ask for Isaac Newton." Devon's head emerged in the mirror. "Huh?"

"Tell him I sent you," instructed Kamau.

Devon couldn't hide the incredulity in her voice. *"Find Isaac Newton and tell him you sent me?"* A laugh escaped. "Is that a joke? I don't feel like jokes."

"I never joke," Kamau said seriously.

"You're telling me," Bree grumbled.

"You know Sir Isaac Newton has been dead for . . . what . . . a few hundred years?"

Kamau brushed it aside. "We should hurry. The shadow walker won't be far behind."

Devon strode across the room and snatched her torn shoe from the floor. "Unless you brought this back, he's already been here."

Bree hissed and went to the window. "He must have hidden when we arrived."

Kamau hurried into the hall. A moment later, he came back with a blank, serious expression. "He'll have gone for help." He turned gravely to Devon.

"Every minute you stay you're in danger. He'll kill you and everyone you care about." Not wasting another minute, Bree began to morph. Her face shifted, elongating until it was hound-like. She sniffed the air and followed the scent to the dresser.

"What are you doing?"

Bree yanked open Devon's drawers. "Picking up your scent." Leaving Devon's roommates' belongings untouched — Bree emptied the contents onto the floor.

"Thanks," Devon grouched and scooped up her things.

"Do you have a pen and parchment?" Kamau asked.

"No time, Kamau," said Bree testily.

"Never mind then." Kamau reached into the air and plucked his wand from it. "As you were." It grew instantly. With a gentle wave of his staff, a pen, parchment, and envelope appeared. "Perhaps a desk?" Kamau's eyes fell on Devon's rather cramped desk.

"Kamau! There is no time for papers, and pens, and desks!" Bree eyes bulged frantically. But it didn't matter. Kamau conjured his own escritoire, right in the middle of the room, and seated himself neatly into an elegant chair.

"Ugh!" Exasperated, Bree threw up her hands and continued tossing things in a pile for Devon to pack. "Here." She flung a pair of jeans and a jacket at Devon.

Devon held them up. "What's this for?"

Bree stuck her nose in the air. "You look like you came out of a horror movie —"

Devon gazed down at her ruined dress, dirt-stained knees, and blistered feet. There were bloodstains everywhere. "I guess you're right." She grabbed a bundle of clothes, strode behind the closet door, and changed hastily, while Bree finished packing. When she came out, Kamau stood up and sealed the letter with a tap of his staff. The escritoire disappeared. "Someone is coming."

Bree's head snapped up. "Who?"

"I believe it is . . . , " Kamau tilted his head, concentrating on a distant sound, "the cook."

"We're done." Devon grabbed the last of her things and stuffed them in her bag. "There's an oak tree outside my window. We can scale the ledge and climb down."

"I'll provide the distraction." Kamau swept from the room.

Bree opened the window. Instead of scaling the ledge, she leapt on the sill like a cat. Grinning cockily, she twisted and dove, falling backwards into the night. Flipping once, she landed gracefully on the ground.

"Show off," Devon murmured. Anything she did would look clumsy after that. Feeling foolish, she stepped up onto the ledge and as gracefully as she could, scaled the wall.

Bree snickered from below. "You look ridiculous."

"How old are you again? " Devon shot back, as she climbed onto the tree. "Eight? Nine?"

"Two-hundred and seven," Bree puffed out her chest.

Devon whipped around. With her eyes on Bree (instead of where she was climbing) she slipped, lost her footing, and fell the last couple feet — scraping her hands and snagging her jacket. Finally, she landed with a thud.

"Ugh," exclaimed Bree. "Can you be any louder?"

Devon swallowed a groan . . . and pressed her hand over the tear in her jacket. Luckily, the scrapes weren't deep. "I'm fine thanks."

"Maybe you *are* human," Bree teased.

A hawk swooped out of the Institute . . . and transformed above the grand staircase. Kamau landed mid-stride . . . and hurried over to them. "Look behind you," he said briskly.

Shadows floated across the sky, clouding it in darkness.

Bree clenched her fists. "They're here."

Kamau faced the coming onslaught — his cloak blowing in the wind. Sparkles of light twirled around him in a cyclone of magic. Bree moved beside him —

fearlessly facing the coming danger. "This is where we say goodbye," Kamau said, with his back to Devon.

Suddenly, Devon was afraid for them. *They didn't need to stay and fight alone.* By the looks of it, they were vastly outnumbered. "You can't stay. We can go to New York together."

Kamau turned and faced her, while Bree kept her eyes locked on the coming shadows. "Bree and I must stay. We'll make sure the shadow walkers don't attack the humans. It will buy you time. Find the Blue Moon and ask for *Sir Isaac Newton*. He'll be your guide and your friend. Don't tell anyone else who you are! There will be spies, even if you don't recognize them."

Devon couldn't help wondering if this was the last time she would ever see them. "I can't leave you."

Kamau turned back to Bree. "You know what to do."

Bree faced Devon calmly, despite the fast-approaching danger. A fierce determination set in her face and she begin to shapeshift. She grew taller and sturdier. Her red hair darkened to a deep brown, like the bark of a tree. Her eyes turned ebony. Her prim clothes turned into a ripped jacket and jeans. Fresh blood trickled down her knee, where Devon fell down the tree.

Devon stared at a perfect reflection of herself. It was amazing and terrifying. She leaned in closer and studied the way her eyes glinted darkly, her cheeks hardened, and a firm blush spread across her face — she was fearless. . . . *Is that how I look before a fight*, she wondered.

"Don't worry, you won't rob any banks," smirked Devon-Bree. She tied back the long hair from her face.

"We're out of time." Kamau raised his staff. Brilliant bronze light burst into the surrounding darkness, lighting up the hills. "They're here!"

The shadows amplified in fury. They raged like a storm, covering the grounds in darkness. Just another minute . . . and the attack would be upon them. Encased in blinding light, Kamau touched Devon's forehead with the tip of his staff. Her skin sparkled, and the world swirled. Dizziness swept over her as the ground beneath disappeared, and the Victorian-styled mansion collapsed. Midnight blue skies replaced the black one, dozens of streetlights popped up from the asphalt, and buildings, tall as mountains, were drawn into the night.

The world closed around Kamau as he faded. Like looking through a portal, Devon could still make out the unfolding disaster behind him. The darkness had taken shape. Frightening faces, with gaping holes, came down on them. Bree turned to fight, and Devon screamed. Kamau lifted his staff from her forehead and spun around with a ferocity that expounded his brilliance beyond him. Bronze magic exploded, forcing the darkness back with cries of anguish. Then he was gone, and Devon fell over on a busy street. A hooded man rushed past, unaware that just a moment ago she hadn't been there at all.

Devon jumped up. "Excuse me," she rushed forward and grabbed the stranger's sleeve. "Where am I?"

"Manhattan, kid." Eying her curiously, he hurried on his way.

Unexpected Visitors Are Rarely Welcome

Manhattan? How am I already in New York? Devon stared up at the skyscraping buildings. *Unbelievable.*

"Hey! You're blocking the road, kid!" shouted a taxi driver.

BEEEEEEEP.

A bronze light glimmered in front of her. Devon reached out, with the tip of her finger, and touched the flickers. The shimmer took the shape of a velvety pouch that clinked, midair. Devon closed her fingers around it and hurried out of the road. The taxi whizzed past, still honking, and Devon examined the pouch. A black envelope appeared on top, from the remaining flickers (sealed with the stamp of a five-headed dragon). Devon flipped it over. In gold ink, it read: *Sir Isaac Newton.*

CHAPTER FIVE

The search for Sir Isaac Newton and the Blue Moon

Devon shivered, but not from the breeze. Though well lit, the wide span of paved sidewalk was mostly empty, except for late night stragglers. It appeared to be a city that was usually busy — but the dark windows and loneliness of the massive streets and buildings gave the feeling that the hour was quite late — perhaps even later than where she came. Hasty was nothing like this. Block after block stretched as far as she could see, and the duplicate streets were disconcerting. Had she not been attacked by a murderous shadow, she might have been frightened of strolling alone through the big city, and no one would have blamed her, but instead, she took a shaky breath and wandered forward, through the unknown streets.

Upon finding a rather shabby café that met the criteria of being open, Devon slipped inside and waited for the sun to rise. The first few hours were quiet and restless. She worried about Kamau and Bree constantly. What if they needed help? What if they didn't make it? Devon forced the thoughts from her head. They were strong. They had to make it.

To pass the time, she washed up in the restroom, scrubbing the bloodstains from her knees and stomach as best she could, and then the dirt from her face. As she watched the blood dripping into the sink, her mind became fuzzy. She tried to remember how she got hurt. There were flashes of images: fighting, Bree's body turning into hers, Kamau's face, full of hope as he transported her here. *But where did the blood come from?*

Frustrated, Devon turned off the water and crept to the back corner of the café. She slept fitfully, crammed into a hard booth next to the cold window. A series of terrifying dreams overtook her, and she awoke, just as the sun peeked over the horizon. With a full day of possibilities ahead of her, she opened the leather pouch.

Glittering gems in ruby, sapphire, and citrine sparkled inside. Beneath those, sat a large stack of U.S. dollars, British pounds, Canadian dollars, and Euros. Jumbled at the bottom, a heavy lump of peculiar coins clinked together.

"I see you're awake," said a cross woman with a square jaw, wide shoulders, and dull brown hair. By her apron and notepad, Devon could tell she was the clerk, or possibly even the owner, as it didn't look like the dingy café could afford many employees. She eyed Devon from behind the counter — looking her up and down with speculative interest.

Devon's throat ached from the fitful sleep. Yawning, she brushed her hair out of her face. The back of her hand bumped against the gold band, and she wondered if the woman noticed the crown. It had always felt simple. Inconspicuous. But now, it felt awkward and heavy, like an ostentatious treasure. Devon patted her hair back over it.

The clerk frowned disapprovingly, making her jaw thicker than it already was. "This ain't a hotel, and you ain't allowed to sleep here. I shoulda woke you up and chased you out," she huffed, cross with her own charity, "but you looked like you needed some good sleep." Her expression turned hard, and then she threatened, "Don't let me catch you sleeping in here again. You don't want me calling social services —"

"I won't," Devon promised, cutting her off. "I mean, I won't sleep here again." She hoped to never set foot here again. With any luck, she'd find this Blue Moon, get Sir Isaac Newton to help her, and sleep peacefully in a warm bed by tonight. "Could I have some water . . . ?"

"Just water?" The woman clapped back. She wiped her hands on her apron and came over . . . then, stuck her hands on her hips. "Where are your parents?"

Devon grimaced. One thing that sucked about being an orphan, was other people always assumed you had parents. They assumed everyone had a mom and dad — forgetting a lot of people didn't. And while Devon knew they weren't trying to be rude, sometimes, she just didn't want to admit she didn't have any. Eventually, she got good at changing the subject. And spotting a delicious display of croissants and bagels, Devon straightened up. "Orange juice and an egg sandwich. . . . Please."

"And how do you plan to pay for it?" chided the woman, rudely.

Devon pulled several large bills from the velvet pouch. "With this."

The clerk's eyes bulged. Then her face fell into a grim line, and she shot Devon a frosty look. "Don't forget. No more sleeping here." She pulled out a pad and scribbled down the order. Then went back to the counter, poured a cup of coffee, and set it on the table with a pitcher of cream. "That will wake you up."

Devon sipped it and coughed as the bitter liquid seared her tongue. "That's disgusting."

The woman set a bowl of sugar in front of her. "It grows on you."

Devon scooped six large spoons of sugar in the mug, and took another sip, this time blowing on it first. "It's . . . better."

"Anything else?" She tapped her pen against her notebook.

"Do you have a map?" Devon asked, voice hitching. It was too much to hope the day would go by that smoothly. The clerk pointed her pen at a wired rack of folded maps and wordlessly headed back to the counter for the sandwich. "Thanks!" Devon called after her.

By the time Devon's third cup of coffee was cold, and she had finished her second sandwich (another thing Ms. Frances never let her do), the sun brimmed over the city, and the streets were alive with people.

Spread across the booth was the map of Manhattan and a thick copy of an old-fashioned phone book, listing the directory. Devon had searched every business in Manhattan and still hadn't found any place called Blue Moon. However, being that she had a knack for figuring things out, she was confident she would find it by lunchtime.

♛ ♛ ♛

Soon it was well past noon. Really it was much later than that, and Devon had scoured the map — marking it as she ambled through the city. Still, she had not found a street sign, building, nor anything called the Blue Moon . . . and the longer it took, the more anxious she became.

Strangely, there were moments when she had to focus on why she was in Manhattan in the first place — like the memory was fading, and she wandered around, lost, until she overcame it. More time slipped away as Devon roamed street after street. She asked dozens of shop owners, passersby, a street performer or two, and no one, not anyone, had any idea where to find the Blue Moon.

With the map crumpled in her hand, Devon turned down another street. The shops shortened, cramping together, sharing trees and lampposts with their neighbors. Stone cornices brought character to the arched windows, short stoops, and wooden doors. *Where am I?* Devon scanned over the map and sighed. She was lost.

A bell tinkled behind her, and a curious man, with too many pockets, bustled into the street —hidden behind a hefty box. Before Devon could get out of the way, he slammed right into her, knocking her into the street. Trinkets and whatnots spilled in every direction.

"AYE!" he bellowed. "Can't you watch where you're going?" Rushing about, he snatched up the baubles and tossed them as carelessly into the box, as they had fallen out of it.

"You bumped into me!" Devon rubbed the bruised spot on her backside. A strange, metal knob with an eyeball blinked up at her. "Eww." Devon kicked it away.

"Don't do that!" the sour man snapped. He plucked it off the ground and dropped it in the box.

Tired and sore, Devon picked herself up. "Have you seen a Blue Moon anywhere?" she groused, not really expecting someone rotten like him to know. But she asked anyway, out of a newly forming habit.

The man stopped picking up his baubles and raised an eyebrow over the brim of his box. "It's not a Blue Moon," he corrected. "It's *the* Blue Moon. There is only one shop. If you're going to ask for directions . . . start with asking for them properly." He spun around and resumed picking up his knickknacks.

Devon let the map fall to her side. "You know what I'm talking about?"

"A' course I do."

A gasp escaped, and her mouth popped open. "You're a magik then . . . ?"

The man's forehead furrowed, like she was quite daft. "A' course I am."

"It's just . . . I didn't expect to bump into one," Devon confessed.

"You should pay attention." He shook his box at her. "There's loads of us in the city."

Loads of magiks in Manhattan? Devon's eyes widened, and she leaned forward, suddenly. "Where is the Blue Moon?"

"An' why should I tell you?" the man snarled. "You nearly knocked me over and spilled my personal property in the street." He indicated to the remaining oddities, still scattered on the sidewalk. "You didn't help me pick them up, either."

"Sorry." Feeling a twinge of remorse, Devon

scooped up a plaque, with the name *P. Talon* engraved in gold . . . and handed it to him.

"P. Talon?"

"That's me." He snatched the plaque and tossed it hastily in his box. "Don't touch my stuff!"

"But you said —"

"Don't worry about what I said. It's none of your business, is it?" He scooped up the last of the fallen oddities and strode right off, bustling down the street.

Devon hurried after him —

P. Talon shot a glance behind him and sped up. "Don't follow me!" He weaved through the bustling streets . . . but Devon kept tight on his tail, her footsteps falling directly behind his. There was no way she was letting the one magik she'd met, out of her sight.

P. Talon stopped abruptly, right in the middle of the crosswalk, and Devon ran straight into the back of him. He scowled around the corner of his box.

"Just point me in the right direction and I'll be on my way."

"No," P. Talon growled.

"Please," Devon tried.

P. Talon scrunched his face, stubbornly. The traffic-light blinked, and the remaining pedestrians hurried off the road.

"I'll follow you all day," Devon vowed. "I have

nowhere else to be." The Blue Moon was her only lead to finding Sir Isaac Newton. Unless, Kamau miraculously showed up in the city and found her wandering around New York — which she wasn't counting on.

The crosswalk light turned red.

HONK.

A car drove around them. Then another followed, weaving through the line of traffic.

P. Talon threw his head back impatiently.

With his eyes averted, Devon slipped her hand into his box of oddities. Her fingers closed around something heavy — and she slipped her hand away, just as P. Talon glared down at her.

"I said I wasn't gonna help you. Now if you please, I have somewhere to be . . . even if you don't! You can take this as a lesson. I expect you need one on manners." Satisfied he made his point, P. Talon hurried the rest of the way across the street, with Devon on his heels — forcing the traffic to come to an immediate stop.

HOOOOONNNNK.

HONK. HONK. HONK.

HOOOONNNNNNNNNNNNNNNNK.

As they hurried off the street, the cars whizzed past, still blaring their horns.

P. Talon shuffled along the sidewalk, ignoring her.

"What about this . . . ?" Devon called after him. "I'll just keep it, should I?" She held up the heavy, metal device she had pinched from his box.

P. Talon's head shot up. "That's stealing!" He started back . . . and Devon held the bauble out into the street.

"All I want . . . is for you to tell me where the Blue Moon is."

P. Talon clenched his lips tightly, barely suppressing his anger. "That is a one-of-a-kind, electromagnetic module, designed specifically for a special mechanism I use in my lab."

"Then show me where the Blue Moon is," said Devon simply, "and you can have it back."

P. Talon threw his arms up wildly. Strangers shot him suspicious looks as they passed. "Fine! I'm heading past it on the way to the Ghost Tavern. Otherwise, I wouldn't bother." He turned on his heel. "Just make sure you keep up. . . . And don't break it!" He didn't say anything else, as he weaved through the blusterous city. And then, as abruptly as before, he stopped in front of an ordinary, brick building with a painted door.

"This is it." He jabbed a thumb at the door.

Devon inspected it, doubtfully. It didn't look like

a place for magiks. It didn't look like anything but a typical, brick shop, crammed in the city like every other building in Manhattan.

P. Talon took advantage of her distraction to snatch the device.

"Hey!" Devon grabbed for the apparatus — but he was too quick.

"I kept up my end. This is the place." P. Talon tucked the device safely away and hurried down the street, with hardly a glance back or kind word to spare.

"Jerk!" Devon called after him. She turned back to the building. Paint chipped around the edges of an old-fashioned door. In the center, a glittering, blue crescent sparkled in the sunlight. *A moon.* Her heart raced. *This is it. It has to be!* She took a deep, unsteady breath, hurried up the stoop, turned the handle, and stepped inside a dimly lit room full of cobwebs, that shrouded the ceiling like sheets.

Crammed directly in front of the door was a worn, wooden staircase that creaked as she climbed it. Beneath the dust, peeked intricate moldings and at the top of the staircase was the most unexpected thing: A brightly painted, indigo shop with shutters and windows and a perfectly cut lawn of grass. It was like she had stepped outside again. Only, the stairs behind her were proof that she hadn't. On the lawn, stood a lamppost, illuminating a petite sign that read . . .

Sugar and Cinnamon Bread Shoppe

Unable to resist the impossibly fantastic sight before her, Devon crossed the lawn. Displays of sugary tarts, golden croissants, custard Danishes, and fruit strudels filled the windows. Each dessert was so intricately decorated, they resembled tiny toys rather than sugary delights. The sweetest smells of warm, baked bread wafted through the walls, and the whole enticement made it quite difficult to tear herself away. But after a moment, Devon dragged herself from the window and headed for the other door, across the wide banister.

It did not own a charming sign, nor possess a tiny lawn. It was merely a door with an old-fashioned lock, and a narrow frame that stood a bit crooked (if you looked close enough or paid attention to those sorts of particulars). Painted in the center was a glittering blue moon.

This was what Kamau had sent her for. The mysteriousness of it made her nervous and fidgety. It would be better to get the whole business over with. Find Sir Isaac Newton and ask him what to do with the crown.

The door opened to yet another staircase, this one knobby and broken with random steps missing altogether. Faded pictures of magical things were painted along the ceiling — among them, glowing moons steered down the stairs and out of sight. *This was it.* Devon scampered down the haphazard steps. Edgy and tense, she threw open the door at the bottom....

Blinding sunlight flooded in. When her eyes adjusted, she stood facing the busy street — exactly where she started.

Miserable, Devon let the door shut and slouched against the wall. Had this all been a waste of time? She ran her fingers through her hair, worried and on edge. How was she supposed to find a place that wasn't on a map? ... Even the glowing moons above her had disappeared. They trickled down the ceiling, through a deep crevice in the wall, and out of sight.

Through a crevice, thought Devon. *They didn't disappear, they went through the rift in the wall....* Devon scooted closer and pressed her face against the jagged crack. Sure enough, faint blue moons continued along the inside. She wasn't lost — yet. She ran her fingers over the wall for a way through, to the other side. There had to be a latch or lever somewhere —

After searching the entire length of the wall, Devon

stood back to think. If there was not a hidden button that opened the crevice, then how did she get to the other side? Either there was another entrance, or she had to go straight through. The only problem was the crack was much too thin. Not even a child could do it. . . .

Devon clapped her hand to her forehead. That was it! The best way to keep humans out was to make sure only *magiks* could get in. If she shapeshifted, she could get through easily.

Devon pressed against the crack. Nothing happened. "Focus," she muttered to herself, and leaned into the rough edges.

Still, nothing happened. Devon pressed harder, so the crevice pricked against her skin, but it didn't widen, and Devon remained herself, exactly as she was. "Ugh. Stupid wall!" She could imagine Bree taunting her now. *Maybe you are human*, Bree had said. Bree would have shapeshifted inside, turned into some tiny thing, like a bee, and buzzed right through. Kamau would have used his magic staff. Even Niko could have turned into a shadow and slipped past the crevice.

Devon pondered, pacing in front of the cave. Maybe she was thinking about this all wrong. If she couldn't focus enough to take on the shape of a single thing, maybe she could focus enough to become nothing.

Hadn't Kamau said the crown allowed the wearer to use the magic of both changers? Sure, it was a long shot. But Bree's lesson on shapeshifting hadn't helped at all. What if turning into a shadow was easier? All she had to do was overcome the curse, which she already had, and if it didn't work, then at least she tried. Besides, no one was around to see how stupid she looked, pushing her face against a crack in the wall if nothing happened.

Be a shadow. Be a stinking shadow. With her face pressed against the rock, she imagined floating through it. But all she could see was the shadow that hunted her. It hid in dark corners — it flew across the night sky — it brought death. She could see it, like it was here.

By the tiniest bit, the crevice widened. A bit more. Then it happened. The strangest sensation as she squeezed inside the crevice. The weight of her body disappeared, and she floated, grazing the inside of the fissure. Then she stumbled through the other side, knees wobbling. It took half a minute before she returned to her old self.

"Wow!" said Devon shakily. *"That was amazing!"*

Devon stared back at the tiny crevice. She had done it — she controlled the Crown of Guilledon! *Imagine the possibilities.* Any magik that could do that was extremely powerful. With one last glance at the crevice, Devon turned around, ready to find Sir Isaac Newton —

A trim, grassy lawn with a painted sign and a funny lamppost, illuminated the path to a purple shop with aged shutters, steep dormers, a smoking chimney, and arched windows caked with dust. Finally, she'd found it.

Blue Moon

The novelty shoppe for every magical occasion

Notice: Location likely to change at any time.

Apologies if you are still inside.

Transportation will not be provided. Shop at your own risk.

Devon hurried across the lawn, her palms sweating, and pushed inside.

A chime jingled ... and echoed through an extraordinary store, overflowing with all sorts of goods and wares. It was unlike any novelty shop she had ever seen. Not that she had seen many, never having money to buy anything anyway. Captivated, Devon stepped quietly through an aisle of peculiarities.

Instead of t-shirts, postcards, and snow globes, there were rickety wooden shelves laden with the strangest-looking mechanics. Old compasses, sundials, binoculars with extra knobs, and all sorts of peculiar inventions filled the shelves, toppling on top of one another. Some continuously moved — spinning, chirping, and burping without any encouragement. While rust coated the others . . . many of which, were clearly broken.

Swords and shields flourished the walls like artwork. Daggers dangled from cords above her head. Jars of crushed herbs, spices, roots, and exotic plants filled three whole aisles. One wall was devoted to books. Devon picked up a leather one and blew a thick layer of dust into the air. Grease caked the side of the bind, sticking the pages together.

"Why are you touchin' that like it's already yours?"

Devon's dropped the book. "Huh?"

"I ain't said you could buy it yet, did I?" A short, squat woman with a wrinkled face and cat eye spectacles bustled over, scooped up the book, and gave Devon's hand a stinging slap.

"Ouch," screeched Devon, taken aback by the old woman's abruptness. "I thought it was for sale —"

"It is for sale. Can't ye see straight? But it ain't yer book, is it? And I ain't said I would sells it to you, did I?"

"Um no," Devon gawked . . . and then said with the tiniest bit of sarcasm, "but isn't the point of a store to sell the things in it?"

The old woman glowered, not liking her cheekiness

at all. "What you want here, missy? It's gettin late and I was jest about to close up. Now I'll be late fer supper."

Devon blinked. *Why am I here? . . .* She scrunched her forehead, concentrating. *Why do I keep forgetting things?* Frustrated, she pushed back the fuzzy cloud blurring her thoughts and focused on the strangely dressed woman glaring at her. Odd trinkets, vials, and even a book were strapped to her waist beneath a high-collared cape. "Is this the Blue Moon?"

"Can't you read none, girlie?" The woman tapped on the wall with her knobby fingers. Half-hidden behind a net of dead snakes, peeked the corner of a sign. "It says right there, Blue Moon Novelty Shoppe."

"If it's so obvious," Devon seethed, "then why is this place so hard to find?"

"What do you expect, miss smarty pants? For some-on' to jest post one of them ads in the paper? Maybe I should put us on one of them maps on that internat?" The woman wobbled off, leaving her behind. One at a time, she shut the lids of dozens of jars and canisters, all filled with questionable ingredients. "Next thing yer gonna tell me is that my shop should stay in one place, too."

"Listen," Devon tried again. "We started out on the wrong foot. I'm looking for someone. His name is . . .

," she shifted her feet, feeling a bit ridiculous. "Sir Isaac Newton."

The woman gave Devon a sharp look . . . before ducking behind a shelf. "I ain't neva heard of em."

"Are you sure?" Devon pressed. "He's famous — you know, wrote the Laws of Motion — English guy — probably wears a white wig."

The woman reappeared from behind the shelf. "What did you say yer name was, missy?"

"It's Devon."

"Devon what?" The woman glowered, suspiciously.

"Devon Connor."

"I ain't never heard of you neither." She leaned in close, squinting at Devon with one eye.

"That's because I'm not famous."

"Don't you get all smarty-pants with me. I ain't lookin my age fer nothing." She poked Devon with her cane. "Now get on. I need to lock up so I can eat my dinner befer it's cold as snow."

Devon caught the cane as the woman poked her again. "I've been wandering all over Manhattan searching for this Blue Moon shop, and the only thing I find is a stupid crescent painted on some door through a crack in the wall." Devon shoved the cane away and it clacked against a shelf. "Now, if you know something, tell me!"

The woman clamped her mouth shut stubbornly.

"Ugh." Devon sighed loudly. "What a waste of time, Kamau!" She swiveled for the door. Kamau and Bree should have come with her. At least then, she would know they were safe.

"What did ye say?"

Devon swung back around. "I said this was a waste of time! I spent all day looking for this stupid place! And came all this way for nothing!" Devon flared, angry heat burning her face. This woman was off her rocker.

"No. no. The name, missy."

"What name?" Devon bit back.

"Well, they sure do make 'em bright these days, don' they? . . . The name . . . you said a name."

"Kamau?" Devon clapped her hand to her forehead. *Of course.* Kamau had told her to mention his name. How could she have forgotten?

"Yes. . . ." The woman's eyes narrowed. "You know him, do you?"

"Yes! . . . I do!"

The woman twisted her lips into thin lines. "Well, I still don' know no Sir Isaac Whatsit."

Devon's shoulders slumped. Kamau and Bree risked their lives for her, and the old woman obviously knew more than she was saying. In fact, Devon suspected she knew exactly who Sir Isaac Newton was and how to reach him. Maybe she thought whatever Devon had to say wasn't important. Devon slowly gazed up. What if she had been going about this all the wrong way? Instead of asking for help, she should give the old kook a reason to help —

"Oh well. Kamau was *counting* on you. You do own the shop, right? He said you were the only one I could trust." Devon turned for the door. "I guess I'll go back and tell him you couldn't help." Of course, this wasn't true at all. Finding Kamau again might not even be possible. Besides, she couldn't go back to St. Frances. Not that she wanted to anyway. If this didn't work, she didn't know what she'd do. Devon cringed at the thought.

"Wait." The woman grabbed a fist of Devon's knapsack and held on tight. "Kamau sent you here, you say?" Still clinging to Devon's knapsack, the woman scrutinized Devon from her secondhand boots all the way up to the tangles in her hair.

"Yes. Kamau sent me," Devon repeated, heat burning in her cheeks. Brushing her hair, after sleeping in the diner and scouring the city all day, hadn't been a priority. "He told me to give this," she held up the sealed letter, "to Sir Isaac Newton. But if I can't find him, I can't give it to him. Can I?" Devon started for the door again. The woman darted in front, so they were nose to nose. There was a strong smell of ginger, cabbage, and something else — the fish paste Duke used as bait. Devon stopped breathing.

"Well, why didn't ya say so in the first place?" Grinning devilishly, the woman dropped her cane and straightened like a brick. "Come on then." She hurried off, walking just fine. "Don't stand there all day. We need to get a message out befer the day is done and night is come."

Devon's mouth fell open. She plucked the cane off the floor.

"Hurry, girl," the woman's voice echoed, from somewhere in the winding aisles.

Devon hurried after her. When she caught up, the woman had hauled a squat, wooden stool to an antique cash-register. Without a word, she climbed up and rang a heavy brass bell.

Ding-dong. Ding-dong.

Then, the squat woman scrambled down again and began to write. When she was finished, she dripped wax over the letter and sealed it with a stamp from a gaudy ring on her finger. "Lazy boy," the woman griped, after hardly a minute. Climbing back up, she rang the bell so forcefully it teetered from the wall.

DING-DONG. DING-DONG.

Devon covered her ears as the bell echoed through the store. "No good help these days," the woman grouched.

A lanky boy stumbled down a rung of stairs and hurried over. "Yes, ma'am?"

"Take this and deliver it straight away." She handed over the letter, and Devon caught a glimpse of a five-headed dragon on the seal. The boy stole a curious glance at the address and then at Devon. "Hurry," the old woman barked, and he jumped into an unsteady sprint, tripping as he bounded through the shop.

The wrinkle-faced woman turned back to Devon. "I should've introduced myself. I am Miss Cornelia Plunkett, but I don't like anyone to call me that. You should call me Elsie."

"Thanks for getting Sir . . . umm . . . Newton for me."

"He'll come tomorrow."

"What? What am I supposed to do until tomorrow? I need to see him today. Didn't that boy just go get him?"

"Yes, he did." Elsie folded her hands with pretended patience. "You want to buy something?"

"No. I want to see Sir Isaac Newton!"

"How about a nice necklace?" Elsie pulled out a glass case with several valuable-looking amulets, that certainly were not new — then again, neither were most of the things she sold.

She held up a chain with several jagged teeth, and Devon cringed. "Gross."

Elsie put the necklace back and eyed Devon's knapsack. "How about a new bag instead?" She pulled out a stained satchel from behind the counter. "Well, maybe not new . . . but it's new for you," she said, showing several gaps in her teeth.

"I need to see Sir Newton today. I can't wait until tomorrow."

"Buy something first." The woman pouted.

"Fine!" Devon agreed. Maybe if she bought something, she'd get to see this Newton guy today. "Give me that book from earlier." Devon crossed her arms. She wanted that book — it had earned her a smack.

"No. No. That's not for you. It's fer borlaugs. 'The Mastery of Magical Metalsmiths,' Elsie recited. "You ain't a borlaug — so there ain't a single thing you could do with it!"

"Fine." She just wanted to get this over with and see Sir Isaac Newton. "How about that scope?"

Elsie shook her head. "No. No. No. That's no good."

"Well, how about you tell me what I should buy?"

Elsie clapped her hands together and grinned, not catching the sarcasm. "What a good idea." She disappeared behind a dusty cabinet and came back carrying a dirty, red-velvet pouch. Inside was a scabbard.

"What is that?"

"A voltaic dagger. 17th Century. Made with real gold . . . It's one of the finest I've put me eyes on." She unsheathed a gold handle . . . and handed it carefully to Devon. Apprehensively, Devon took it and flipped it over in her hands. "This is just a handle."

Elsie let her breath out in a huff and snatched the hilt back. "You're not holding it right." Elsie adjusted her grip, and a soft shimmer of light twisted from the handle, forming a short blade. "You never know whos you're gon to run into these days. . . . More magiks are carrying 'em then you think." She winked a thick, fleshy eyelid.

"What does it do?"

"Paralyzes a shifter, don' it? . . . How come you don't know nothin?"

Bree and Kamau hadn't mentioned anything about a dagger that paralyzes changers from shifting. And Devon doubted that anything in this store was as good as Elsie made it sound. Still, she didn't have much choice. "I'll take it, but . . . ," Devon pulled out the wad of U.S. bills Kamau had given her, "I don't know if I have enough for something like that —"

"I'll give you nice price," Elsie said, lips curling into a greedy grin. . . . She spotted Devon's wad of cash and her face turned glacial. "No. No. NO! I don't take none of that paper here. It's no good for nothing 'cept burning to cook me dinner. You give me Gubbins." Elsie whisked the handle away. The light disappeared, like magic. "I tried that paper stuff before, and it ain't no good."

"I don't see how it's not any good?"

"In 1722, I lost all I had in a fire trying to escape the Troll Guard. For 157 years I didn't touch it, and then on one blighted day, I traded my finest sword and best trained Laphak to an old gent with a real handsome face for that paper. I known I shouldna done it. I known it, I did. The next day, my pet Snapper got to it and ate every . . . last . . . bit. Might as well have traded it all for a smooch." Elsie grinned, showing a smudge of lipstick on her teeth. "Of course, I got talked into taking some of them paper bonds not eighty years ago. A fine lady with perty clothes told me I could double my money in just two years. Then just six months later that blasted market broke. That darned paper was worth more to wipe my hinny than buy a loaf of bread."

Devon tried to block the image from her head.

"So, you can pay me in Gubbins, or you can go right on out of me store!" Elsie insisted. Her eyes landed on the thin, gold crown, and Devon held her breath. "What's that yer wearing —?" Elsie reached for the crown.

"It's not for sale." Devon stepped back so fast she bumped into a shelf.

Elsie's eyes narrowed suspiciously ... but Devon dumped the strange coins and gems on the counter ... and Elsie's greedy eyes gleamed. By her expression, Devon could tell this was what she wanted.

There were three sorts of round coins: pewter, silver, and bronze. Two sorts of square coins: light gold, and dark gold. Then, scattered between the jumble of coins were sparkling gems in ruby, citrine, and emerald.

"How much is the handle?" Devon asked, anxious to get this over with.

"Dagger girl. And it's four kepplers, three nuggets, and one waffle." Elsie licked her lips.

Kepplers, nuggets, and waffles? Devon scooped up a handful and held them out to Elsie, hoping she would count the money for her.

Instead, Elsie glowered back. "Four nugg-ets." Elsie pointed a knobby finger at the golden squares. "Three keep-lers." She jabbed at the silver coins. "And one waff-le." Elsie pointed to the bronze coins.

Devon counted out the money and handed it over.

"Put the rest of that there away, missy, and don't yous take it out again!" Elsie's warned, dramatically. "If some magik were to see yous carrying them baubles around so easy, they might be too tempted ter try an take 'em from a little thing like yerself."

"Baubles?"

"Them gems yous carryin' around. Bad enough yous got so many nuggets, and then yous carrying them baubles too." The old woman gave her a suspicious look. "How come you don't know none of this stuff already?"

Devon bit back a retort. It was best if Elsie didn't ask too many questions. "Miss Cornelia, when will Sir Newton be here?"

Elsie clicked her tongue and snatched a wool sweater from behind the register. "I told yous it's Elsie . . . and he'll be here *tomorrow!*"

"What?" Devon blanched. "You're joking."

"Come back at noon sharp and don't be late. He's a busy man with important things to do."

Devon stepped in front, blocking Elsie. "I bought your silly knife, so I want to see him today."

Elsie leaned in, unafraid. "Voltaic dagger, girl. It's

not no knife . . . and it's not no handle neither. It's magic . . . mixed with e-lec-tricy," she said, struggling with the word. "Was invented by borlaugs you know."

"You don't understand . . . I *need* to see Sir Isaac Newton. Now."

"Listen, missy. He won't get that message until after I'm gone asleep, dreaming about something prettier than you. Now out you go, and if you're late, don't come at all."

The old woman gave Devon a feeble shove . . . then, like an invisible lasso of magic, Devon was pulled backward and slammed against the brick wall, shaking the shelves of tonics, and knocking the wind from her chest. Just as she felt the shelves would crash down on top of her, the wall swallowed her up and spat her out onto the street, where she began.

Clutching the useless handle, Devon gazed up at a plain wall on an abandoned building — no door in sight. She ran around it . . . but the blue crescent had vanished. There was no proof that there had ever been a Blue Moon Novelty Shop, or a strange, mean, old woman.

CHAPTER SIX
Meanwhile, In A Place Not So Far Behind...

Two dusty, old cop cars sat parallel to the orphanage, and Ms. Frances bustled around her office, complaining. In the state of her hysterics, she didn't notice the lurking shadow that hung above. It had been following her for some time — listening — watching, undetected by the cavalier woman.

"I can't stand the indignity of it. Police! At my grandmother's institute!" Ms. Frances threw Duke a sideways glance. "The way the town will talk."

"Let them talk." Duke turned to the window, with a determined hardness beneath his calm look. "We knew this day would come. We always knew. You were eager for the day the girl would be gone."

"You're right. After three generations, she is finally gone." Ms. Frances slumped in a chair, relieved. Fanning herself, she glanced up at a large painting of a stately woman. "I can't believe my grandmother took her in."

Meanwhile, In A Place Not So Far Behind...

The shadow crept down the wall — restless to hear more.

Oblivious, Ms. Frances flipped pointed to the lamp. "Turn that on, please Duke."

Duke paced to the table and flipped on the lamp. "She is not your responsibility anymore. You've fulfilled your grandmother's promise."

"That should bring me happiness, Duke," she flared, "but look at the mess she left behind. Tell me how I'm supposed to explain that giant crater along the hill?" Ms. Frances threw up her hands. "My grandmother didn't leave instructions on how to handle that!" She swooped up, dramatically, crossed the office in a huff, and snatched her shawl from the hat-stand, nearly toppling the whole thing over.

Duke came to the rescue and tipped it straight again. "Sinkholes," he said simply.

"Sinkholes? Nonsense." Ms. Frances swatted the notion away. "It would take a missile to do that sort of damage. Dirt blasted away to bits more like, and shambles of grass carried from one side of the lot to the other. What a catastrophe!" Ms. Frances stopped by the window. "Look, Duke. There they are — inspecting it."

Duke opened the door for Ms. Frances. "Then perhaps we ought to go say hello."

Meanwhile, In A Place Not So Far Behind...

Ms. Frances put on her best garden hat. The one she wore when sashaying through the village, impressing others with her sophisticated taste. "I don't know what I'd do without you, Duke," she admitted, as she bustled past. The shadow slipped into the brim, just before she swept through the door and led the way down to the gardens.

By the time they reached the demolished fields, that had once been a beautiful landscape, Ms. Frances had recovered every dignity she had been taught. "Good evening officers," she said to the two uniformed men surveying the damage with incredulity.

The closer officer, with skin as light as his hair, removed his hat. "We're uh . . . sorry to be interrupting Ms. Frances . . . but there was a call." He nodded to the mass of overturned mud and dirt with embarrassment.

"It's all right, Walter," Ms. Frances managed with calm politeness. "You see we've had a sinkhole."

"A sinkhole?" Walter scratched his white hair. "I've never heard of a sinkhole in Hasty before."

"We're as surprised as you, though these things do turn up," Duke said smoothly.

Ms. Frances studied the other officer. A tall, dark-skinned man with a design etched into the side of a tapered fade. His crisply ironed uniform appeared brand new. "You seem familiar, but I'm certain I've never met you before," said Ms. Frances.

"This is officer . . . ," Walter scratched his head again, confused. "This is officer . . . well . . . pardon me, but I've forgotten. I rarely forget a person." Walter flushed, embarrassed. "What is your name again?"

Ms. Frances's eyes turned to slits.

The officer plucked a wooden stick from thin air, and it grew, interweaving around itself. The wind swirled around him, picking up dust in a cyclone of magic. A long, high-collared cloak that rippled with the breeze, replaced his uniform, and the second police car vanished. Kamau waved his staff, and it burned with light.

"There is no need for you here, Walter."

Walter's expression went from suddenly frightened to stoically calm. "I can see there is no need for me here," he repeated, mechanically. His eyes passed over the giant crater like there was nothing but soft hills and grass. "Everything looks in order. . . . Ms. Frances — ," he said, tipping his hat, and headed for the remaining police car.

With Walter leaving, Ms. Frances turned suspicious. "Who are you?" she demanded, taking a step back. Duke steadied her, unafraid of such peculiarities by now.

Meanwhile, In A Place Not So Far Behind...

"I am Kamau," he said politely. "We've have met before — though of course, you wouldn't remember."

A gray wolf jogged up the path and transformed into a fiery-haired girl. "No sign of him anywhere," Bree said to Kamau. Hidden, securely in Ms. Frances's hat, the shadow listened —

Meanwhile, In A Place Not So Far Behind...

"As expected," Kamau returned.

"Sign of who?" demanded Ms. Frances, unable to mask the tremble in her throat. She shook her finger at them. "You're one of those magik people. This is your fault! Isn't it?" She pointed to the giant crater. "Explosions. The garden turned to bits. Three children missing — two of them from my own Institute!"

"What do you know of magiks?" Bree blinked, surprised.

Kamau motioned towards the institute. "Let's speak inside. It's been a terribly long day. I wouldn't mind a cup of coffee."

"I'm not letting strangers into my home," Ms. Frances protested indignantly.

Bree rolled her eyes and started for the Institute. "As if a snobby old bag, like you, could stop me," she muttered, under her breath.

Before Ms. Frances could protest, Duke interceded. "Perhaps we should hear what they have to say."

Ms. Frances puckered sourly after Bree (getting further and further away). "If they murder us all, it will be on you," she warned Duke and hurried up the path. "It's locked!" she panted after Bree.

Bree snorted. At the door, her finger faded silver, hardening into a key that molded to fit the lock. The door clicked open, and without pause, she headed past the foyer into a grand room with stuffy, straight-backed chairs, sewn with those irritating fabrics that itched. Ms. Frances scampered after her, hanging her shawl in the foyer, along with her hat. Free to move again, the shadow slipped to a dark stretch of wall.

Kamau strolled in after and took a seat. Without bothering to suggest coffee again, he subtly waved his staff and a steaming cup appeared, along with a short table and all the condiments necessary, such as cream and sugar and even warm blueberry muffins. "Would you like some?" He offered, pleasantly.

Ms. Frances sat in a huff. "No!" To keep herself from glancing at the delicious tray of food, she straightened the hem of her skirt. "Ahem. . . . Where is Leni?"

"She has fully recovered," said Kamau, after a sip of coffee. "She will be returned within the hour and with no memory of the attack. As there were no other injuries nor witnesses, this should be fairly easy to sort out . . . at least as these things go."

Ms. Frances tapped her fingers, disapprovingly. "And what about my institution? A place like this has a reputation you know."

A hint of bewilderment crossed Kamau's face. "Are you not going to ask after Devon?"

Meanwhile, In A Place Not So Far Behind...

Ms. Frances turned pink. "I assume she's quite all right."

Bree crossed her arms, and shooting daggers with her eyes, she let out a loud huff.

"Devon was attacked at the Festival," Kamau said. "Leni stumbled upon it, unfortunately. She is recovering as I said and will return to your care shortly. But the attackers followed Devon here. She is on the way to a safe haven, as we speak."

"I told her not to go to the festival," said Ms. Frances, crossly. "She snuck out. So it seems to me, this whole mess is her fault . . . where are these attackers, now?"

Seeing the uneasiness in Ms. Frances's face, Kamau answered kindly, "A long way from here, I suspect."

"And will they be back?" asked Duke.

"Not likely." Kamau set down his cup, and eyed Ms. Frances, carefully. "Do you know anything about why Devon was attacked?"

"How should we know?" Ms. Frances's ears reddened, and her eyes darted to Bree, who had declined to sit. She stood with her back to the wall and a muffin in hand. "Devon is a naughty child. Always was. I regret my grandmother ever allowed such a nuisance in this establishment."

"Your grandmother?" Kamau puzzled.

"I suppose she was in a bind," Ms. Frances rambled on. "Trapped really, into taking her."

"Who — ?" Bree stared fixedly.

"My grandmother."

"I apologize for my confusion," interrupted Kamau. "I thought *you* were the headmistress of this institution?"

For a moment, Ms. Frances stared back, as confused as Kamau, and then suddenly laughed. "Oh, did I say my grandmother? I meant my grandmother's institution. My grandparents were the founders you see. They're dead of course. I didn't mean my actual grandmother. That would be . . . impossible."

Kamau held his composure but forgot all about his coffee and muffins. "Could you tell how Devon came to be here?"

"Well, I'm not sure," Ms. Frances said, wringing her hands together. She shot a look at Duke.

Bree straightened off the wall and leaning forward, sniffed the air.

"How old is Devon Conner?" Kamau asked bluntly.

"Thirteen," said Ms. Frances, automatically. "Well, I'm glad to be rid of her if that's what you want," she said hastily, changing the subject. "I can sort out the whole business officially. I'll get the legal papers." Ms. Frances strode out.

Duke reached for a muffin. "May I?"

"Please." Kamau lifted the plate, and Duke twiddled over which one to choose, deciding on the largest. He opened his mouth to say something —

"I always have a few of these ready." Ms. Frances walked in with a crisp stack of papers. "Official release forms of said child. Blah . . . blah . . . blah . . . I'll sign here." Ms. Frances scribbled on the document with an elegant stroke and handed over the papers. "That's where you'll put the institution that will be taking her, and the bottom signature is for whom will be responsible for her supervision. Her guardian I suppose."

Kamau took the papers. "You would give her up so easily?"

Bree kicked off the wall, eyes flashing.

"Why yes," said Ms. Frances surely. "There may be a few more official things to sort out . . . but I'm quite pleased. My mother was fond of her, not I."

"Your mother?" Kamau said skeptically.

"You do want her, don't you? That's why you're here?" Ms. Frances asked flatly.

"Well, yes," said Kamau. "It seems she belongs with us."

"And once you take her, you cannot bring her back," insisted Ms. Frances.

"She won't be coming back!" snapped Bree, finally losing her composure. She hurled her muffin at the table. It hit the end and bounced —

Kamau waved his staff. Before it hit the floor, it disappeared. He stood with the unsigned document. "Thank you for your time, Ms. Frances. If there is anything else, I'll be in touch."

Ms. Frances didn't bother to get up. "You don't mind seeing yourself out," she said, without asking. "I have a few matters to attend to."

Kamau managed a polite nod and left. Bree stomped behind him — seething. No one noticed the shadow creep above. At the door, Bree stopped Kamau. "Shouldn't you do something . . . ," she nodded to Ms. Frances, "she knows too much."

Kamau shook his head. Quietly, so that neither Duke nor Ms. Frances could hear, he said, "If I erase her memory of this encounter . . . I may tamper with the memories we need."

"You think she knows something!" Bree whispered back, confirming her own thoughts.

"She most certainly does," he replied, solemnly.

"I knew she was lying — I could smell it."

"You should trust your instincts, Bree. They are rarely ever wrong."

Bree opened the front door. "Do you think Devon

found the Blue Moon? . . . I wasn't as nice as I could've been — breaking the bed on her and stuff." Bree jabbed her thumb towards Ms. Frances. "I didn't know she lived with a woman like that."

"We'll know soon enough." His faced hardened, and there was an urgency filled with concern. "We'll travel east, to be sure we're not followed, and then I'll transport us to the city. With any luck, by the time we arrive, she'll have already found our friend." With one last glance at Ms. Frances (who plopped promptly back in her chair, so as not to be caught eavesdropping), Kamau left, with Bree right behind him.

Ms. Frances hurried to the French window and from behind the velvet curtains, watched as they walked out into the garden. A glowing, bronze light swirled around Bree and Kamau . . . and they disappeared.

With her attention engrossed on the happenings outside, Ms. Frances didn't notice the shadow that slid up the wall, clinging to the ceiling above her. It twitched, fighting the urge — the craving — for death. It towered over the despicable woman. Selfish. Cruel. And even jealous of the magic she didn't possess. Beneath that, she was the essence of what the shadow detested most of all — ordinary.

Meanwhile, In A Place Not So Far Behind...

Niko's face, dark and twisted, appeared within the shadow, and loomed over the oblivious woman. It was unnecessary to murder her — but it would please him. *No.* He shifted back to a shadow, letting the dark blade in his hand disintegrate. *The woman was safe for now. She might have a purpose.* The warlock believed there was more to the girl's story, and so did he. He may need the loathsome woman one day. For now, he'd let her live. Quick as the breeze, the shadow slipped through the crack beneath the oak door and down the pipes.

CHAPTER SEVEN
Ghost Tavern

Night came swiftly, and the cool, harsh wind prickled against Devon's skin, sweeping her along as cruelly as the old woman had shut her outside. Her only option now was to find a place to stay ... and wait until tomorrow. A place without magiks preferably, as only humans could be trusted. At least not to kill her for a crown, anyway. That shouldn't be hard. How many magiks could she possibly run into in a big city like Manhattan? More likely she'd get lost or robbed. Then again, with the magic crown, she could turn into a shadow and frighten off an ordinary mugger. The thought brought a mischievous grin to her face. Perhaps this crown could be of use, or at the very least, a bit of fun.

Devon straightened the thin gold band on her head. Then she bent over and tied the intricate handle to her ankle — cursing the old kook that tricked her into buying it. With the crown and dagger secured, Devon headed back the way she came.

Not having slept, nor eaten since the morning, weariness began to set in as she stumbled along the cold sidewalk. First, she would find food . . . then, she would find a place to sleep. Perhaps one should concern themselves with the second matter first, and the first matter second, but Devon was tired, and when one is tired, decisions are made with less thought and more doing.

Fortunately, she didn't have to go far to find a cluster of well-lit restaurants. They filled the bleak night with warmth and aromas that gave the illusion of safekeeping. It was the oldest place that drew her attention. Not as brightly lit nor as lively, but as she stood there, deciding what to do, it glimmered and then flickered, like a lenticular picture. From one angle the restaurant was there, and from the next, it disappeared. Curious, she hurried up a neat doorstep with a hanging sign that read . . .

Ghost Tavern

This was where P. Talon was headed! Excited (and deeply curious), Devon pushed open the heavy door and stepped inside. *I'll only stay for a few minutes,* she said to herself. *Just long enough to eat.*

It was a strange place. From the entrance she could go downstairs or upstairs, and the split-level tavern was packed with people. They huddled together — talking and laughing — all of them trendy, in an urban grunge sort of way. Almost everyone wore high-tops, fingerless gloves, and multiple rings. They went from booth to booth greeting each other, fist knocking and shaking hands all over the restaurant as if everyone here knew everyone else.

A pretty girl with straight blonde hair, striking blue eyes, and gold rings, on every finger, came up to the podium. "Ahem."

"Is there a wait?" Devon asked. Exhaustion from the long day was taking over, and

she was looking forward to a short rest.

"Let me see." The pretty blonde leaned over a chart on the podium. "I haven't seen you around before." Her eyes followed Devon, as she scanned the lively tavern. When Devon turned back around, the girl's gaze dropped to the chart again.

"That's because I've never been here before."

The pretty blond raised her eyebrows. "Really? Then how did you see it?"

"See what?" Devon asked.

The blonde's face turned sour. "The illusion — how did you know we were here if you weren't invited?" She shrugged impatiently, like her question made sense, though it didn't."

"I heard some loony with a box of baubles, that bumped into me, mention a Ghost Tavern —then I saw the name on the front."

"So . . . it was an accident." Her forehead wrinkled crossly.

Behind them, the door opened, and a sandy-haired boy in torn jeans walked-in. Flashing a brilliant smile, he leaned on the podium in a familiar way. "What's up, Abigail?"

"Hey Seth." The pretty blonde beamed.

"Hex should be back tonight," Seth teased with a wink. Abigail punched his arm playfully — but he ducked around her with a grin and disappeared into the crowd. With forced pleasantry, Abigail turned back to Devon. "I think we're pretty full."

"Oh." Devon surveyed the tavern again. Several tables were empty. Still, she didn't have the energy to argue — she just wanted to eat. She took a wavering breath, fighting back the urge to start trouble.

"Have a good night." Abagail's lips twitched in a tight-lipped grimace. She ducked around the podium and followed Seth, with a menu tucked under her arm.

Devon turned to leave, swearing, under her breath. But with Abigail distracted, there was no one to stop her from finding her own seat. Why should she have to leave anyway? There were obviously tables. Without thinking twice, Devon shot past the podium (grabbing her own menu on the way) and headed for an empty stool at a table beside the bar. A sturdy man with gray in his red beard, and a friendly face, despite the scar above his temple, gave her a polite nod. "G'day," he said as he wiped down glasses with a dishtowel.

Warily, Devon opened the menu. "Hi. . . ."

The sturdy man came out from behind the counter. "What can I get ya?"

Devon's stomach rumbled. "Um —"

A sharp pinch on Devon's arm made her eyes burn. "I told you we're full," hissed Abigail.

Devon yanked her arm free and stood up in one

swift move. She had never let anyone bully her, and now wasn't a good time to start. "Looks like I found an empty place."

The scarred man thumped a tall glass of water next to Devon's menu, startling them both.

"Alrigh' there, Abigail. Let the gel alone."

"She doesn't belong here, Archie," Abigail argued.

Devon scrunched up her face. *What did she mean by that?*

Archie steered Abigail away from the table. "It isn't the first time we served one a' them, and it sure as blazes won't be the last. They get in on accident, you know that."

"I can hear you," Devon grumbled. . . . *If P. Talon could come here, then why couldn't she? This was a tavern for magiks, right?* . . . Then it dawned on her. There was an illusion on the tavern! And somehow, inviting you in allowed you to see it. They thought she got in on accident, which meant they thought she was human. This was all just a misunderstanding. She just had to explain. "You don't understand —"

Abigail whipped around, eyes blazing dangerously. And changing her mind, Devon clamped down on her teeth. Kamau had warned her not to trust anyone! She was supposed to find Sir Isaac Newton without drawing attention to herself or the crown. "I . . . uh . . . just want to eat."

Abigail's face turned purple. She opened her mouth, ready to lash out, when Seth appeared from nowhere, wrapped his arm around her, and led her back to the podium.

"Don't worry about that one. She's a bit touchy," said Archie. "Thinks she runs the place."

Devon sat down again with one eye still on Abigail.

"So what will ya be having?"

"Um . . . Is it too late for breakfast?" Breakfast had always been her favorite, but she usually slept in too late to get it.

"Brekkie it is. How 'bout fried eggs and waffles?"

Devon's stomach rumbled louder, and Archie waved down one of the waiters. For a while, that was the end of their conversation. Archie returned to wiping glasses, and a handful of troubles occupied Devon's thoughts.

What if someone recognized the crown that she daringly wore on her head? Was it safer if she took it off? And did it really erase memories? She seemed to remember everything just fine. . . . Deciding to keep it on for now, her eyes darted anxiously around the tavern as she thought of Bree and Kamau. Were they all right? . . . And what happened to Niko? If he managed to escape Bree and Kamau, would he come after her again? Devon snorted. Of course he would. If he survived, he was already on his way. And now, Devon could add Elsie's attempt to swindle her, *and* her refusal to get Sir Isaac Newton, to her growing list of troubles. *What a mess.*

To distract herself, Devon glanced around the bustling tavern, but after a moment her thoughts wandered back to tomorrow. Would she be able to find the Blue Moon again? And if she did, would the door even come back? It had just vanished. Worst of all . . . what if she went through all this trouble, and Sir Isaac Newton didn't come to meet her?

Archie set down a steaming plate of cheesy eggs and buttery waffles. "Dig in."

"Thanks." She scarfed it down before it cooled and immediately felt better.

"I see you were hungry." Archie chuckled, as he straightened up behind the counter.

Devon grinned, not the least bit ashamed. "I've been walking a lot today."

Though he seemed to want to ask about it, Archie took the plate instead. "You want some more?"

"No thanks." Devon reached for the stack of bills inside the pouch. "What do I owe?"

She was getting tired at an alarming rate. If she

didn't hurry, she might be too tired to find a hotel. Of course, she hadn't ruled out crashing on a bench for the night. It wouldn't be a bad idea to stick close to the Blue Moon. Her eyes drooped as the door opened, and a large group of people walked in all at once. Silence trickled across the tavern until only a light chatter remained. Then that died out too. Devon and Archie turned to get a look at the cause of the stir.

"It's on us for the trouble," muttered Archie. "It'd be best for you to head off now."

Without waiting for a response, Archie strode to the other end of the restaurant, where Seth stood, clenching his fists and barely restraining himself from approaching the newcomers.

There were nearly ten of them. Each dressed in immaculate clothes. Even from her seat, Devon recognized the designer labels. Contrasting with the trendy grunge, they lounged about the entrance completely at ease, bored even, despite the agitation they caused. Behind them, partially concealed, a sturdy boy with dark-brown hair watched the room. His gleaming eyes lingered over the growing tension.

It wasn't long before the 'lovely' Abigail was arguing with the newcomers.

Devon slipped closer, hoping to catch a drift of the conversation — She was nearly in range when rough hands lifted her from the floor and pushed her towards a back door. "It's time for you to go," crabbed a boorish waiter with calloused hands and a bad haircut.

Devon's eyes flickered back to the brown-haired boy and found his piercing eyes on her too. His expression darkened with agitation.

What had she done?

"I *said* it's time to go!" The burly waiter shoved her towards the back door (so there was no mistaking which door she was supposed to use).

"Maybe you should try asking nicely." An angry flush spread across Devon's face, and her eyes glossed over with heated adrenaline (the way they did right before she found herself in a scuffle).

The waiter pointed to the door. "Get out!"

Satisfied he'd made his point; he strode off to confront the unwanted intruders.

But why weren't they welcome? Devon's curiosity got the better of her, and instead of leaving, she ducked behind a table. From there, she could see everything.

At the podium, an argument ensued, and it was getting more animated by the second. An unruly waiter (much like the boorish one, though younger and not as ugly) was reacting to the newcomers' presence by cursing at the lot of them. Testing his limits, the young waiter darted forward threateningly, and a boy (perhaps eleven or twelve) with light-brown skin and curly black hair shoved him back. It was a ridiculous thing to watch someone so small shove someone twice their size, but the force behind it was strong, and the waiter stumbled back.

Archie grabbed the waiter, just as he made for the boy again. "Not tha' one mate. He'll pummel you."

"He won't beat *me*," Seth said, vaporizing. Thick flakes of skin dusted off, darkening, and blew around him into a shadow.

Devon covered her mouth, swallowing a scream.

There was only one thing that could do that — A shadow walker. All around the tavern, people began to shift. Billows of shadows blocked out the lights, dulling the room.

Devon backed away from the crowd. *Now is a good time to go*, she decided. The back exit was suddenly looking good. In fact, the sooner she got out, the better —

Devon slipped to the back door and tugged hard, but it didn't budge. "Of course it's locked," she said, scowling. *Nothing else had gone right*. Not since the Festival of Gondolas.

Devon swung around to the podium. The only way out now was the way she came in, and, at the moment, it was the center of the commotion. There was no way for her to get past unnoticed, which put her and the crown at risk. Devon cursed under her breath. She had made a disastrous mistake by coming here.

"WE'VE COME FOR BRAXUIS." A commanding voice bounded across the room. The shadows condensed — metamorphosing back to their human forms, and all heads turned to the boy with piercing eyes and brown hair.

"Ryker. It's Ryker Beurguard." Whispers spread through the room.

"There's no need for fighting. Give us Braxuis, and we'll leave peacefully."

"And if we don't?" asked Seth. His shadow rippled around him, threateningly.

Ryker's piercing eyes flitted around the room and landed on Seth. He huffed. "Ah, it's Seth. Where is Hex or Puxley? I thought you were lower in the chain. Give me Remy at least. It's insulting to negotiate with you."

Seth seethed.

Ignoring him, Ryker addressed the crowd. "Give up Braxuis. He is not one of you. He is a murderer."

The crowd muttered. News of Braxuis's charges were a surprise. "A murderer?" they murmured. "Can't be!"

"That's what he said," spewed another shadow walker, pointing at Ryker.

"Why should we listen to you?" Seth spat. "If it weren't for your father, no one would look twice at you."

A growl rumbled from Ryker's chest, and he closed the distance between them. "Don't start something you can't finish."

Suddenly afraid, Seth fell silent. His chest rose and fell with each breath as he sulked back, angrily. Ryker, however, turned back to the tavern, ignoring Seth again, as if he were beneath him. "We will be searching the tavern." He motioned, and those with him spread out, searching the restaurant.

"By whose authority?" someone from the crowd demanded with audacity.

The small boy with curly black hair pulled out a scroll and held it up for everyone to see. Devon took advantage of the distraction to slip closer to the front exit. She darted from one table to the next, crouching low, so that she easily hid behind the booths. "This is a warrant for the arrest of Braxuis Baumbach the Assassin," declared the boy. "By order of the United Governance of Magiks, any establishment that may be harboring the criminal Braxuis Baumbach, also known as Braxuis Baumbach the Assassin, is subject to search, and must concede and abide by Magik Law."

"Oligarchy!" cried a pudgy woman, just feet away from Devon. Startled, Devon darted for the next table and ducked behind it. "Nonsense from a bunch of hoity-toity, puffed up politicians!" the woman jeered.

The crowd catcalled and heckled in agreement.

Ryker's face hardened, and he strode to the center of the room, completely at ease, despite the angry crowd. "These are laws that *all* magiks are subject to . . . Laws that *you* are subject to. Braxuis is charged with leading an assault of shadow walkers against magik and human civilians in peaceable land! We're giving you the opportunity to hand him over without harm to anyone. The favor won't be given twice."

Abigail's face blotched red. "Do you think we'll hand over one of our own to a bunch of dirty skin thieves?" Stupidly, she charged — just as she reached Ryker, the young boy slipped in front, protectively — and flattened, shapeshifting into a brick wall. Unable to recover in time, Abigail bulldozed into it — knocking herself unconscious.

An outcry spread across the tavern as angry shadow walkers griped and groused, resulting in heated skirmishes. Devon bolted for the door.

"HALT!" boomed a new voice that silenced the room. Only a few continued fighting.

Devon crouched behind a long buffet table, slipped down the length of the food bar, and spied from behind it. She was nearly there. All she needed was one more distraction and she'd be out of here. She fought back the curiosity that normally led her into trouble. This wasn't her fight. She had her own problems, and she couldn't afford to get dragged into this one. *Find the Blue Moon, keep the crown safe, and get as far away from Niko Throntropt as possible.* That was her plan.

"Go and break it up!" the new voice commanded.

Two hulking figures moved through the room and yanked apart the last of the skirmishes.

Devon peeked around the buffet table and quickly found the owner of the voice. A black-haired boy, in a faded leather jacket, was flanked by two boys the size of bulldozers. He stood with his arms across his chest, and judging by the look he gave Ryker, they were not friends.

"It's Hex. Hex is here!" The name spread through the crowd just as Ryker's had, who now had Seth pinned on his stomach.

"I heard a rumor that you were back." Hex dared closer to Ryker. "I didn't believe it, but here you are. The great General Beurguard has sent his prodigal son back to Beorgburg." Hex sneered. "It seems we will be classmates after all."

"Classmates? . . ." Devon mouthed, under her breath. *What is Beorgburg anyway? No*, Devon chided herself. *You have to get out of here!*

Ryker tightened his grasp on Seth. Blood trickled down his ear and he hung over forward, fighting consciousness. "Give me Braxuis, and I'll let the kid go."

Hex's face hardened. "You'll let him go, anyway."

"Care to test that?"

Seth groaned as Ryker flexed, bending his arm behind his back.

Abigail regained consciousness and rushed forward. "Wait. Let him go. Braxuis isn't here."

Two waiters moved to silence her . . . but Ryker shoved Seth forward on his face, busting his nose.

"Oww!" Seth moaned. He started to shift — darkening into a shadow.

"Try it and I'll bust your nose again," Ryker warned. Seth stopped.

"He hasn't been here for weeks," Abigail promised.

"All right." Ryker nodded (towards two of his own friends that were being restrained by shadow walkers). "Let them go, and we will be on our way."

"Let them go," Hex repeated, dismissively. Immediately, they were released.

Ryker pulled Seth up, and nudged him forward. He stumbled over to Hex.

"And the girl," Ryker added.

Devon looked around, and all the eyes in the room fell on her.

"You think I didn't notice?" Ryker snorted. Then his voice turned suspicious. "Why do you have a human anyway?"

"It's her own stupid fault she's here," spat Abigail. "I told her to leave!"

Hex's wide-eyed expression fell on Devon. He quickly recovered. "She can leave any time," he said dryly. "She's no one important."

Devon huffed. *No one important?*

With there being no point to hiding anymore, Devon stood up and glared back at them. Anyone who hadn't spotted her before, now saw her clearly — but she was too offended to care. She might not have parents, or know much about magic, and she hadn't had a bath since before the festival — but that didn't mean she wasn't important.

Misunderstanding her frozen state for unwillingness to leave, Ryker leaned against a booth — making himself comfortable. "We're not leaving until she does." A couple of his friends chuckled.

"She's leaving." Abigail's voice loomed from behind Devon.

The hairs on Devon's arms prickled . . . but it was too late. Abigail grabbed Devon by the shirt and hurled her into a booth. Anticipating the coming crash, Devon tensed — and shifted. Instead of smashing into the booth, an airy feeling of weightlessness overcame her, and she floated above the floor — before she landed with a thud.

Dizzy, Devon sat up. The tension in the room had finally broken into chaos.

Inhuman and frightening sounds tore through the room as it was ripped to pieces. Bits of ceiling fell in crumbles, making it cloudy and dim. An earsplitting crash brought down an entire rack of bottles, littering the floor with shards of glass.

A cold, wet trickle of blood ran down her ear and dripped on the floor beside a heavy, medieval crown, laden with enormous emeralds and blood-red rubies. It was nothing like the thin band of gold that it once was. *This was made for a king.*

Then something strange happened. Like tuning the radio so the station is clear, everything around her became amplified. Her senses sharpened, distinct and pronounced. She could hear gasps and whispers from across the room, smell bacon burning in the kitchen, and see the tiniest shimmers of colors in the jewel-encrusted crown. They swirled together like stars glimmering in the moonlight.

While she lay there mesmerized, she knew where everyone was without looking up. The fuzziness she struggled with was gone. Her mind became clear (like everything had been blurry before, but she never noticed).

A flicker in the crown caught her attention. A thin crack snaked down the metal. Devon scooped it up to examine the damage. The gold crown transformed back into a thin band, but the crack remained. Disheartened, Devon slumped against the booth.

A loud thrumming on the floor bounded towards her, sending vibrations through the wood. Devon yanked off her knapsack and carefully zipped the crown inside.

The air above dispersed as billions of molecules were sent into disarray by two hands that shot for her throat.

"You don't know what you're messing with," Abigail snarled, as she lifted Devon off the floor.

"You don't either," Devon rasped. She peeled Abigail's fingers back, releasing her grip.

Swift as a fox, the curly-haired boy appeared, and Abigail dropped Devon. She took a step back and ran.

"Need a hand?" The boy grinned slyly.

"Hah." Devon laughed, though it sounded more like choking. "Not anymore."

The boy spun and swept the feet out from a waiter as he charged them. "I think I'll hang around . . . just in case," he said, dusting off his shirt. "I'm Kian."

The waiter scooted up and ran.

"Devon," she said, impressed. He looked about as old as Bree, though who could tell anymore. Bree said she was two-hundred and seven. Still, it didn't stop her from feeling a tinge of jealousy. Kian was strong, and for the first time, as far back as she could remember, she was the weaker one. Thrown into a world of magic she knew nothing about, she felt dependent and powerless. It wasn't a good feeling.

A swift movement behind her blew a soft breeze against her back, and Kian froze. Unblinkingly, he peered behind her. She sensed the sudden proximity of something hovering, and goosebumps shivered down her arms. Slowly, she turned around. Hex stood very close.

Kian twitched, like he wanted to get between her and Hex but was unsure how to do it. Hex caught the movement and turned away from Devon, giving Kian the opening he needed.

Kian lunged.

Maybe it was the immediate camaraderie between them, or the distasteful feeling of sitting on the side and doing nothing . . . but when Kian attacked, Devon did too.

Kian was fast and strong, using his small size as an advantage. He darted around Hex, evading his swings. Devon went for Hex's back and tried a knee sweep she had once used on a neighborhood bully. But even together, it wasn't enough. Outmaneuvered, Hex dumped Devon on the floor and pitched Kian into the wall. He staggered and collapsed as his friends rushed to help him up.

Then Hex was beside Devon, towering over her, alert and thoughtful. His eyes flickered to the dagger, exposed at her ankle. A frown spread across his face

—

Devon scooted away, but when Hex didn't move to stop her, she jumped up . . . and ran straight into Ryker.

"Ready yet?" Ryker asked sarcastically.

"I've been ready," Devon mumbled. *Everyone else was just getting in the way.*

Ryker leaned in. "What was that?"

"Let's go," she said clearer. She peeked over at Kian — relieved to see he was all right.

Solid masses came from all sides, surrounding

them. An impressively quick assimilation. It was strategic, and they were protected from all angles as they left the tavern. The outside air was a blast of cool relief, but no one around her relaxed.

"Spread out!" Ryker ordered. "If he's here, find him."

Like trained soldiers, they broke off in calculated formations. Shapeshifting, they blended into their surroundings better than chameleons. And without a sound, they disappeared into the night.

Devon turned to leave. If there was a shadow walker assassin on the loose, then she didn't want to be anywhere in the vicinity. . . . But leaving was apparently the wrong thing to do. The next second, Ryker had her by the collar. Her feet dangled above the pavement. "Did you think you would sneak by me?"

"I wasn't sneaking."

He shoved her against the wall, knocking the wind from her lungs. Before she could crumple to the ground, he had her by the collar again.

"Who are you? Are you a spy?"

Still grasping for air, Devon rasped, "No!" Obviously, she wasn't a spy, or she wouldn't have teamed up with Kian, but this wasn't the time to get cheeky.

He leaned in close, so his face was level to hers.

"I'll give you one chance to tell me the truth," he said quietly. "Are you working for the Shadow Reign?"

"I don't know what you're talking about," Devon blurted. Though of course, she did know — She knew very well. The Shadow Reign was after her. But she wasn't going to tell him that. He could be just as deranged as Niko. Kamau had said not to trust anyone.

"What's your name?" Ryker demanded.

The second Devon took to decide whether to answer was a second too long. "WHO ARE YOU?" Ryker roared, more lion than human, and punched the wall so hard that it shook. Large chunks of cement crumpled to the ground.

"Devon," she rasped. The pounding of Ryker's fists drowned her out. "DEVON!" she shouted.

Ryker stopped, and the last few pieces of cement crumpled and fell. "Devon what?" Catching her hesitation, he leaned in, so they were nose to nose.

"Connor."

"Are you a spy?" he emphasized.

"Obviously not!" she said, her courage biting back. "I don't even know what a *Beorgburg* is."

"Beorgburg is a school," he said skeptically, "that every magik has heard of, and you are a magik. You may have fooled them, but not me. I sensed it."

"Sensed it?" Devon asked without thinking. "What do you mean?"

Ryker narrowed his eyes, till they were practically slits. "I sensed your form when you shifted. Shadow walkers are light and fluid — while shapeshifters, at their core, are incredibly dense. You may have hidden as a human," he leaned back coming to a realization, "something I've never seen done before, but I felt you shift when that shadow walker threw you. A human would have hit the booth — hard. And you didn't hit it at all." He glared, accusingly. "But your metamorphosis was blurry — why?"

Devon stayed silent — thinking very fast. The curse on the crown must be the reason he mistook her for a human — it hid magic. It was likely what caused her metamorphosis to be blurry. But Kamau hadn't mentioned it was possible to sense a shadow walker from a shapeshifter. Neither did Bree. It would have been useful though. "I didn't know that was possible."

"Only very few magiks can do it. So few, that many don't even know it's possible." A glint at her ankle caught his attention. In a swift movement, he swooped down and unsheathed her dagger. Fury gleamed in his eyes. "Proof you must know something of what I'm talking about." He crossed his arms. "Where did you get this?"

"I bought it."

"So you're admitting you are a magik — but not that you've heard of Beorgburg?"

"I just found out," Devon confessed, grudgingly.

"No friend of the Shadow Reign would *dare* carry one of these." He raised his brow suspiciously. "So why are you here?"

"Why wouldn't a friend of the Shadow Reign carry one of those?" she countered, with more courage than she felt. If she kept asking questions, he couldn't ask them himself. The last thing she wanted was him to find the crown in her knapsack. As soon as he touched it, he would realize it was special.

Ryker's face creased, trying to decide what to believe.... "You really don't know?"

"I didn't know I was a magik until *very* recently." Hopefully, by admitting this much, his skepticism would ease. "I didn't know the Ghost Tavern was full of shadow walkers either. I'm a shapeshifter." *At least, I think,* she finished in her head.

"There are not only shadow walkers in the Ghost Tavern, " Ryker corrected, not showing any surprise that she just discovered she was a magik. "It's a hangout for supporters of the Shadow Reign. That's why I'm here. To find a murderer."

"I swear I didn't know." Since he continued to glare

suspiciously, Devon pointed at the dagger. "What's the big deal with that?"

Ryker sighed. "I'll show you." Sliding a pocketknife across his palm, he sliced a thin cut. Blood ran in a smooth stream down his hand. Devon cringed, but Ryker didn't. Already he was healing. Before it healed completely, he pricked the voltaic dagger against the smooth skin on his arm. The dagger pulsed, coming to life. Blood ran down his hand again. Ryker clenched his jaw, in pain from the magic tremors.

"Are you crazy?" Devon grabbed the dagger and pulled it away from his arm.

The shocks stopped and the blood dried. A moment later the cut began to scab.

"This blade slows down changers from shifting," explained Ryker. "I couldn't heal until it was removed. It's dangerous to shapeshifters, but even more to a shadow walker who relies on transforming to attack and defend himself. They're especially vulnerable as it freezes their state of transformation completely."

"You're lucky no one caught you with this," Ryker reprimanded. "There is no reason for you to carry a dagger, and this particular blade has been outlawed by Magik Law. I could arrest you for carrying it."

Devon thought of Hex who'd seen it. Why hadn't he exposed her? "Are you the police?"

"Police?" Ryker laughed loudly. "Humans have police. . . . No. I'm not part of the Magik Guard, but . . . I'm not a civilian either. A smirk slid to the corner of his mouth, "As part of an elite unit of the Magik Military, I'm allowed special privileges, including the ability to detain law-breaking magiks."

Devon silently cursed Elsie for selling her an illegal weapon. "I'm not a spy."

Ryker's eyes flickered across her face. "All right. I'll bite. But I'm keeping this." He sheathed the dagger.

"Why? It's mine."

"All right." Ryker grinned mischievously. "Here." He unsheathed it and held it out to her. "But then I will have to arrest you for having an illegal dagger."

Devon shrugged. "You can keep it."

Ryker grinned bigger. "I thought so." He sheathed the dagger again. "Now tell me where you got it —" Suddenly, Ryker straightened, listening. "Shh!" he put his finger to his lips.

Devon swirled around. She heard it too. A rustle somewhere in the dark. The air thickened. Darkness spread above them and the stars disappeared. Ryker signaled to the guard hidden around the perimeter. "Check the door."

Kian came back carrying a limp figure over his

shoulder and carefully set one of the guards at Ryker's feet. "He's just unconscious," said Kian.

"Still here?" Hex's voice sounded from the sky above them. "I didn't think we would get past your friend so easily," the invisible voice taunted. "You should have left while you had the chance."

"Run," Ryker whispered.

Devon took a feeble step towards the parking lot as darkness spread around them. The bleakness condensed into outlines of shadows and the stars above them reappeared.

A roar rumbled from Ryker — loud and wild.

"GET OUT OF HERE!" Ryker shoved Devon towards the empty parking lot. She stumbled and then ran into the dark alone.

CHAPTER EIGHT
Creepy Shadows

Devon raced through the city streets. She turned down a slightly busier one, where the sidewalk opened up to an underground tunnel, with signs that pointed to the subway. Hurriedly, she raced past, weaving between the stragglers that were catching the late-night train. For the first time, she didn't tire. Her movements were light and airy — making her fast, lithe, and eerily quiet. Without the crown, her memories were sharper, and her senses weren't clouded. It was *fantastic*. The crown had been a chain, weighing her down. It had made her human and slow. But now, she was free.

It wasn't until her fear ebbed and adrenaline ran out that she slowed to a walk with her mind racing. There was a whole other world with magic and war (besides the ordinary one she lived in Hasty). And the distrust between shapeshifters and shadow walkers went deep. How had it stayed hidden? By the way Abigail acted, it wasn't likely that many humans got past the lenticular illusion at the Ghost Tavern. The Blue Moon hadn't exactly been easy to find either. But, if Kamau and Bree would risk their life so she could escape with the crown, then it must be dangerously powerful. Keeping it safe was the most important thing right now — along with staying alive, of course. She *had* to find Sir Isaac Newton. He was the only one that would be able to help, and perhaps the only one she could trust.

Which meant right now, she needed to find a safe place to stay until tomorrow. She had already made a mess of this whole day. All she was supposed to do was find the Blue Moon and speak with Sir Isaac Newton. So far, she had annoyed P. Talon (the very first magik she ran into), wandered aimlessly around Manhattan, gotten swindled into buying an illegal dagger, stumbled into a dangerous feud over a wanted criminal, and cracked the infamous magical crown she was supposed to protect. To top it off, she learned absolutely nothing about Sir Isaac Newton. Devon groaned. She wouldn't feel safe now, parked up on a bench somewhere. Well maybe it would be all right, but she'd still rather not.

She dug out the crumpled map from her knapsack. Earlier that morning, she had passed an entire block of hotels and according to the marks she made, they weren't too far from the Blue Moon. It was as good a place as any to spend the night.

As she walked, Devon tried not to worry, but she couldn't shake the flashes of terrifying images that haunted her. Two nights in a row, she had found herself mixed up in a fight between shadow walkers and shapeshifters. Two nights in a row, she had been unimaginably outmatched. And two nights in a row, she was forced to run. It didn't sit well with her. It wasn't *who* she was. If war and fighting was the norm here, then she would have to learn how to fight, and she was going to have to learn how to shapeshift — without the crown.

Devon checked the map again and redirected, taking a shortcut through a residential street with stone apartments. A flickering lamp cast momentary illusions. As she passed it, every shadow made her heart pound and her hands sweat. She half-expected Niko to appear, hovering in the dark street. If he managed to escape Bree and Kamau, then he would find her.

Devon checked her map again. "Almost there," she muttered to herself.

THUMP.

Afraid to move and afraid to stay put, Devon *slowly* turned around. The only light came from the flickering lamppost and the soft glow of the moon that crept past the tall buildings. Shadows draped over the walls like blankets. Except ... there was another shadow that moved along the building, coming closer. It shrank and disappeared behind a metal trashcan.

Devon took a step back, pressing softly on the pavement so there wasn't any sound. Something was definitely there ... perhaps ... Niko had already found her. And now she was alone. There was no one here powerful enough to face him.

The trashcan shook.

Devon jumped back as the trashcan rustled, spilling remnants of leftover food onto the street. She ground her toe into the cement and shifted her weight. One more twitch ... and she'd run ... she wouldn't stop until she was surrounded by people. *Ordinary* people.

A soft shuffling nudged the fallen garbage, and just as Devon coiled to run, a furry head peeked around the corner. Even from here, there was no mistaking a raccoon. It sniffed in her direction, and Devon exhaled noisily. If she didn't calm down, everything would start spooking her. Not one to linger in a place so dark, Devon hurried off —

Just before she reached the end of the block, the raccoon scuttled out from its hiding place and transformed into a young boy with curly, black hair. "She almost spotted me," he mumbled to himself. "I nearly blew my cover." He squinted, as Devon whirled around the block, taking note of which direction she ran. Ryker wouldn't have liked it if he'd been caught. *Spying is meant to be discreet, after all.*

♛ ♛ ♛

Devon reached the block of hotels as the first drops of rain fell. Unlike in the alley, there were plenty of brightly glowing lampposts, and night-goers hung about — giving life to the late-night hour. This time she would choose a place to rest more carefully. Devon scanned the line of hotels and stopped in front of the most mundane, humdrum, ordinary-looking, bed-n-breakfast on the street. Just as the rain began to pour, she hurried across the road, ran up the steps, and went inside.

The unattended counter was partially obscured with stacks of travel brochures, and a furry, white cat lazed across the only cushioned chair in the lobby, shedding on the velvet.

Ding. Ding. Ding.

She rang the bell.

Ding. Ding.

A sleepy-eyed, messy-haired boy, maybe sixteen or seventeen, in a wrinkled t-shirt, came around the corner (where he must have been sleeping) and placed his hand on the bell. "Can I help you?" he emphasized — so she would know he was annoyed.

"I need a room," Devon said. "Just for tonight."

The young attendant sat down at the computer and began typing lazily. "Are your parents coming to check-in?"

"I'm old enough."

His eyebrow quirked over the side of his computer. "You don't look old enough."

"And neither do you," Devon pointed out.

The young attendant shrugged. "Well . . . we only have one room left." He drew his bushy eyebrows together doubtfully . . . ,"and it's pricey."

Devon pulled out the thick wad of cash, and pinching it between her fingers, let it swing back and forth. "I have money."

"Ahem." The attendant cleared his throat and clicked the mouse. . . . "Name?"

"You don't need it."

He looked over the computer and insisted, "I need a name to check you in."

Devon unfolded a few bills and slid them across the counter.

The attendant perked up, slid the bills off the counter, and tucked them in his pocket. "I do need a name . . . but it doesn't have to be yours —"

The cat leapt onto the desk and poked his head between them, curiously. A shiny nametag caught the light. "Poo-kie," Devon read from the collar.

The boy glanced over at the cat . . . and then back at Devon. "That's terrible." He shook his head, jabbed at the keyboard, and smirked amusedly. "Last name?"

The cat pawed at the wet drizzles on her jacket, and Devon leaned against the counter, trying to be patient. She didn't care about names, just a decent place to sleep. "Toes."

"*Toes?*" The attendant's mouth fell open stupidly. "You're not very good at this, are you?" Devon opened her mouth with a retort, but he cut her off. "I got it —"

He stretched his fingers out in front of him. Then clicked away at the keyboard. "Waldgrave," he said without looking up. He typed a minute more, printed off a form, and pointed to a blank line. "All right . . . Pookie Waldgrave . . . sign here —"

"Hmph. Like that's better . . . sounds like a name from a haunted tombstone." Devon scribbled the fake signature and pushed the paper back across the counter.

"Ahem." The boy held out his hand expectantly.

Devon handed over a few large bills, and he rubbed his fingers together for more. Frowning, she handed over one more bill. "Last one."

Satisfied, he stood up stiffly and stretched. "This way," he said, yawning. On the second floor, he unlocked a room and handed her the key. "Check-out is twelve o'clock, sharp."

"No problem." Devon scooted past and closed the door, making sure it snapped shut as he sauntered off.

The room was neat as a pin and unsettlingly quiet. For a moment, Devon stayed put with one hand still on the doorknob. From there, she inspected every nook, corner, and shadow. When nothing moved, she hurried from the door and turned on every light in the room. Still not satisfied, she bolted the locks and then dragged the armoire in front. Finally, she pulled the towels from the closet and stuffed them around the gaps under the door.

Unable to settle, she unpacked and rearranged her knapsack. When she was finished, she sat with her back against the wall. Tonight had been a disaster. But at least she was safe, and she hoped that, somewhere out there, Kamau and Bree were safe too.

There was only one thing to do. Niko said she was a shapeshifter . . . so it was time to start learning how to be one. She needed to learn how to shapeshift. The obvious problem was that if she *did* manage to morph into something else, she might not be able to change back. But determined to give it a go, Devon walked around the hotel room and tried to turn into different objects. The lamp. The table. The coffeepot. She tried staring at them — lifting them — playing catch with them. She even tried meditating . . . but still nothing happened.

Feeling ridiculous, Devon sat down again.

After a moment, she took the crown out of her bag and studied the gold band with the sparkling green gemstone. How ironic that one of the poorest orphans at St. Frances owned one of the most priceless treasures in the country — a magic crown.

Well . . . If she couldn't shapeshift on her own yet, maybe she could overcome the curse and control the magic in the crown. She had already done it. So, it must be possible. If only she knew *how* she'd done it in the first place.

Devon placed the crown on her head and stood

in the middle of the room. A cloud overtook her thoughts, choosing which ones she should remember. For a moment, she was confused as to where she was.

Devon blinked.

How did she get here? . . . Where was Ms. Frances? . . . There was something that she was supposed to do —

Devon fought back against the fuzziness and ambiguity overtaking her thoughts. Slowly, a memory came back . . . and then another. . . . *She was searching for something . . . the Blue Moon . . . she was being chased . . . Niko nearly killed her . . . Elsie was expecting her tomorrow.*

"Noon sharp, and don't be late," Elsie had said.

Yes — that was it. Niko was after her. He wanted to kill her and take the crown. She needed to find the Blue Moon quickly, before Niko and the Shadow Reign caught up to her. Furthermore, she needed to learn how to control the magic crown — so she could protect herself.

Devon took a deep breath — and focused on the weightless sensation that had gotten her through the crevice outside the Blue Moon. For a while, she stood there, and still nothing happened. Then, a lightweight feeling fluttered in her chest. It spread to her fingertips, and suddenly she slipped into a shadow. Floating weightlessly, she stretched and shrank as fluidly as air. Emboldened, she shot up the wall and soared around the room before softly landing in the exact same spot, human again —

Devon yanked off the crown. A wide grin spread across her face. *She had just controlled the Crown of Guilledon!* It was only for a moment — but she had done it! And for tonight, that was enough — no, it was more than enough! It was incredible!

Exhausted, Devon sat by the door where she could hear an intruder. Bree had been right. The crown messed with her mind. It tried to control her memories, but why? What kind of curse would do that? And why would someone use it? It must be a very powerful spell — which only further proved how special the crown was. Her eyes fluttered to the window, and then the dark corners of the room. If Niko survived, he would never stop until he found her. She sat there for hours, thinking about everything that had happened. It wasn't until early morning when she finally fell asleep, curled up, under the writing desk.

CHAPTER NINE
A Secret Meeting . . . Shish!

A car alarm outside the hotel window woke her. Feeling rather foolish, Devon climbed out from under the desk. Last night had been a nightmare. She barely slept a wink, and it was consumed with vivid dreams of spies that turned into ghastly figures. Rubbing her eyes, Devon crossed the room and yanked open the curtains. Foggy streets hid behind a dreary cloud, and the sun had risen long ago. Her eyes flashed to the clock, but it's hands weren't working.

"Shoot." Devon hurried to the phone and dialed the front desk.

"Receptionist . . . ," said a curt woman.

"What time is it please?"

"The time . . . let me see . . . it's eleven-thirty."

"Oh no!" Devon cried into the receiver.

"Can I help you with something?"

"No . . . thank you." Devon dropped the phone on the receiver, grabbed her bag, and ran down the stairs, through the lobby, and didn't stop or slow for anyone

A Secret Meeting . . . Shish!

— not even the sleeping boy, who strangely looked just like Kian.

Outside, muddy, brown puddles speckled the ground forcing pedestrians to weave humorously around the street, but Devon raced straight through them. She sprinted the entire way and didn't stop until she was standing in front of the glittering blue crescent — her shoes soaked, and her jeans splattered with mud. The Blue Moon stood in exactly the same spot — like it had been there all along. Devon leaned against the scratchy paint, hugging it gratefully, and sighed.

"Momma, look at that girl," said a young boy.

"Hush!" A podgy woman with pink cheeks grabbed the boy's hand and pulled him along. "It's rude to point."

"But she was being weird," whined the boy, as his mother dragged him away.

Devon hurried inside. She ran up the crooked stairs, past the Sugar and Cinnamon Bread Shoppe, and (with a bit of concentration), squeezed through the tiny crevice.

The shop chimed as it opened, and quiet voices drifted from somewhere in the back. An old grandfather clock read 11:58, and Devon heaved a sigh of relief. She had made it. Glad of another moment to explore, Devon slipped through the tall, dusty aisles and examined the strange things.

Weapons clung to the walls in a semi-organized fashion. Dried herbs and teas, with strong aromas and weird names like garbaloo and honeymoo, filled two entire aisles. Old maps, cages, and exploration gear overflowed onto the floor and packed into corners.

Devon wondered over to a nook by an ancient window. Outside of it, the scenery changed from the familiar, muddy street in Manhattan — to a grassy hillside, where the heat from the sun beat down on her — to a busy street overlooking a canal with loud voices ringing through the window . . . .

Devon peered closer, examining the scenes outside. *It was like the shop was moving. Which wasn't possible . . . was it?*

Crowded around the nook, large baskets of animal furs and pelts topped to the brim and spilled over onto the floor. Devon leaned closer to examine the pelts. None of them belonged to any creature she had ever seen. One fur had six legs, took up three full baskets, and still overflowed onto the floor. Devon picked up a jet-black one (that was hardly bigger than a rabbit) and let the softness run through her fingers. Deep, bottle-green tips made it quite extraordinary. Amazed, she put it down and picked up another. The thin bristles pricked her fingers, drawing blood. "Ouch!"

Devon dropped it back in the basket and rubbed the soreness from her fingertips. As she started to leave, a glimmer caught the light's reflection, and she paused. A million shades of blue emulated an iridescent ocean against the dull light of the shop. It sourced from a pelt of scales that cascaded onto the floor, shimmering like opal gems in the moonlight.

Mesmerized, Devon picked up the soft pelt. Strange images filled her head. Suddenly, she was under the ocean. Dark rifts of water moved with the current. Beautiful sea creatures swam in the reefs, and the sand blew up in tufts on the ocean floor.

The creature dove deeper and Devon could feel the water break apart as it plummeted. Fewer creatures swam here, and with the depth, the ocean cooled. Enjoying the swim, the creature wove through a cave of rocks, gliding easily through the dark channels. A light dawned at the end of the cave and the creature sped up. Just before it reached through the other side, something massive broke in front of it, whipping against the sea and pushing the creature back inside the cave. It was too dark to see the danger. The massive thing broke again from behind. A tumult of water rippled, pushing the creature against the cave, and humongous serrated teeth appeared out of the dark water. A horrifying sea monster closed its jaw

A Secret Meeting . . . Shish!

around the creature's head, and Devon plummeted back to the old, cluttered shop. She dropped the pelt, her pulse hammering.

Devon stared down at the shimmering blues, dumbstruck. *Incredible!* Had she just seen the last few moments of this creature's life? Had this creature died so terribly? Unnerved, she continued to poke through the shop, leaving the rest of the pelts and furs alone.

She passed a wall lined with heads of monstrous beasts. Some had horns, some had fangs, and some had a hideous mixture of both. A particularly ferocious one was smudged with blue smears, that were likely blood.

Beneath a nameplate that read, *Snapper*, sat the largest stuffed toad Devon had ever seen (over a foot high and nearly as wide as it was tall). Since it was dead, Devon crouched beside it and admired the reddish-orange colors. It had three horns, a shiny black belly, funny purple legs, two rows of tiny black spots down its spine, and two saber teeth that hung past its squished, orange jaw.

"You're kinda cute." Devon poked its belly.

The toad twitched. Both eyes popped open, and SNAP . . . it just missing her face.

"AAAHHH!" Devon jumped back, falling over.

CROAK. The toad belched indignantly. It hopped from its perch and crawled away.

A Secret Meeting . . . Shish!

"Where have you been, missy?" barked Elsie, appearing just as suddenly as before. "You're late!"

"You said noon. I'm right on time."

"I said no such thing! He's been here since sunrise. Never in my life has he come so early. Said he would wait for you. Never heard of such a thing!" Elsie shooed Devon towards the back of the store. "Through that door there and don't forget to mind your manners. He's an important man, you know."

Elsie shoved her again, and she stumbled ungracefully into a cramped sitting room with a glowing fireplace. Oddly, or perhaps not (given that this was Elsie's place), none of the furniture matched. A loveseat hung next to a china cupboard, a birdhouse (with several colorful birds fluttering around it) stood in the corner, a baroque table sat in front of the fireplace, and a giant chandelier lit the room with hundreds of tiny, glowing lights that appeared to be buzzing. Nearly everything was chipped or broken, but it all came together somehow and was cozy (in an odd sort of way).

Next to the brick fireplace, sat a tan-skinned man with a styled, black beard. He wore a black-silk sherwani with golden, floral motifs and a tired, gentle expression. Beside him, a somber girl with skin like snow and jet-black hair stood expectantly.

A Secret Meeting . . . Shish!

Devon entered, lingering by the door, and Elsie gave her a sharp nudge forward with her bony knuckle. "In you go," croaked Elsie.

The man stood up beside a dull lamp, his gold broach catching the light. "Miss Connor? Please — have a seat."

Devon sat in an upholstered chair of bright-yellow stars — but didn't relax. She was expecting someone older. Maybe with wrinkly skin, fragile old bones, and a wig. "Are you Sir Isaac Newton?" she asked skeptically.

"You may go," the wigless man said to Elsie. He remained standing as Elsie shuffled out of the room, and when he sat, he folded his leg comfortably across his knee (like Ms. Frances said proper gentleman do). He eyed Devon curiously. "I was told Kamau had a message —"

"Uh . . . ," Devon mumbled. Now that she was here, all the things she wanted to say became jumbled up and were forgotten. "I was attacked, and I ran away from home. It's not really my home, but I live there — lived there. I don't live there anymore. I live . . . well . . . nowhere."

"I see —" He combed his beard with his fingertips. "Perhaps we should start from the beginning."

Remembering that Kamau said not to trust anyone,

A Secret Meeting ... Shish!

Devon swallowed dryly. "I have a letter — but I am supposed to give it to Sir Isaac Newton. I really should only talk to him."

"Ah." The man leaned back in his chair. "Forgive me, as I haven't introduced myself, or my associate. I am Hammad Mustafa, Head of the Department for International Magical Communities and Affairs of the United Governance of Magiks. Sir Isaac Newton is my alias. It is only used among particular friends. . . . In this case, I believe it was to help you reach me quickly, as I am normally much harder to get in touch with. This is my personal assistant, Miss Amy Gray." He indicated to the somber girl (poised with a pen and leatherbound book). "You may speak freely in front of her. I trust her above all others. Now, continue if you please, as I'm terribly curious why you were sent to me . . . and by code as well."

Being that Sir Isaac Newton was actually a high-ranking, government official of a magic world made Devon slightly more nervous. She tried to concentrate on something other than the imposing official and his stern assistant in front of her. "How do I know you are who you say?"

"Well . . . ," Hammad paused, thinking, "I believe you may have to have faith in us. Kamau sent you here, didn't he?"

A Secret Meeting . . . Shish!

"Well . . . yeah," Devon agreed.

"So tell me what you can, and I will try to earn your trust."

"I'm not sure where to begin."

"Why don't you begin with who attacked you?" Hammad encouraged.

"It was a shadow walker named Niko. He tried to kill me and nearly murdered my friend. Kamau and Bree saved us, and I don't know if they're okay —"

Hammad's eyes tightened, and he shared a troubled look with his assistant.

Restless, Devon pulled out the letter. "This should explain."

Miss Gray moved across the room, politely took the letter, and handed it to Mr. Mustafa.

Hammad held the letter in front of the fireplace and examined the five-headed dragon seal. When he was satisfied, he fumbled around in an old-fashioned writing desk and pulled out an ornate, gold lighter. He held it up to the seal and began clicking it. A flame shot out and the seal caught fire, engulfing the wax.

Devon jumped up. "NO!"

POOF. The flame went out with a puff of smoke. A red cloud floated up and took the shape of the five-headed dragon from the seal. It breathed fire . . . and then remolded into the silhouette of Hammad . . . and finally faded away. The letter, now a glowing ember, remained in perfect condition.

"Proof of who I am." Hammad smiled, amused. "The wax is magicked. All of it is — always." Hammad explained. "So I can be sure of whom this came from, and the letter can be certain of who reads it. I'm sure you didn't attempt to tamper with it, but if you had, the words would have vanished. No matter how many times I see it, I'm always captivated like a child." Hammad broke the seal and proceeded to read the letter. When he finished, he slipped it into his pocket. "Kamau and Bree will be all right. They're both unquestionably powerful. All the same . . . Miss. Gray, please send a search party to find them as soon as we're finished here."

"Of course," said Miss. Gray, and Devon let out a deep breath, relieved.

"May I see it?" Hammad asked.

"See what?" asked Devon.

"The Crown of Guilledon," he said simply. "You do still have it?"

"Oh." Devon sat for a moment — unsure of handing the crown over to anyone. But, Kamau had sent her to Hammad, and since she trusted Kamau, she unzipped her knapsack and handed over the thin gold band. The moment it was in Hammad's hands, it changed.

A Secret Meeting . . . Shish!

The large emerald melted away. The gold liquified and wove into a soft velvet lined with precious jewels. Pearls, rubies, turquoises, sapphires, and diamonds sprouted from the crown, and regal feathers drooped back majestically at the top. The three of them leaned in, mystified.

"Magnificent!" Eyes sparkling, Hammad held the new crown up high, admiring the workmanship and fabulous jewels. "This headdress is from the Mughal dynasty."

"Mughal dynasty?" asked Devon

"The Mughal dynasty ruled in the sixteenth and seventeenth centuries in what is now modern-day Pakistan and India. It was the empire of my ancestors." Hammad glanced back at Devon. "This isn't the crown you were just holding —"

Devon shook her head. "No, I've never seen that crown before —"

"How intriguing . . . it must change for each magik that touches it . . . perhaps if I . . . ?" Hammad set it down on the baroque table. The moment his hands were free, the crown metamorphosed again into the heavy, medieval crown, laden with emeralds and blood-red rubies.

"Spectacular," Mr. Mustafa breathed. . . . "As a child, I grew up hearing stories about the Crown of

Guilledon. Never in my wildest dreams did I imagine that I would hold it with my own two hands." A look of longing glazed over. Then, like waking from a daze, Hammad's eyes fluttered, and focused on Devon. "Have you told anyone else about this?"

Devon shook her head. "Why would someone curse it?"

"The legend of the Crown of Guilledon is a fascinating one. Many years ago, there lived two brothers. Both were mighty kings of their own kingdoms. The crown was a gift bestowed in an elaborate ceremony from King Kazar, king of the shapeshifters, to his brother King Zaeg, king of the shadow walkers. It symbolized peace between the two kingdoms of changers and was crafted by one of the greatest warlocks to ever have lived. Before the ceremony, King Kazar secretly had a curse cast on the crown, and King Zaeg fell under its spell. When King Zaeg finally learned he had been tricked, nearly a century had passed, and King Kazar had taken over his kingdom."

"Wow. He betrayed his own brother?"

"Yes. King Kazar knew of his brother's growing thirst for power and used it to lead his brother into his trap. Since then, many magiks have spent their lives seeking it. Some simply for its rich history, others for the price it would fetch — wealth beyond dreams. The more ambitious would have wanted its magic."

Devon fidgeted in her seat. "The ability to change between shadow walker and shapeshifter?"

"Yes. The legend says the beholder can change between a shapeshifter and shadow walker at will — possessing the abilities of both changers at once. But how did you know?"

"Because Kamau told me . . . and I've done it."

Hammad's eyes tightened, and he leaned forward, no longer subduing his interest. "Have you done anything else?"

"No . . . why?"

"It's also said the beholder can manipulate magical properties contained in other forms . . . like perhaps, a wand or staff."

"Are you saying whoever wears that can become a wizard?"

"Not quite. Only a wizard born a wizard can be a wizard. But a magik in possession of both the Crown of Guilledon and an object containing magical properties could control the magic of that object. At least to some extent. Which is why it would appeal to King Zaeg who sought power."

Devon bit her lip. "And Niko." With the power of both changers, and the ability to control other magic, no wall could stop the Shadow Reign. There was still the problem with the curse though. "How does the curse mess with your mind?"

Hammad locked eyes with Miss Gray, apprehensively. "Well . . . nobody knows *exactly*," said Hammad, "but the one thing everyone does know of, is its tendency to cloud the wearer's thoughts, obscuring time, erasing memories, and blocking magic. It's said . . . that an unknowing magik is most likely to be bewitched by its enchantment."

"I don't know what you mean by *unknowing*, but that sounds like what happened when I had the crown on," agreed Devon. It made sense of times when an eventful memory was forgotten, or a peculiar incident became fuzzy.

"I meant . . . that if one doesn't know about the curse when putting it on, they have no chance of conquering the spell and can fall deeper into its sorcery. How long has this been in your possession?" Hammad asked.

A memory flashed of the crystal-eyed woman, with the braided hair and cloak, that gave it to her. "A couple years ago — I'm twelve now."

Hammad's eyes softened. "I find it . . . unlikely that you've been wearing this relic for so short a time, though it may seem that way to you. That's part of its remarkable magic."

A Secret Meeting... Shish!

"I don't understand."

"You see, when you wore this, you were here physically. You could be seen and heard and so on, and you lived life normally... but a part of you was not here... as if you were frozen in time, caught between dimensions. It dulled your senses and erased your memory. It should have concealed your magic entirely, but according to Kamau you overcame it — perhaps, more than once."

"You're saying that I was here, but I wasn't... like I was in some other dimension?" Devon snorted. Just saying it aloud sounded crazy.

"Not quite. More like you were caught between two dimensions. Of course, some theorists say that's all hooey. You could be twelve as you say... or a few years older... or... you could be a few hundred years older." Seeing Devon's startled expression, Hammad hurried on. "If it helps, our kind don't age quite the same way as humans do. I'm celebrating my three-hundred-and-eighty-seventh birthday this November."

"*How is that possible!*" Devon massaged her temple.

"Time passes differently for us," said Hammad. "Mostly, we age like ordinary humans until our first transformation. Then, some changers go through rapid growth and, for a time, age quickly, while others

A Secret Meeting . . . Shish!

will stop at that precise moment and won't change again for years. It's important to understand that magiks don't age the same as humans, and not the same as each other."

Devon picked up the crown, and watched it transform into a thin, gold band. "If I stopped aging, Ms. Frances would have noticed."

"Quite right," agreed Hammad. "Something I will be looking into personally. It should be a remarkably interesting conversation. I would like to know how you came to be at the institute. Then, perhaps we'll learn where you picked up such a distinguished piece of magic."

Devon fiddled with the crown. Her whole life had changed in just two days. She was wanted by an assassin for having a notorious crown. Now, a magik government official was telling her she may have been living as a twelve-year-old for years without ever noticing.

"I know this may be a lot to take in," Hammad said kindly. "But . . . as we said . . . with this on, you still showed signs of magic — which leads me to believe you may be a uniquely-strong magik yourself."

"Niko said that too." Devon returned the crown to the table.

"Very clever of him."

"But I wasn't strong enough to beat him. He hurt my friend."

Hammad's eyes softened. "That is expected. Niko had training, and you have not."

"I ran." As she said it, the guilt she had buried, resurfaced. "Kamau said if I didn't run, Niko would kill my best friend."

"You made a difficult choice," said Kamau. "One that, I can tell, goes against your very nature. But if I may offer a bit of advice . . . if Kamau ever says you should run, you should run. He is one of the most respected warlocks I've ever known, and he would not lead you astray."

"Thanks," Devon said, feeling slightly better.

"Well then." Hammad clapped his hands together lightheartedly. "According to the letter, the shadow walker, Niko, believed you to be a shapeshifter?"

"I hope so — I don't want to be a shadow walker."

Hammad raised his brow in surprise. "Why ever not?"

"A shadow walker nearly murdered my friend! Shadow walkers want war — and I don't want to be a part of any war."

"Some of them, yes, are trying to tear our way of life apart. But I have many friends that are shadow walkers who only want peace. They're an incredibly

A Secret Meeting . . . Shish!

powerful kind of magik. To believe they are all evil is to misunderstand them and to misguide yourself. Every living soul has the choice of good and evil." Hammad turned to his assistant. "Miss Gray . . . would you please?"

Amy faded into a shadow. The darkness crept over the ceiling, spreading across the room, and then instantly, it converged, and she changed back again. Miss Gray stood, perfectly still, with a pen and paper in hand.

Devon tensed momentarily . . . and then, slowly relaxed. "You're right. Everyone has a choice." As an orphan, she knew this as well as anyone.

Seeing that she understood, Mr. Mustafa began to pace. "Right. . . . The best thing to do now is to hide the crown somewhere safe — somewhere it won't break — or fall into the wrong hands."

Devon hesitated. "The crown is . . . already broken." She clenched, guiltily.

Hammad picked up the crown — it transformed into the brilliant headdress — and he studied the thin crack. "I wouldn't say it's broken," he assured her. "I doubt it's quite that fragile. You may find that, in time, it will heal itself like all things do. But for now —"

Hammad picked up the ornate, gold lighter, and with a gentle rub of his thumb, a sliver of metal carvings *absorbed* into his skin. His thumb shimmered, and he lightly touched it against the crown. The crown smoldered as the gold flowed into the crack, molding back together.

"How did you do that?"

Hammad smiled. "Shapeshifters, powerful ones, can do a little more than morph into other things." His thumb stopped glowing. "Now, as I was saying, we need to get this crown someplace safe — somewhere the Shadow Reign won't get it."

"I'll take it," Devon blurted.

Hammad's dark eyes twinkled. "Are you sure? You were very brave to get it this far. But keeping it in your possession will put your life at risk — Kamau told me in the letter, that Niko plans to use the crown to invade Thysia. Until now, there has been nothing I can think of that would allow a magik to sneak past the magical walls around Thysia. This crown, might actually do it — for one, very dangerous magik. And once inside, who knows what a shadow walker assassin might do? There are many ways to topple an already precarious city."

"This started with me. I want to finish it."

"But sir!" Miss Gray interrupted. "Surely the crown would be safest with us!"

"Perhaps. . . ." Hammad eyed Devon skeptically

A Secret Meeting . . . Shish!

and then said, "But consider this Miss Gray. Being that I work in a high-level position for the magik government, and you work for me, we are constantly watched. No part of our lives is private. We wouldn't get past security without it being discovered. And by whom?"

Miss. Gray sucked in air, tensely.

"You know as well as I, there are spies for the Shadow Reign within our own government. What would we do if they got their hands on it? Niko may be chasing her, but with us, it will certainly be found — and confiscated. Not even I could prevent that."

Miss. Gray gritted her teeth but remained quiet, which was likely the best approval Devon would get. Kamau turned back to Devon. "If you can get the crown into Thysia, it will give me time to arrange a safe place for it. We'll have somebody meet you inside."

Devon let out a deep breath she didn't know she was holding on to. "I'll get it there." She knew if she kept the crown, she'd never stop being a target, but she wanted to hold onto it a bit longer. She was learning from it — she had *controlled* its magic. And now that she knew of the curse, she was more likely to beat it, right? This was the moment to tell Hammad how much she had controlled the crown's magic, and what she planned to do with it, but the words never came —

"Then forgive me for sounding like a parent, but I must leave you with a final warning. The curse is very powerful. Don't put it on and don't show it to anyone. The shadow walker killed without mercy just to keep it a secret. If word gets out that the Crown of Guilledon has been found and someone so defenseless has it, there will be no safe place for you."

Devon stiffened at the word *defenseless*. Was that how he saw her? She zipped the crown back in her bag. "I won't tell anyone," she vowed, making one promise, but not the other. She'd keep the crown safe — but in the meantime, she'd learn everything she could from it. She didn't like being seen as defenseless — whether it was true or not.

"Now, there is the matter of what we should do with you," Hammad said. "Most obviously, you cannot return to Hasty." He waited, giving Devon a moment to accept this, but there was no need. She never wanted to go back there again. "I'll address Ms. Frances directly and inform her that her ownership of your care has been terminated. Perhaps, Kamau has already done so." Hammad turned to Miss Gray. "When Kamau and Bree have been located, check in and see what's been done already."

A Secret Meeting ... Shish!

Miss Gray scribbled in her book. "There should be no problem getting these done straight away."

"Good." Hammad returned to his seat across from Devon. "Now, the only place for you ... if you'll consent to stay ... is Thysia. It's inhabited solely by magiks, hidden away in the valley of the Bearded Mountains. You'll meet others like yourself. As you have no family, and I assume ... no offense ... ," Hammad smiled apologetically, "no money, it will be difficult ... but not impossible."

"What will I do in Thysia?" Devon sat straighter and pulled the knapsack in her lap. Since she had left St. Frances, her only thought had been to find the Blue Moon. She hadn't made any plans of what she should do next. How would she keep this a secret? And if she was a magik, what did that make her parents?

"Like all youth, you'll learn. Education is essential to improvement, and improvement is the only path to growth. ..." Hammad tapped his finger against his chin and added, "There's a school called Beorgburg. You can apply for admission."

Miss Gray stifled a cough. Hammad glanced over his shoulder and she dipped her head, suddenly engaged in her scribbles.

"Beorgburg?" Devon repeated. That was the school Hex had mentioned. Those kids from the Ghost

A Secret Meeting . . . Shish!

Tavern went to school there. She couldn't imagine facing them again so soon —

"Beorgburg is the most elite school for magiks in the country," Hammad said, interrupting her thoughts, "perhaps even the world. However, getting in will be difficult. It takes a great deal of money, talent, and connection to get accepted. Many promising magiks are turned away." Hammad thought for a moment. "You'll need a benefactor."

"A benefactor?" asked Devon.

"To ensure your acceptance, you'll need someone with not only a great deal of wealth, but someone who has influence. Because of my current position with the United Governance of Magiks, I cannot personally do it. It will attract too much attention. For now, it would be best for you to go along unobserved. . . . Does this sound acceptable to you? You do, of course, have a choice . . . if there were somewhere else you would like to go perhaps?"

Though she hadn't thought much about it, she felt certain she didn't need too. "No. I want to live with other magiks, like me."

"Good." Hammad's approval shone on his face. "Now. A private institution will be expensive, Beorgburg the most, so finding a benefactor will be difficult —"

"I may be able to attain a shortlist of possible candidates." Miss Gray flipped a page in her book and continued to scribble.

"Very good." Hammad nodded warmly. "In the meantime," he said to Devon, "I'll enroll you in one of the smaller academies. Perhaps Gordimer is best. As it happens, I know the Headmistress well. I'll reach out to her and request she take you on as a special case. Room and board will be financed by me." Hammad's expression turned solemn. "I expect you to repay me for my assistance with excellent grades and new friendships. And I'm confident you'll conduct yourself in a manner relative of someone receiving my notice — one that would not embarrass yourself or me for recommending you."

Feeling like she was already being disciplined for something she hadn't done, Devon mumbled, "I'll try my best," and then added, "but I'm not sure about new friends." She was never particularly good at making friends. Leni had been an exception, and she already missed her.

Hammad laid a hand on her shoulder. "Friends will come and go. Some will become part of your past, and others will steer your future. But you must always face the next day. You must always be willing to try again and not let the world bare down on you." He handed

A Secret Meeting . . . Shish!

her the ornate, gold lighter. "That being said . . . with exception to the Headmistress, myself, and Miss Gray, no one will know that I've assisted you, in any way."

"Thank you . . . ," Devon admired the scrolls curving delicately down the lighter, except for a small edge where the gold was missing, "for everything." He was right. Somewhere out there was a whole world of magic, and she was going to live in it. The thought made her heart beat faster.

Hammad pulled out a gold timepiece with three clock faces, extra dials, and knobs jutting out everywhere. "It's best not to waste any more time. The next ferry departs this evening. If you leave within the hour, you should make it."

Miss Gray continued to scribble, pausing only to lean forward and whisper to Hammad. He nodded in silent agreement. "Miss Gray will accompany you to the dock. After that, you'll be on your own, I'm afraid. The ferry will take you through the underwater passage straight into Thysia. There shouldn't be any trouble. . . . Send a letter to Miss Gray once you've settled in and then one regularly with an account of your progress."

Devon handed over the money pouch. "Kamau gave this to me. I used some for food and a room last night. Can you return it to him?"

A Secret Meeting . . . Shish!

Hammad glanced inside the pouch and handed it to his assistant. "Double that amount and return it to Kamau. Devon can keep what is left inside."

Miss Gray emptied the coins, plates, gems, and folded bills onto the weathered table by the fireplace and rummaged through them. Then she scribbled the sum on her notepad and pocketed the pouch to return to Kamau. Hammad rang a bell.

A moment later, Elsie came waddling in and bowed awkwardly. "Do ya need something sir?" Her eyes twitched towards the pile of Gubbins on the table.

"Yes. Please supply Miss Connor with a new money pouch, along with any other essentials she needs for travel and school. Miss Gray will take care of the bill."

A toothy grin spread across Elsie's face. "Yes, sir. It'd be my pleasure, sir." She bowed sloppily. "Anything ya need, I'm the one to do it — sir." She bowed twice more as she backed out of the room.

"Oh, and Cornelia," Mr. Mustafa pointed to the ornate lighter in Devon's hands. "Would you please add that to the bill."

"Oh — ah — but," Elsie stuttered and rethinking it, ducked out of the room. "O'course, sir."

Hammad checked his pocket watch again. "I should be on my way. I don't believe there is anything else . . . but if you need something, address it in the

A Secret Meeting . . . Shish!

letter to Miss Gray. Remember . . . once I've left this room, we will have no connection whatsoever. Sir Isaac Newton is dead. You must forget that name and never again repeat it to anyone. Can you do that?"

Devon stood up to leave. "Not a problem. Your secret is safe with me." She was curious why a magic politician needed a secret alias, but she'd keep his secret. "I'm not sure how to thank you —"

"You just did." He held out his hand, and she shook it. His hard expression locked on hers, deciding if she was trustworthy. "I'll be watching for something spectacular from you." He dipped his head in farewell. Then, without warning, he metamorphosed into a fluttering, black bird and flew straight at the brick wall. Just as he reached it, the wall opened up and rearranged itself. Mr. Mustafa flew through, and Devon barely caught a glimpse of the street before the wall closed again.

"Woah," said Devon, wishing she had assured him somehow. There was no one at St. Frances more trustworthy than her. Leni had been the closest.

Elsie returned barely a moment later and seeing that Mr. Mustafa was gone, dropped all formal civilities. "Gone out the back, did he?" She dumped a dusty box of pouches on the table and then left again. There were a dozen different varieties — some new, some old, some large or small, and others oddly shaped — all in various colors from murky brown to dull blue.

While Miss Gray waited for Elsie to return, Devon rummaged through the pouches and picked up a leather one. It was a little worn but sturdier than the others. She flipped it over and traced her finger over the gold stitching on the back: a five-headed dragon like the one Kamau stamped on the letter.

"What does this mean?" Devon pointed to the dragon.

From her position across the room, Miss Gray's eyes flashed to the pouch. From the way her eyes narrowed, Devon was sure she recognized it. "It doesn't mean anything."

"It's the same dragon as the one Kamau used to seal the letter," Devon pressed.

"I'm sure you're mistaken," Miss Gray said shortly, ending any invitation of probing further.

Elsie returned and dumped an ugly and large, brown valise with an old-fashioned lock on the table. It clunked loudly against the wood.

"What's *that* for?" Devon's mouth fell open.

"Yer trunk," Elsie replied, matter-of-factly. "To put yer school things in."

A Secret Meeting . . . Shish!

Devon made a face. "No thanks." She was fairly sure she had seen it earlier full of grain. Elsie must have dumped the grain to sell the case.

"Don' be ridiculous. Made in England, it was — by one of the finest trunk makers. It's even got a lock and key." Elsie shook it so it rattled. "Very strong."

Devon eyed it doubtfully. "It looks like it's fifty years old!"

"No, no," said Elsie. "At least a hundred. I've had it meself for eighty."

Devon turned to Miss Gray for help — but she only shrugged. After all, Mr. Mustafa had requested Devon be outfitted with everything she needed, and that included a trunk.

Elsie took her silence as a confirmation and spotting the leather satchel in Devon's hand, hurried on, "You've chosen one then? Ah. That's a fine one, it is. It belonged to the house of DuVingnaud — one of the oldest families in Thysia. No descendants. Dreadful affair. . . . Good quality though," she added, perking up.

"What happened to DuVingnaud?" Devon asked.

"We're on a schedule," Miss Gray cut in. "I'm sure we can talk about these bedtime stories another time." Miss Gray strode around the table, took the pouch, and began filling it with the coins and gems. "Elsie . . .

A Secret Meeting . . . Shish!

I'll need a gift. Something *nice* . . . and a thermos of honeyed milk."

Elsie's eyes dawned with understanding. "Ah. I have just the thing. I'll just add it to the bill, shall I?"

"That will be fine."

Elsie unlocked the trunk and handed a rusty key to Devon. "Come. Come. We'll fill the trunk." Without waiting, she strode off with a hop in her step and a gleam in her eye. Devon tucked the key in her pocket and hurried to catch up.

Elsie darted around the store, pulling odd things off shelves, and muttering to herself like a crackpot. Before long, Devon's arms were laden with magical baubles, gadgets, and doodads including, a heavy metal compass, a self-heating rock that turned ember when you smashed it, several musty books with no covers, and boots that had proved to be fireproof when the old kook set them aflame because Devon turned them down.

"Here, take this," Elsie said, handing Devon a worn, leather jacket.

"That's a man's jacket." Devon handed it back.

Elsie gawked. "Don't be a half-wit. It's made with Afanc hide. And it's lined with the skin of a chimera."

"So?" Devon pushed it back at Elsie again.

"Afanc hide is nearly indestructible." Elsie unzipped

the jacket and jabbed her thumb inside. "This one has a secret pocket."

Devon rubbed the fine lining. There were no pockets anywhere. She snorted. "You're trying to swindle me."

Elsie's eyes flashed dangerously. "I'd never cheat any—" she cut off abruptly. "I'm not cheating *you* — and that's all that matters." She hugged the jacket delicately. "You're lucky I'm offerin' to sell it at all. Mr. Mustafa will pay what's fair, that's why. Would hav' kept it for me'self but it doesn't fit."

Elsie stuffed it back into Devon's arms. "Put it on, and when you need it, you'll find the pocket." Elsie shuffled over to a shelf and lifted the top off a large jar. She pulled out several pieces of spiced jerky. A strong smell of meat and salt filled the air, making Devon's nose itch. Elsie stuffed them in a paper bag, that immediately soaked with grease, and handed it to Devon. "Klug," she said. "Good protein."

"Eww." Disgusted, Devon pushed the bag back at Elsie. "You're supposed to give me things I *need* for school. This stuff is completely useless. And don't think I'm going to let you take advantage of Mr. Mustafa."

"USELESS? . . . TAKE ADVANTAGE!" Elsie turned red and dropped the bag of greasy meat in Devon's arms. "You ungrateful lot! Nothing I sell is

A Secret Meeting . . . Shish!

useless. Maybe unnecessary, but NOT useless!" Elsie strode off, leaving Devon with the Klug, and both of them seething in frustration. Still grouchy, Elsie returned and handed Devon a box of vials with gold lettering.

KIT FOR YOUR BASIC ROOTS, POWDERS, AND TUNDERS

Tiny labels read: Dindle, Milkweed, Fluxroot, and Bottercress.

The old crow added several sachets of powders and roots to the box.

"What are tunders?"

"Grains and bugs. All the little ingredients in your craft-making kit."

"I don't need this, Elsie." Devon handed the box back."

"You *do* need it. Every magik is taught the basics of magical remedies and brews. Not just mages and wizards." Elsie handed the box back to Devon. "This is a good start but if you need more," she lowered her voice to a whisper, "come see me." Elsie grabbed a handful of sapphire rocks and threw them into a dying fireplace. It burst into a blazing blue light. Instant warmth and sweet aromas spread, making the shop cozy and homelike.

A Secret Meeting . . . Shish!

"What was that?" Devon's eyes popped open.

"Fire Crystals. Can blaze a room anywhere, and the colors last for hours." Elsie sniffed, so her nose crinkled. "I smell peanut butter and sugar cookie — think I smell a dab of toasted pistachio too. It could be something else though."

"I want some," Devon blurted. They had to be more useful than the rest of this junk.

"You do, do you?" Elsie grinned smugly. "Alrigh' then, but it will cost ya."

"I'm sure it will."

Unperturbed, Elsie filled a satchel and handed it to Devon. "Keep 'em in the bag. The bag is fireproof. You don' want to go aroun' settin' things on fire —"

Elsie shut the cupboard before Miss Gray could get suspicious. "Now, let me see. . . ." Elsie tapped her temple. "How about a light?" Elsie hurried off, forcing Devon to play chase. By the time Devon caught up, Elsie was clicking her teeth impatiently in front of a long row of lanterns. Lifting one by one, she inspected them carefully, checking their weight and sturdiness. She swung them, tapped them, and even sniffed a few. Frowning, Elsie examined a rustic, green one and finally satisfied, handed it to Devon. "This will have to do."

"Do for what?"

A Secret Meeting . . . Shish!

Elsie gave her an exasperated look. "For light . . . duh."

Devon flipped the lantern over. "Where is the bulb? . . . Or wick?"

Elsie scrunched her face. "You don't know nothing!"

Devon grumbled a place where Elsie could stick it.

"What did you say, missy?"

"I said how is it supposed to light?" Devon said loudly.

"Boewood of course!" Elsie pointed to a humongous, glass cage on clawed feet, and for the first time, Devon noticed the brilliant source of light: It wasn't a bulb, candle, or lantern, but a huge, glass cage with thousands of tiny creatures zooming around inside. Elsie pulled on thick gloves that extended past her elbows.

"Are those bugs?"

"Boewood. I said that, didn't I? Stand back a bit. Bit more. Child, they have teeth like razors, and they're hotter than coal . . . lit-tle more." Elsie slid the glass open just a crack and dropped her net inside.

A dozen fiery Boewood flew into the net, and Elsie emptied them into the lantern. Then she dipped the net back into the cage. After a few minutes, hundreds of tiny, glowing boewood zoomed around inside the rustic lantern. Elsie replaced her gloves to the table and hurried back around the glass cage.

"How come they don't burn the net?"

"It's tempered, girl," Elsie tapped the cage with her cane, "just like the glass." She pointed to two metal caps on the green lantern. "You put sugar in one and syrup in the other. They eat it as it drips to the bottom. No water." Elsie handed Devon a sack of sugar. "They don't need nothing else."

"What if they die?" Devon asked.

"All things die, missy. You jus' got to come back an' get more. They should last you a year. I expect, I'll see you then for more things anyhow."

Devon doubted it, but she didn't say so. Instead, she followed the old woman around the store, while

A Secret Meeting . . . Shish!

she piled one oddity after another into Devon's arms. Finally, when she was satisfied, Devon stuffed them all in her trunk, while Miss Gray took care of their debt.

Now that she had a destination, a newish trunk, a bunch of used things, and enough money to start a new life, Devon relaxed. The Ferry would take her straight to Thysia, where she would be safe. She would help hide the crown so Niko and the Shadow Reign couldn't steal it. Thysia would be safe and then, this would all be behind her. It was simple. For the first time in days, Devon breathed easy.

Miss Gray handed over an impressive sum of coins, not bothering to haggle over the absurd price (something Devon wouldn't have done). Obviously, Elsie had a sly knack for business.

"Good day." Elsie patted her pocket gingerly, liking the sound of the jingle.

"Good day," Miss Gray returned politely.

The brick wall scrambled into a door, and using her best manners, Elsie politely saw them through it. "Come back *any time*." She flashed a toothy smile.

As soon as they were through the wall, the door vanished without a trace. Cars whizzed by the busy street in Manhattan, and Amy Gray was already on a phone, speaking quietly.

CHAPTER TEN
The Fairy Ferry

There was only a moment of foolishness — standing on the sidewalk with an ancient valise while cars whizzed by — before a spacious, black sedan pulled up with tinted windows and shiny silver handles. Jumping out of the car, the driver raced to the front passenger side and opened the door for Miss Gray. Briskly taking the valise from Devon, he heaved it into the trunk and hurried back to his seat, leaving Devon to open her own door and climb in.

The stiff leather didn't help settle her nerves as they drove. She had a million questions. Perhaps she would have asked one or two, but Miss Gray had settled into silence, and the driver, used to her quiet ways, didn't bother to disturb the tranquility of the trip.

Once they were out of the city, they picked up speed, and the passing scenery became blurs. With nothing else to do, Devon slumped against the window and fell asleep simply out of boredom.

It was well after dark when Devon awoke. Groggy, it took a moment to assess that the car had slowed and was traveling through a winding road with nothing but trees in sight.

They turned down a steep, inconspicuous drive they could have passed a dozen times, and nobody would have noticed. The spacious car kicked up a light layer of dust, and finally stopped. Like before, the driver rushed to the passenger side, opened the door for Miss Gray, and left Devon to open her own.

"I'll be back shortly," Miss Gray directed, tucking her short, black hair behind her ear.

The driver, silent as a mouse, heaved Devon's valise from the trunk, hurried back to the driver seat, and shut the door with a snap.

"This way." Miss Gray started gingerly down a path, distinguished only by the dead grass — trampled from frequented footfalls. It jutted into the lining of the trees and out of sight. "It's only a short walk from here."

Aside from the illuminating glow from Devon's boewood lantern, there wasn't a shimmer of light. They walked in darkness, with trees, roots, and shrubs constantly in their way. So that without the lantern, the awkward path would have been treacherously impassable.

Through a clearing, they came to a dune waterfront, well hidden in a secluded cove. A layer of fog hovered near the entrance, and three ferries sat along the shore — illuminated by lamp posts with bright flames of molten gold.

Mesmerized by the flickering colors (from warm honey to sunset yellow), Devon hardly noticed the steep path had ended, and the soft sand caved beneath her footsteps. "Why is the fire gold?" she wondered aloud — though she wasn't expecting an answer, since Miss Gray had hardly spoken at all.

"It's Fairy Fire," Miss Gray replied shortly, surprising Devon.

"Fairy Fire?"

"Yes. Fairy Fire burns forever. It need not be tended and provides infinite light."

"Why don't they make the lanterns with Fairy Fire then?" asked Devon, holding hers up.

"Put Fairy Fire in that —?" Miss Gray snorted. "Too dangerous." She hastened to the ticket booth, where a balding man with oval rimmed spectacles that barely fit his large nose, sat hidden behind a purple newspaper — which read, in bold letters, Enchanted Chronicle. Miss Gray rapped on the window, startling the man so much that he would have fallen from his chair had there been enough room inside for him to do it.

"Blasted to hell, dag nammit —" The man adjusted his spectacles and spotting Miss Gray, cut off abruptly. . . . "Oh. Excuse me, Miss Gray. I didn't see you there," he recovered awkwardly. "What can I do for you? . . . Is Mr. Mustafa here with you as well?"

"No. Today's business is unrelated. I need one ticket for the Gates of Thysia. Next departure."

"Well, let's see then . . ." He opened a dusty book, smeared his thumb across his tongue, and flipped through the pages. "The next departure . . . the next departure . . ." His finger stopped, and his balding head popped up. "The last departure would be the Fairy Ferry. Perhaps you'd rather —"

"It will do fine," Miss Gray said shortly and glanced down at her watch — though Devon expected she knew the time to the exact minute already.

"Right'o." The man snapped the book shut and pretended to be interested in something on his desk. "Are you traveling today, Miss Gray?"

"No. An acquaintance of mine." Miss Gray dropped a few coins into a silver tin.

"Ah." His eyes settled on Devon. With a calculating look, he tore off a ticket the size of a mango and slid it through the window. "The ferry departs in three minutes. Give that to the cap' and he'll give you a room."

Devon took the ticket, and the man turned to Miss Gray. "Is there anythin' else I can do for you, Miss?"

"Not today, thank you."

"Always a'pleasure . . . and . . . uh . . . I'd be pleased if you didn' mention me swearing."

"I wouldn't dream of it." A smile peeked through the corner of Miss Gray's mouth, and she led Devon down to the short docks where the three ferries were anchored. Soothing waves rippled across the sand beneath the glow of the Fairy Fire. A rustic, orange ferry with purple trim, floated between two grander ferries — one crystal blue (reflecting light like a glass sculpture), and the other yellow (like daisies in the morning sun). It didn't take long to reach them. Hardly a minute and not nearly two. Barely enough time for Devon to prepare herself for what came next.

Halfway along the middle of the dock, three men huddled together, but as Devon approached, it became apparent that two of them (which were half the height of the third), weren't men at all. Short tusks stuck out from their lower jaws, and they had reddish-orange skin with long pointed ears. They laughed jovially at the captain of the rustic, patchwork ferry (a thin, frail man whose trousers fit much too small).

"Hobgoblins . . . ," Miss Gray warned quietly. "Best not to agitate them. They get a tad vengeful."

Devon's mouth fell open as she eyed the swords hanging from their waists. *Hobgoblins?*

"I bet my ol' dory could outrun that bathtub," said one hobgoblin, who was portly, shorter than a tabletop, with a long, crooked nose that nearly reached his chin. He laughed so hard that he held his belly like it hurt.

"Look at it leanin'," teased the second hobgoblin, who was thin as a twig (though just a short, and just as orange).

"How yeh get that totter to go?" the portly hobgoblin jested, his voice carrying the length of the docks. "Push or pull?" He animated with rowing motions, and the two burst into a renewed fit of laughter.

The man, neither as orange, nor as short, steamed red as an iron stovetop. He whipped his captain's hat from his head threateningly —

"Excuse us, gentleman," Miss Gray called, interrupting them. The three quarreling men paused. "You have a passenger —"

Miss Gray nudged Devon forward, implicating the need for their assistance.

"A'course, ma'am." The portly hobgoblin tipped his hat.

"This is where we part ways." Miss Gray reached inside her jacket and pulled out a ruby amulet. "Give this to the captain once you take off. Absolutely *not* before!" she insisted and then handed over the amulet along with the thermos of milk and honey.

The Fairy Ferry

"Why am I supposed to give these to the captain?"

"The ticket paid the ferry fees," explained Miss Gray, "but the captain will want a gift for the trip you'll require. He prefers treasure to coins."

This utterly stumped Devon. Gubbins, gold, coins — they were all money, and Miss Gray had already paid for a ticket. "I don't understand."

"You will. . . ." Miss Gray lowered her voice to a

whisper. "Remember your promise. Hide that crown, and Sir Isaac Newton is dead. You must get to Thysia as fast as you can! If Niko is alive, and the Shadow Reign catches you, you're as good as dead — and Thysia is lost. The Shadow Reign will invade the city and kill every magik that stands in their way."

Sweat prickled down Devon's neck, and she tugged at her collar.

"I'll send a letter once Kamau and Bree have been found. And as soon as possible benefactors are located, you'll be notified." Miss Gray slipped a piece a parchment in Devon's hand with a handwritten address. "I'll be expecting a letter in two days.

"Right." Grasping the thermos tightly, Devon headed down the rickety dock. The wood creaked under her. "Thank you!" She spun around, but Miss Gray had already climbed back up the path, into the woods, and disappeared from sight.

Alone, Devon walked down the narrow dock. With each step, the tiniest ripple threatened to sink her beneath the surface. She stopped beside the luminescent ferry with rustic orange paint and blue trim that glowed against the dark sky.

Recognizing the overly large ticket, the infuriated man calmed down. "Ah. You'd be with me then," he said smugly. "Welcome to the Fairy Ferry." He waved dramatically to the sinking ship behind him, patched together with mismatched parts from other boats. "I'm Gnuld, Cap'n of the Fairy Ferry," the frail man boasted, and pulled a ladder down for her to climb aboard.

Devon managed a doubtful smile. At best, the ferry was unimpressive, but if she were being honest, the hobgoblins were right in making fun of it. "Will it sink?"

At this, the two hobgoblins bent over and laughed with uncontrollable snickers so that their long noses touched their bellies.

Gnuld turned red. "Course it won't. Tis the fastest ferry in a thousand leagues."

"Gah. Hah. Ha." His companions burst into a renewed fit of laughter so that tears leaked in their eyes, and they had trouble breathing.

Ignoring the hobgoblins, Gnuld gritted his teeth and held out his hand. "I'll take your ticket."

Devon handed it over and tried her best to be brave. She was fine going to Thysia alone. She preferred it even. . . . But riding that ferry didn't feel like a good idea at all.

"Oy there! This is your last chance," the portly hobgoblin cried between gasps. "You don't want to be riding that totter. Come back whilst you can and purchase a ticket for another ferry."

"I can't wait for the next ferry to Thysia," explained Devon. Reluctantly, she reached for the ladder.

"Hang on . . . ," cried the portly hobgoblin, "least take a life vest with yeh."

"Or some floaties." The other hobgoblin balled with laughter.

Quick as lightning, Gnuld shoved both hobgoblins off the dock. They fell backwards into the water. Icy splashes soaked Devon's shirt, and she shivered.

"Bloody hell!" The portly hobgoblin spat water from his mouth.

"We'll get you back for this," growled the twig hobgoblin as he swam for his ship. "I'll sink your ferry before the night is done."

"Gaff!" Ignoring the shouts of obscenities, Captain Gnuld shoved past Devon. "You comin' or not?"

With nothing else to do, Devon hurried after him. Meanwhile, the two hobgoblins reached their own ferries and climbed out of the water. Remembering what Amy had warned her about hobgoblins, she asked, "Would they really sink us?"

"Gah." Gnuld slapped away the notion. "Let 'em try." He pointed to another passenger, already waiting for the ferry to depart. "Wait there whilst I gather the crew."

"But —" Devon started. . . . Gnuld, however, had already strode off.

Devon joined the dark-haired boy, with a backpack slung across his shoulders. "Are you headed to Thysia too?"

He tossed a rock in the water, watching it skip over the waves. "No."

"Ahoy!" Gnuld hailed, across the ferry.

No one answered.

Gnuld clumped across the deck and untied the ropes himself. "AHOY!"

A moment later he returned, slightly shorter than before. He guffawed at the hobgoblins, rushing to untie their ferries from the dock. A wicked smirk spread across Gnuld's beard.

Wait. Had he had a beard before? Devon narrowed her eyes. As she studied him, he continued to shrink. His reddish-brown beard grew, weaving into three beaded braids.

Devon held out her hand, measuring her height to his . . . he was definitely shrinking.

Gnuld scurried across the empty ferry. "Come on ye' scallywags," he yelled to a non-existent crew. "Ready the ship!"

"He's mad," Devon snorted.

The captain returned again — so short, he had to climb a stool to spy over the side of the ferry at the hobgoblins, who were now rushing about their ships.

Aghast, Devon stared down at a bearded man (no

The Fairy Ferry

taller than a foot or two) with long, slender ears, bony arms, and gold earrings beneath a pointed hat. He grinned up devilishly. "Best hold on.

The hobgoblin ships circled in front and fired at the Fairy Ferry. The air exploded.

Gnuld shot his arms above him. A sphere of magic erupted from his stubby hands and encircled the ferry in a silver bubble. Two cannonballs ricocheted off the barrier and exploded, propelling them forward.

"Gahh haha." Gnuld laughed, with a gleam in his eye. "Thought they would get us, did they?"

A blast of light burst across the ferry. Tiny men popped into existence (each apparition cracked and fizzled like the fuse of a bulb blowing out) one after another, until the ferry was full of life. The men scuttled across the deck. Some had beards with no hair, and others had hair with no beards. Most had either pointed noses or boney chins, but not both, and all had beady eyes and gold jewelry of some sort. The last flash of light popped, the ferry began to drift, and the crew sang in deep voices, like a hum.

"Row. Row. Row."

Magic swirled from their hands, dancing in the breeze, and the ferry picked up speed, in rhythm with their song.

"Hoist the sails, and here we go
Fast as kettle, and sure as Gin,
Lift the anchor, and here we go
Across the sea, around again."

The air thundered as another cannonball hit the barrier. The force from the explosion recoiled, and the two hobgoblin ferries blew off course. Devon barely steadied herself as the woozy sway of the boat lurched forward, knocking her off her feet.

"Thought they could blast us from the sea, did they?" scoffed Gnuld. He lept off the stool and flew several feet before landing softly on the deck.

"Are you a fairy?" Devon asked, standing up.

The boy beside her, who had also fallen, snorted.

"By the dragon's eye, I be no fairy. A brownie I am."

The wind raced around them, and they shot out of the cove, into the open sea. With the hobgoblins still recovering their ships, the Fairy Ferry quickly left them behind.

"And that's not a fairy?" asked Devon, scratching her head.

Gnuld rubbed his chin. "Well . . . a type, I suppose . . . if you're being technical. But not the sort you're thinkin'. Listen well, cause fast I'll tell, the story ye be seekin'. . . Ahem," he cleared his throat and then recited.

The Fairy Ferry

"When searching for treasure, imps cause mischief
As guardians of earth, sprites be impish.
Pixies glow the brightest, while
bringing seasons to solstice.
The most beautiful be fairies tall, or very, very small
But be warned, brownies cause
the most trouble of all."

"Fairies are tall . . ." Devon raised her eyebrows, "or very, very small?"

"Yes," explained Gnuld, without explaining it. "But that wasn't the point of the verse was it?"

"What was the point then?"

"I'm not a fairy!"

"Hah!" The boy beside her guffawed. *"You don't know what a brownie is!* Oh. That's a good one. Hah. Ha."

Devon ground her teeth. There was no point in trying to explain herself. Mr. Mustafa was clear. She shouldn't tell anyone who she was or what she was doing. Spies were everywhere. "I've just never met one. That's all."

Gnuld's frustration subsided. He rubbed his hands together and said in an eager rhyme, "To get this settled we best hurry. Time passes in a fury. Soon we'll dip in the sea. Then too late it'll be." He clapped his hands together. "So, who ye both are, and where ye both be going?"

"Bulwark," the boy rattled off. "Axel Snevets, and I need to get to Bulwark."

"Devon Conner. And the Gates of Thysia."

"Bulwark and the Gates of Thysia, huh?" Gnuld tapped his finger to his lips. "Not quite in the same direction . . . and there is another boy headed for Brume Gate."

"I answered first," interrupted Axel. "So, I should get off first. Besides, Brume Gate is another route to Thysia. Just a short walk. So they can get off together."

"What gift do you have?" Gnuld wriggled his fingers together greedily.

"Well," Axel said awkwardly. "I don't have anything with me . . ." He patted his empty pockets and glanced up at Gnuld, whose expression was quickly turning sour. "But . . . when we get to Bulwark, I'll bring you whatever you want. . . . I have gold. Lots of gold!"

Gnuld's face fell into a frown. Quick as a wink, he shoved the air in front of him. An invisible blast of terrific wind expelled Axel from the ferry. The barrier of silver magic opened up, and he shot through it, into the open sea.

"AHHH!" Axel cried. Thrashing wildly, he yelled, "I CAN'T SWIM!"

Gnuld twirled his finger, and Axel shot back to the dock (skidding across the water like a pebble). His

The Fairy Ferry

greedy eyes turned to Devon. "Did you come without a gift too?"

"No! No! Of course not. . . . Devon rummaged in her knapsack before remembering the thermos of milk. Shielding the contents, so Gnuld wouldn't see the jewel-encrusted crown, Devon handed over the thermos.

Gnuld sniffed the milk and licked his lips. "Milk and honey. Oooh hoo hoo. I *love* milk and honey." He took a sip and sighed, drooling. "Delicious!"

Devon breathed a sigh of relief.

Gnuld snapped his fingers and the thermos disappeared, leaving a trace of magic that slowly dissipated. "Anything else?"

Devon took the ruby amulet from her pocket.

"Ooh!" Gnuld's eyes lit up, and he tugged the chain from her grasp. "Hehe," he giggled and draped it around his neck. "Follow me. The Fairy Ferry will take you speedily."

Wisps of magic spun into the night as the crew of brownies sailed the ship. Gnuld waved his fingers, and a hole appeared in the middle of the deck, with a dark staircase that led deep below them. "After you."

Devon hesitated. "Uh — Perhaps, I can stay up here?"

Gnuld shook his head. "Best to hurry. Soon we'll dive in a fury."

Before Devon could decipher his meaning, the ferry

reeled back and dove forward beneath the surface. Dark water rose around them. Magic shot from the crew of brownies, encasing the ship in a bubble of air, and the water swirled past harmlessly.

Devon, who had crouched at the sudden dive, steadied herself as the ferry leveled off deep beneath the ocean. In a burst of speed, it launched forward like a bullet. Devon glimpsed the water break apart in enormous waves as she toppled below.

The steps were steep and short, allowing no way to stop once the momentum picked up. She curled into a ball as she fell. Finally, she bounced off the last stair and hit the bottom.

"Ugghh." Devon rolled flat onto her stomach. The cool floor felt good against her face. At the top, Gnuld cackled. The door shut with a snap, and Devon was left in a dim hall beneath the deck.

"You okie dokie?" asked a red-haired brownie, with a nose down to his chin. He leaned over Devon's face.

"Yeah —"

"Then up you get, to your feet. Soon your cabin, you will meet," the brownie said in a singsong voice.

"Right." Devon ached terribly as she stood up, and a large bruise was already purpling on her arm. After she checked that the crown was safe, she picked up her trunk, and followed the brownie down the hall.

Thick walls lined a narrow passage that led to half-a-dozen cabins. Another staircase led to more floors below. "This ferry is bigger than it looks from the outside," Devon noted.

"Brownie magic is best — better than all the rest, " sang the red-haired brownie. The ferry took another steep dive — veering to the side, before righting itself.

Devon smacked into the wall. "Ouch!"

Chuckling, the brownie opened a cabin door. Inside, a seasick boy retched over the side of his bunk into a bucket. Unfortunately, not all the vomit made it inside.

"Gross." Devon pinched her nose. "Erm, do you have another room?"

"Not to worry. Easy to fix. I'll right the room with just a flick." He wiggled his fingers and the vomit disappeared. The wood floor sparkled clean, the sheets were changed, and the boy, suddenly overcome with sleepiness, yawned, and fell asleep on his pillow.

The brownie started to leave.

"Wait. How long will it take to get to Thysia?"

"Just one night, you'll see. Fast as fairies we will be," the brownie promised and shut the door, leaving Devon with the sleeping boy.

Devon took the furthest bunk. From the window, she watched the water sweep past harmlessly. Finding herself with a moment of peace, Devon pulled out the crown, and it transformed in her hands. It was astonishing that such a simple band of gold could possess such incredible magic. She wanted to practice with it — but it was too risky. The curse might overtake her thoughts and more, if the boy woke up, he might guess what it was. So, she would practice shapeshifting without it until she was alone. Reluctantly, she returned the crown to the knapsack and tried to clear her mind.

Searching the cabin for ideas, Devon's eyes fell on the sleeping boy. Bree had turned into her . . . so it was possible. Devon scooted to the edge of her bunk and studied the boy carefully. He wasn't athletic looking like her, and he was perhaps a year or two older. Using her reflection in the window, Devon tried to take on his appearance. First, his trimmed, blond hair . . . then, his perky nose . . . and finally, his plump, rosy cheeks. Some time passed, and the ship sailed on — but no matter how hard she tried, nothing happened.

"Ugh!" Devon sank back in the bunk. "Nothing is happening," she grumbled. Bored and frustrated, she sank further down, one arm cradling the knapsack. As soon as her head touched the pillow, she fell asleep.

Being that she was deep beneath the surface, and the dark water cast an eerie gloom about the ferry, there was no telling the hour when the first explosion hit. WHAM. CRACK. BOOM!

The force of the blast plunged the ferry on its side, and the underwater ship flipped over and over, spinning like a top. Devon was thrown from the bunk. She hit the wall of the cabin, then the bunk, then finally, rammed into the bed post and held on. Her roommate got the worst of it. Unable to grab on to anything, he continued to roll and bang against the walls and floor until the ferry came to a stop, entirely upside-down. The ship floated along the currents lifelessly, before righting itself. Devon fell back on her bed, but the boy, now suspended midair, hit the floor.

"Ouch," he cried, as he struggled to get up.

"Are you all right?"

"Not really." The boy rubbed his backside. "W-what happened?"

"I don't know." Sore and aching, Devon climbed tenderly up the bunk and looked out the window. A slim eel slithered past. Unable to see anything else in the bleak water, she squinted closer, pressing her nose against the glass. Two giant whales, circled around the ferry — one crystal blue like a glass sculpture and the other yellow, like daisies in a morning sun. Devon stilled. *Those aren't whales!*

"WATCH OUT!" Devon dove, but she never made

it back to the bed. The ship exploded again. Harder than before. Wood above them creaked. Water leaked through the roof in dribbles. Anything that wasn't anchored or hitched to the floor toppled over and crashed against the wall, along with Devon and the unexpecting boy.

Dazed, Devon sank in and out of consciousness. Slowly, her vision came into focus —

Everything was on its side, and the beds (bolted into the wood floor) now jutted out precariously above their heads. Through the window, she could just make out the hobgoblin ferries circling closer.

Devon crawled over to the boy and found him, facedown, several feet away. Carefully, she nudged him. "Wake up. We need to get to the deck."

His eyes fluttered and opened.

"Oh, good." She let out a deep breath. "Can you stand?"

"Yeah." He rolled on his side and cried out. "My arm. I think it's broken."

Devon gritted her teeth. "I know it hurts, but if we stay here, we'll sink with the ship." She ducked under his good shoulder and helped him up.

"What happened?" he fumbled.

"Hobgoblins —"

"Hobgoblins?" the boy scrunched up his face. "But why would they bother us —?"

"We agitated them," Devon grumbled, remembering Amy Gray's warning. A red light shimmered through the window, illuminating the cabin. "I'll be right back."

Unsteadily, Devon scrambled back to the window. What would have taken only a second or two, now took precious time they didn't have. But the risk had proven worth it. The silver barrier was gone. Without the shield, there was no telling how long the ferry would last. And they were deep beneath the water. Frantic, Devon swung her knapsack over her shoulders, grabbed her valise, clambered back to the boy, and ducked under his shoulder. "We have to go. The ferry is going to sink."

He allowed her to help him across the cabin. "Thanks."

"Thank me later . . . if we're still alive."

With the ferry on its side, Devon had to kick the door open. They hastened across the hall, with the boy lumbering heavily against her shoulder. When they reached the staircase, he moaned sickly.

"Hold it in," Devon urged, though with everything on its side, she felt woozy too. "We only have a little further to go," she encouraged. As they plodded down the wall, a silver glow seeped in through the ferry . . . then the walls started to turn.

"Oh noo," groaned the boy.

"Jump!" Devon screamed — but it was too late.

The boat righted itself. Devon landed flat on her stomach, sprawled out across the stairs. The boy, however, fell curled in a ball (trying to protect his arm), and trundled back to the bottom. "Ouch. Ouch. Ouch."

"Are you okay?" Devon called down the stairs, winded.

"No!" he groused.

Devon clumped down after him, "Come on." She dragged his arm over her shoulder and helped him, reluctantly, climb the stairs. Once on deck, he collapsed against the rail.

The crew dashed about the ferry, humming a deep, urgent tune, and weaving silvery tendrils of magic. The blue and yellow hobgoblin ferries snaked threateningly around the new barrier, scouting for weaknesses with an arsenal of firearms and cannons. Nearby, Captain Gnuld howled out commands. The lighthearted singsong in his voice was replaced with a steely tone, "Friog, check the stabilizer fins. Dossgoll, steady the rudder. Erodin, load the cannons for counterattack!" Gnuld stopped two brownies hurrying past. "Get below and bring up our guests."

"Sir. Yes, sir." The two brownies hurried for the stairs.

Stopping one, Devon pointed out the boy, slumped against the deck. "He needs help."

"Safe and sound he'll be — a bubble spell in a jiffy." Coils of magic weaved from the brownie to the boy. A colorful bubble, like the ones made of soap, encased around him, and he floated up, off the deck. Flushed pink from his injuries, he started to heal, and the brownie flew after his crewmate, past more bubbles of injured passengers that wafted up the stairs.

Devon slid past them, retrieved her valise, and then hurried over to Gnuld. "How far are we from Thysia?"

"Hmmm," Gnuld grumbled and turned to the brownie beside him, who was closely studying a map with a pair of spectacles. "What port are we closest to?"

"Brume Gate."

"How many passengers get off at Brume Gate?" asked Gnuld.

"Only one, sir."

"Me too," said Devon in a rush. "I'll get off at Brume Gate." Getting off at a different port might give the Shadow Reign a chance to catch up, but it was a risk she was willing to take. The Fairy Ferry was being attacked by hobgoblins. And she had no desire to stay aboard a ship that was likely to be sea decoration. "Brume gate can get me to Thysia, right?"

"Yes. . . ." Gnuld clasped the amulet at his neck fondly. "But ye paid for Thysia. And there are no take-backsies —"

"I don't care about the blasted necklace," said Devon. "I'll get off at Brume Gate."

SWOOSH.

Cannon fire lit up the sea and shattered against the barrier. Waves surged through the ocean, and the ferry shuddered under the impact.

Gnuld reached in a pouch, strapped across his chest, and pulled out a gold coin. "The amulet I keep . . . and a trip you reap." He tossed the coin in the air and Devon caught it. On one side, a jaunty brownie lounged in a lavish room, and on the other, another brownie winked mischievously.

"Flip it high in the air — anywhere you need to be — a special trip I will heed." Gnuld swirled his arms and dipped his head in an elaborate bow. "A brownie's vow — I give thee."

"Deal." Devon patted the Afanc jacket for a pocket, before remembering it was useless. But just as she did remember, a zippered pocket appeared along the lining. Devon patted it again, doubtful, but there it was — a pocket. *Elsie was telling the truth.* Devon scoffed as she tucked the coin inside. But as she pulled her hand away, the pocket vanished again. Swearing under her breath, she patted the lining — but it was gone. *Well, there goes that.*

Tendrils of magic swirled from Gnuld's fingertips. "Until we meet again, Devon Connor."

Before Devon could say farewell, light flew past like shooting stars. The last thing she saw was a swirl of glittery magic. Then she was pulled from space, stumbled, and fell back on a bank of sand. From the ground, she blinked up at the sun, just peeking over the sky. And straight ahead stood a brightly painted ticket booth.

CHAPTER ELEVEN
Shadow Walkers Chase

Somewhere not too far away . . .

Across the horizon the shadows raced, bringing darkness with them. Niko didn't need to look to know the killers following behind him. He could feel them. Feel their shapeless bodies as they soared like ghosts blocking out the sun.

What they needed was a warlock. Cursed that they didn't have a warlock. The dirty skin thieves had one, and that tipped the scales in their favor. The Shadow Reign must find one too.

But would the council listen? There had been other instances when they ignored his advice. Tactics. Diversions. Infiltrations. All would have spread the war like fire in the desert. His patience with the council had long burned out. This was why he must keep the crown for himself. With the Crown of Guilledon, the council would bow to his will. He would bring war across the world and Thysia would no longer be able to hide from it.

There was one question that ate at him. It grated his soul. Infuriated him whenever he had a moment of quiet. *Why her?* Why had the crown fallen into the foul hands of a vile, disgusting shapeshifter? One that hid in the human world. Its magic was meant for a king! A spur of bitterness and contempt pushed him faster. She would die. The thought brushed a wicked smile against his lips.

Beside him, one of the shadow assassins caught up, disrupting his pleasurable thoughts. His gaunt, angular face formed from the shadow billowing around him. Turning his black, hollow eyes on Niko, he spoke in a raspy voice that carried with the wind, "Where are we headed?"

If any other shadow walker dared question him . . . Niko would have cut off their head, but Braxuis Baumbach had earned his right. They were equal in rank within the Shadow Reign. Though, not for long. Not once he possessed the Crown of Guilledon.

Niko pulled his shadow around himself, transforming, so his head and torso took shape beside Braxuis. "The only safe haven for her . . . ," he hissed, "Thysia."

"If she makes it there, the crown is lost." Braxuis threatened. "The Shadow Council won't be pleased." He flashed his razor teeth, menacingly. "Perhaps then, they'll put me in charge of the next mission."

Niko glared back, meeting Braxuis's threatening gaze with one of his own. It was true Braxuis liked to tear out the throats of his victims with his teeth, but he didn't frighten Niko. Niko was a monster too. And he was more than a match for Baumbach — if ever he dared challenge him — which they both knew, he wouldn't.

"She won't get away," Niko gritted.

On his other side, another shadow emerged from the rank — a sour and disgusting thing, to assume he was equal. Niko ignored the intrusion and raced on, letting his shadow billow behind him.

"Uh," said the boy, as he struggled to keep up. "We're getting a bit tired —"

A surge of anger twisted, and Niko shifted. Grotesque shapes erupted from his shadow as he soared through the wind. An anguished screech cried out. One slash and the gangly boy was dead. Niko didn't even know his name. Pete perhaps. Paul. Something with a P. . . . It didn't matter. Spying had been his purpose, and he had served it already.

Niko whipped around to the remaining shadow walkers behind Braxuis. "Do you need rest too?"

"No," they spat.

"Then hurry," he growled and took off with the wind. For now, they must fly and fly swiftly.

CHAPTER TWELVE
Brume Gate

Six rows of docks jutted out into greenish water, and all of them were occupied with ordinary sailboats and yachts. Not a trace of magic was anywhere. There was no fairy fire, nor hobgoblins, nor oddities of any sort that gave Devon the indication she had landed in the right place.

Along with the early morning chatter of fisherman, the sounds of the waves lapping against the boats filled the port. Nobody, however, seemed to notice that Devon had suddenly appeared.

Overwhelmingly relieved to be on solid ground, Devon laid back on the cool sand, sprawled out, like it was the best bed in the world. Somewhere out there, deep in the ocean, Gnuld and the Fairy Ferry were trying to escape the hobgoblins. Had they managed to block the attacks? Or, had the hobgoblins blasted their way through the magic barrier and sunk the Fairy Ferry? . . . Hopefully, they had escaped . . . and were far away by now.

Devon sat up. There was no point worrying about them now. She had to find the Brume Gate and get to

Thysia. She made a promise to deliver the crown safely and keep it out of the hands of the Shadow Reign . . . no matter what. And now, she had made her promise a lot harder to keep.

After checking her knapsack and finding everything as it should be, Devon scouted out the dock for Brume Gate. But the only thing that wasn't perfectly ordinary was the gaily painted ticket booth, squeezed between a cluster of boat rentals, merchants, and fisherman hauling their morning catch up the beach.

Dangling from the ticket booth, a sign read CLOSED — but inside, a thin man, with grey hair sprouting from his ears and nose, was snoozing with his face pressed against the glass, and his warm breath fogging up the window.

"Excuse me." Careful not to startle him, Devon tapped on the window. "I need to get to Thysia." Hopefully, he knew of it. If he didn't, this would be an awkward conversation.

The ticket man peeked through one eye. "Take Brume Gate to the Repository. From there, you can either ride a borbach or go on to the Shipyard." He yawned, and his warm breath fogged the window.

"Is there a more direct route? One that takes me straight into Thysia?"

The ticket man narrowed his open eye. "Naw."

"Do I buy the tickets here?"

"Obviously."

"Um —" Devon scratched her head, unsure what a borbach was, or if she wanted to go to the Shipyard instead.

The ticket man huffed and opened both eyes, with his face still pressed against the glass. "By all means, take your time. You're not keeping me from anything."

"I don't know which one to choose —"

He pinched the bridge of his nose (like she was giving him a headache).

"I'll take a ticket for whichever is faster. I need to get to Thysia quickly."

"The Shipyard then —" He fumbled around the booth and clipped a ticket from a scroll. "It'll be twenty-seven Gubbins."

Devon pulled out a few different coins and dropped them in the tin. He huffed, counted the coins, and returned several through the window, along with the ticket.

"Can you tell me where Brume Gate is?"

The ticket man leaned his head back against the glass and tried to get comfortable. "Four miles west."

"Is there a ride?" Devon asked. Walking through an unfamiliar forest, at dawn, with vague directions didn't seem like a good idea —

Not bothering to lift his face from the glass, he replied, "There's no transport at this time a' year. The coachmen come at the start a' school term and the end a' it — not enough business to keep 'em runnin' all year."

"But there must be a bus or something. I could get lost walking west for four miles, and I *really* need to get to Thysia right away —"

"Agh." The ticket man sat up and scowled at her like she was quite slow. "Naw, there's no bus! There's no taxi, no train, and no trolley. There's no ride. You got legs, don't you? I see you do! You got two feet, then?" The ticket man stomped his feet as if to demonstrate how they worked. "Whatcha need a ride for?"

"Um . . . ," Devon grumbled. She had just told him she could get lost.

"Well . . . then it's four miles west." The man jabbed his finger due west, leaned his head back against the glass (harder than he meant to), and grunted. "Sheesh. Yon kids today are so *lazy*." His eyes drooped as he settled comfortably against the window.

Devon fumed. She had hoped to start over in Thysia, making friends rather than enemies. But why was every magik giving her a hard time? It wasn't like she could say *Hey, I'm carrying a magical crown that puts everyone in danger!* She had a few choice words that neither Hammad nor Ms. Frances was around to hear. . . .

Instead, she lifted her fist to the glass. THUMP. THUMP. THUMP.

Startled. The man racked his head against the window. "OH. My head. You wretched girl! Wretched."

Unbothered, Devon strolled around the ticket booth, for the woods.

"I hope you get eaten by a knucklerbuff!" he shrieked after her.

But Devon didn't mind walking anymore, knucklerbuff or not — whatever that was. This was just a small hiccup in her plans. If she walked fast, four miles wouldn't take too long. And soon the sun would be bright and shining. No shadow walker would be able to sneak up on her.

She pulled out the metal compass Elsie had sold her and set off on the trail — due west. It took her up and down slopes, through forests, and past streams. Twice, she lost sight of the trail, but after retracing her steps, she found it again. Dawn came and went, and the sun beat down through the trees. After some time of fumbling along, the forest path hit a dead end at a large, gray lake. Too tired and sore to retrace her steps, Devon sat down on a rock overlooking the murky water. Her stomach, long past the rumbling stage, grouched unhappily. Reluctantly, she unwrapped the Klug.

First, she nibbled on the end, letting the salty meat sit on her tongue. . . . Finding that it was somewhat pleasant, and not entirely disgusting, she chewed off a chunk, savoring the instant warmth of energy as she watched the gray clouds blow past.

She could have sat on the rock overlooking the water for hours and never noticed how no fish swam beneath it. Tiny water spiders did not dance on the surface, and when the wind blew, ripples didn't form against the shoal. All went unnoticed until a black crow swooped above the gloomy lake and smacked straight into the blue sky. Bouncing off it, the crow tumbled from the air, but instead of splashing into the murky lake, it dipped through, sending up tuffs of cloud.

Devon jumped up . . . *Birds didn't just hit the sky and fall out of it —*

She scrambled down to the lake, and as she reached it, the crow flew out again (with a wobbly sort of beat). Edging closer, Devon crouched beside the lake and gathering her courage, dipped her hand inside. A cool mist swirled around her fingertips, light as air. This wasn't a lake at all . . . it was fog and vapor.

"Brume," Devon whispered, though nobody was

around to hear. *Didn't brume mean . . . fog? So if this was Brume Gate . . . where was the entrance?* Excited, Devon followed the edge of the fog all the way around, searching for a way inside. Half an hour later, she circled back to where she started, having found nothing.

Warily, she gathered her things and waded into the fog. For the first twenty yards or so, the mist swirled harmlessly around her ankles. Another twenty yards and she began to have trouble. The fog had reached her chest, and there was still no sign of an entrance anywhere.

Then the ground vanished.

It dipped so suddenly that one moment it was there and the next it wasn't. With the added weight of her trunk, Devon fell fast, and deep, beneath the surface. She gulped the murky air in giant mouthfuls. Retching, she choked back the moldy flavor (like rotten milk) as she hit the bottom.

Though it hurt terribly, she scrambled up anyway. Beyond the length of her hand, she couldn't see anything! Heart pounding, Devon felt around blindly and stumbled against something sharp, scraping her shins. Recognizing the shape of a corner, she scrambled up a staircase, frantically dragging her trunk behind her. When she reached the surface, it was the sweetest breath of air she had ever taken.

It was several minutes before Devon calmed down

enough to scope out the unusual fog. This was not at all like her trip to Thysia should be. First a hobgoblin attack and now she was in a forest, alone, in the middle of a fake, gruesome lake made of horrid fog, with no gate in sight and no way down — except perhaps, falling again — which hurt. She was supposed to be there already, safe within the city.

Once she had fully calmed down, she carefully moved one foot and then the other, and stood up, so slowly, she couldn't possibly loose her footing. Even from the middle of the fog lake, the platform remained invisible — so that she appeared to be floating. Unable to see the platform meant one wrong step . . . and she could fall back to the bottom, with no one around for miles.

She had just decided how best to move, when the sky opened up, and a blond head popped out. "Um. . . . Hello?" said a familiar boy, with chubby cheeks and a perky nose. He leaned out further, blocking the hole in the sky and called again. "Heeelllllo!"

"Down here!" called Devon.

"Ah. There you are." His face lit up as he spotted her. Waving frantically, he lost his balance and tumbled out of the sky.

WHOP. He landed on his backside, dangerously close to the edge of the platform.

"Are you okay?" she exclaimed, thoroughly startled. It wasn't every day that someone fell out of the sky.

The boy stood up, blushing furiously. "Oh, yeah. Happens all the time. My pa says it's 'cause I don't think before I do things, like I should."

"You're the boy from the Fairy Ferry," Devon blurted, recognizing his plump face and rosy cheeks. *The one who threw up all over the floor.*

"Bet you don't think the best of me." He strode over, less concerned by the precarious edge, and held out his hand. Noticing it was dirty, he wiped his hand on his trousers. "My name's Beoc. Beoc Hobbart. Thanks for uh . . . helping me out before."

"Devon." She beamed — happy to meet someone else way out in the middle of nowhere. "It wasn't like I was going to leave you behind."

"Yeah. Well . . . dreadful trip wasn't it," he said, his cheeks tinged pink.

"What happened to the ferry and the rest of the passengers?"

"Oh . . . well . . . right before Gnuld sent me on ahead, the crew was preparing a counterattack. No one else was supposed to get off. So, I guess they stayed."

"I hope they're all right."

"Me too," he said solemnly. Then perking up, he

added, "I'm sure they are . . . the Fairy Ferry had a load of cannons too. I bet the hobgoblins regret attacking by now."

"Well . . . I'm glad you're here. I've been wondering around for hours . . . I must really have gone off-trail."

Beoc's face turned the tiniest bit smug. "Well . . . I thought you might be up here. Checked the bottom entrance first, you see."

"Bottom entrance?"

"Yeah." Beoc pointed to the grey mist beneath them. "There's another entrance under the fog. I hung around a bit, but after you didn't turn up, I thought perhaps you made it to the sky door. I really wanted to thank you . . . you know . . . for helping me out." He flushed, embarrassed.

"No problem." It was a relief that she ran into someone at all. Devon's eyes flickered to the bright, empty sky. "Just show me where you came from and consider us even."

Beoc whirled back to the empty sky. "Ah. The door shut. Don't worry . . . I can find it again." He started up an invisible set of stairs. "Where are you headed?"

Devon grabbed her trunk and tugged it after him. "Gordimer."

"You must be joking? . . . What are you headed there for?"

"I'm a new student."

"That's where I go to school! ... I guess we'll be classmates," Beoc bubbled excitedly.

In the middle of the sky, Beoc stopped short ... and reached into the empty air. A handle appeared, taking the shape of a lizard-like monster.

HISSSSSS. The handle snapped at Devon and then curled affectionately around Beoc's wrist. Unperturbed, Beoc turned the handle. The monster disappeared, and the sky opened up revealing a pitch-black hole.

"Come on." Beoc waved for her to follow and climbed in.

Normally, she would have resisted climbing into a dark abyss ... but with as much courage as anyone could muster, Devon clambered in after him.

Everything went cold and dark. Whispers inside the emptiness called like sirens to sailors. Suddenly, she was afraid of getting lost forever. The whispers grew, frantic, pulling her towards nothingness. She tried to scream, but her jaw clamped shut. Then she was through the darkness, standing on a rough pebbled path, blinded by a full sun that beat down on a busy settlement.

CHAPTER THIRTEEN
The Monsters and the Airships

Devon shielded her eyes from the bright sun. Brume Gate had taken them right into the middle of a busy settlement. Surrounding her in every direction were clusters of stables, one after another, and more on top of that. Some were made of wood, some of iron, and others were wrought with roughly mined gold. An advanced water system twisted through the Repository, allowing aquatic beasts to roam freely.

Though the Repository was ingeniously designed, the creatures were no less spectacular. Strange and exotic blended together in breeds she had never imagined. A blue-scaled bunny (with fins rather than feet) popped its head out of a murky-green fountain and splashed them with water.

"That's a Killynox," Beoc said smartly.

"A Killynox?" A bark of laughter escaped, and she reached out to touch the floppy ears. "You've got a funny name for something so cute —"

Beoc grabbed her hand. "Not cute," he warned.

"They lure creatures in the water and drown them ... for sport."

Devon backed away —

Disgruntled, the Killynox shrieked. It's fins shot out in a threatening arc, and it dove back under the surface, splashing them with water.

"They've got terrible tempers — bet that's why it's aquarium is in shallow water." Beoc wiped his face with his sleeve. "

"What is this place?" Devon marveled.

"The Repository," Beoc said matter-of-factly. "It's where magical creatures are housed, traded, and sold. . . . Haven't you ever been to Thysia before?"

"Uh . . . no . . . this is my first time," Devon said, careful not to reveal too much. It was true enough, as she had no memory of ever being here before.

"Whoa!" Beoc darted in front of her. "You've never been here at all!"

"I didn't know I was a magik." She shrugged. It couldn't be that surprising. Hammad had said some magiks didn't transform until later in life. That meant, there were others like her — that lived ordinary lives first. "There must be others . . . that didn't know they had magic?"

"Well, yeah —" Beoc admitted, and started walking again. "It's a bit unusual, but not unheard of. . . . I suppose your parents aren't magical?"

"I don't know. I never knew my parents."

Devon was careful not to show the grief it caused her, but Beoc still dropped his head.

"Oh, sorry."

"It's okay. I don't remember them . . . so I guess that's better than missing them, right?" She wasn't sure that's how she really felt, but it sounded better than being miserable. "Besides, look where I am now. I got to ditch the institute, come here, and who knows what amazing things I'll get to do in Thysia —"

"Yeah." Beoc shrugged. "I guess."

A giant blue and orange toad hopped in front of them.

"Watch out!" Devon pushed him back, remembering a similar toad in Elsie's shop. "Those things bite."

"Ha-ha," Beoc chortled. "That's just a Toallipygian." Beoc crouched and stretched out his arm. Come here buddy —"

The toad remained put, unblinking — Beoc reached closer — and it snapped for his wiggling fingers. Beoc whisked them away — swooped under the toad — and scooped it up. It gnashed it's teeth ferociously. Chomp. Chomp. Chomp.

"Toallipygians are common enough." Beoc maneuvered the toad so it's snapping was harmless. Goo oozed down the toad's back, and Beoc held it further out. " You got to watch out for the poison it excretes though —"

"Ugh! That's disgusting."

"Don't worry ... he won't get me ... will ya, little guy."

Beoc coddled the toad, and then, wondering something, his head popped up. "You're a shapeshifter, right?" Then, answering his own question, he hurried on, "You must be if you're going to Gordimer. Only shapeshifters go to Gordimer. Shadow walkers go to Trumbald."

"I think I'm a shapeshifter ... I haven't officially shifted yet," she said, wondering if that would change their friendship. "Not in front of a magik that can verify it anyway."

"Well that isn't unusual ... it's fairly common actually. It just means you can't control shifting enough to be certified ... I know a girl at Gordimer who hasn't shifted at all —"

That made Devon feel slightly better, but her eyes were still on the snapping Toallipygian. "Maybe you should put that down —"

"Right —" Beoc lowered the Toallipygian to the ground, and it hopped free. "I guess you don't know your way around here, huh?" He dazed off ... and then having an idea, perked up. "Since you're headed to Gordimer . . . would you mind if we went together? It's just . . . Headmistress Wrottesley doesn't really trust me with important errands all that much. I haven't had the best track record, you see. But if I helped a new student, who say, didn't know their way around, she might start to see me as a bit more dependable. Plus, I kinda snuck out this morning, and since I'm getting back later than planned, she'll certainly have found me out."

Devon held back answering, uncertain if she was better off with or without him. "Why did you sneak out?"

Beoc scratched the back of his head, and he pretended to be interested in a beautiful aviary, fully equipped with luscious gardens, fountains, and bird feeders. "I needed a break . . . you know . . . from school and all. There's a lot of pressure on the kids of politicians. We have to be perfect *all* the time . . . and well . . . look at me. I'm not athletic. I'm not super smart. I don't have a rare talent that makes me special. I'm not anything my father wants me to be —"

"You shouldn't be so hard on yourself." Devon watched a golden bird run around the aviary, past the birdfeeders, in search of something else. "If it makes you feel better, I don't have the best track record either. I can't count the number of times I snuck out where

I used to live. Actually . . . I'm kinda impressed." She punched Beoc on the shoulder. "Sneaking out takes nerve."

"Really?" The corner of his mouth perked up.

"Sure," Devon said, grinning now. "Stupid nerve, but still nerve."

"So . . . is that a yes? . . . I could show you around —"

"Sounds good to me. I had a load of trouble getting here," Devon admitted. Kamau had said not to trust anybody (and even made a point to say it twice) but Beoc was going to school with her, and he seemed all right. Besides, it wasn't a bad idea to get a layout of the city from somebody who knew it. She knew every nook and cranny of St. Frances, and she'd like to know Thysia the same way.

"You won't regret it!" Beoc promised cheerfully.

Devon pointed to the luminescent bird (whose golden feathers shimmered, even as he waddled in the shade). "Why isn't that bird flying?"

Beoc's eyes rounded, then he laughed. "That's an Alicanto. They eat ore, like gold and silver — which weighs a ton. So, they're too heavy to fly."

"They eat gold! . . . That's amazing!"

"Yeah. . . . They're native to Chile, so that one must have been imported. Treasure hunters use them to find gold and lost treasures." Beoc pulled her away from the aviary. "Come on . . . I promised to show you around. The Repository has the largest number of magical breeds in the country."

As they walked, Beoc pointed out magical beasts, describing them with a happy naivety that relaxed Devon, making her comfortable. "If I ever get into Beorgburg, I'm going to study Beast Mastery! Some of the best Beast Masters in the world live right here in Thysia!"

"You want to get into Beorgburg too?"

"Ha. Tell me someone who doesn't. The professors at Beorgburg are all great masters. Besides . . . Beorgburg doesn't just teach shapeshifters and shadow walkers — Beorgburg is a school for *all* magiks — borlaugs, fairies, elves, and mages. Since you're new, you don't understand how cool that is . . . but you'll see. With the war between shapeshifters and shadow walkers, it's hard to find a place where everyone can get along. But, at Beorgburg, everyone learns together, and they learn from the greatest masters in the world."

"Have you applied?"

"Thirty-seven times," he said shamefully. "My dad works for the Bureau of Magical Security and Defense — directly under Mildred Everhart. He's a top official, and I still haven't gotten in."

"Thirty-seven times? How old are you?" Devon gave him a puzzled look. He didn't look much older than her, and his face was still rounded in a boyish way . . . "If it's okay to ask?"

"Oh, it's fine. Magiks don't really care about that like ordinary people do. We live for centuries. I'll be eighty-two this spring."

"Wow." Eighty-two was older than she expected . . . but nothing like Kamau, Hammad, or Elsie. Beoc just seemed younger. Perhaps this is what Hammad meant, by gauging magiks by power and talent, and not age. "Well, don't worry about it. I'm sure you'll get in."

"Thanks —" Beoc cut off as a grouchy man scampered past, tugging the leash of a squat, donkey-like creature, with a knobby horn on its head, a broad chest, wide girth, and wings so short it couldn't possibly fly. "That's a Mendaecus." His voice turned somber. "A misbreed." He shook his head sadly.

As magiks strolled along, the owner bustled into each of their paths and urged them towards the Mendaecus. "You sir! Would you like to buy this beautiful creature?" He rubbed his hands together eagerly. "You could make a profit — a clever gambling man like yourself."

"Pfft." The man hastened around the Mendaecus and strode off.

Beoc scoffed. "He called *that* . . . beautiful?"

Sadly, Devon agreed. Of all the words Devon would have used to describe that creature, beautiful wasn't one.

"What about you, ma'am?" The greasy owner turned to a passing woman instead.

"A companion for your children? . . . You've got such lovely children."

"Humph!" She steered her kids forward, sticking up her nose as she passed.

Spotting Devon and Beoc, the owner hurried over. "Hey! You!"

"Let's go," Beoc whispered —

"Wait a second." The greasy owner threw his arm out, cutting them off. "You got Gubbins on you?" A gold tooth flashed in his dirty teeth.

"Why?" demanded Beoc.

The creature nudged Devon dejectedly —

She brushed her hand across his warm muzzle. A flake of mud chipped off, revealing a gray coat underneath. The Mendaecus whinnied, low and gentle, and bumped its head against her for more.

"Oh, look, he likes you!" A broad grin gleamed across the man's face, and he bounced excitedly. "Could still grow his wings you know — he's not full-grown yet. I've been asking for four hundred

Gubbins . . . but, as I see he likes you already, I'll give him up for three hundred and fifty —"

"Three hundred and fifty Gubbins!" Beoc gawped at him. "For a Mendaecus! You're a crook."

The man's smile disappeared, and he gave Beoc a frosty glare. "It's a steal! You'd be robbin' me!" He pressed his hand against his chest, where his heart would be (if he had one, considering how poorly he cared for the sad creature).

The drooping Mendaecus tugged on the leash — trying to reach a sparse patch of grass. But, by the way the owner held the rope, the Mendaecus couldn't reach it.

Devon tore up the grass and offered it to the Mendaecus. He nuzzled against her palm, tickling her fingers, as he chomped happily.

"So what will it be? I can see you like him —"

Devon regretted the words before they came out of her mouth. "I can't. . . . I don't have a place to keep him." She wasn't even certain she had a place to stay yet. Hopefully, Hammad Mustafa had reached the headmistress of Gordimer . . . and hopefully, the headmistress would allow her to stay. That was a lot of hopefully.

"Two hundred and eighty-five," the owner lashed. "Take him now . . . and I'll give him up for just two hundred and eighty-five Gubbins!" He glowered at Devon, like she was deliberately trying to rob him.

"You can't swindle us!" Beoc snapped, pulling Devon away.

"Gaph!" The man whipped around and yanked the leash. "Come on!" he barked at the Mendaecus and hurried off to haggle another passing magik.

"What's a misbreed?" asked Devon.

Now that the man had led the Mendaecus away, Beoc sighed with relief. "Have you heard of a Pegasus?"

"Yeah —" Even the kids at the institute had heard of mythical horses that could fly.

"Well, sometimes they mate with ponies or horses and give birth to misbreeds, and that's what magiks call a Mendaecus. . . . Sometimes, a Mendaecus will grow its wings and fly, but it's rare, and it's a risk. As foals, they all have stubby, miniature wings, so nobody can tell what will happen. But, if your Mendaecus does fly, it's worth a fortune!"

"And if it can't?"

"You're stuck with a useless creature nobody wants."

Devon shouldn't have been surprised that Pegasi were real, but she was. "Could that Mendaecus still fly?" she asked hopefully. If he did, then maybe his owner would treat him better.

"Nah. That one is already too big — he's nearly full grown. Good thing you didn't buy him. From what I've heard, they eat a ton." Beoc puffed out his chest. "Guess you're happy you let me stick around with you, huh?"

"Sure." Devon tore her eyes away from the poor creature. Whether the Mendaecus could fly or not, it deserved better.

"Come on, I'll show you something really cool." Beoc pulled Devon along. They weaved through the Repository like a maze and stopped in front of a giant stable with a fancy saddle that hung above a bucket of wiggling worms. At the end of a chain-linked leash was the most fantastic beast Devon had ever laid eyes on.

Hisssssssss. A shiny, black beast with a stallion-like body, lustrous black wings, and the head of a snake, pawed at the dirt.

"See that?" Beoc elbowed her, barely able to contain his excitement. "That's a Woriax. Nearly as rare as a flying Mendaecus. This one just arrived last week. They have a wingspan of twenty feet and fly as smooth as an eagle." He dropped his voice, and said longingly, "If only I could touch one —"

"Why don't you ask?" said Devon. She wouldn't mind getting a closer look herself —

Beoc sighed. "Trainers won't let you near 'em. They're worth thousands of Gubbins."

As he said it, a stately dressed stable boy came around the corner, and his mouth tightened. "What are you gawking at —"

ROARRRR. A rumbling clamor shook the pebbles around them and filled the sky like thunder.

"What was that?" Devon whipped around.

"I'm not sure." Beoc turned too, but all they could see were stables.

The Woriax reared up, beating its wings heavily, and came down on the stable, battering its hooves against the wood. The stable boy rushed to settle it.

Another roar echoed across the stables.

"That doesn't sound good," sputtered the stable boy.

Devon started forward. "We better go. I don't like the sound of that."

Devon and Beoc hurried through the Repository,

winding through the jungle of stables. At the end, they came to an expansive paddock, and in the center, a monstrous beast (three-times the size of a rhino) with shoulders that arched into a natural spring, and horns that curved down to its snout, had become rampant. Screaming Magiks ran forward and tried to rescue a teen boy that was tangled in one of its leashes.

Devon cringed. "He's going to get killed."

"That's a borbach." Beoc's mouth fell open.

Two stable boys circled around the beast, while a score of others pulled hard on the ropes — attempting to subdue the borbach so the boy could escape.

"They don't have to be so rough. Borbachs are gentle creatures," Beoc grumbled disapprovingly. Catching Devon's expression, he added, "Normally, anyway. I've never seen one act like this."

The borbach reared up, snapping one of the ropes. When it came down, a quake rumbled through the ground, knocking another, tough-looking, boy from his feet. Then, the borbach tried to trample him.

"Gentle —" Devon grunted.

"Well, I didn't say they weren't dangerous. Borbachs are used for transporting magiks. I really hoped I could ride one," he said wistfully, "but Wrottesley forbids her students from going near them. Says it's too dangerous."

"I don't see why." Devon huffed sarcastically. She was perfectly fine not getting dragged by a borbach, even if they were *usually* nice.

"I wonder if he'll get free?" Beoc winced as the borbach charged a group of stable boys, dragging the other behind it.

Devon exhaled, as an utterly stupid idea settled in. "We should try to help —"

"Only trainers are allowed in the paddock."

"We can't stand here and do nothing, while he gets trampled." Resigning to her own absurdity, Devon crouched and climbed through the fence.

In a desperate attempt to free himself, the tangled boy grabbed the rope, jumped, twisted, and spun midair. The leash unraveled from his ankle, he hit the ground hard, and rolled free. Two more trainers rushed forward and dragged the boy away from the borbach. The crowd erupted in cheers.

Beoc clapped with the rest of the crowd. "Guess it's good I'm taking the airship."

As he said it, a humongous ship with sails and masts and all the riggings soared above them, blocking out the sky. Had it not been for their vantage point, and the shadow cast down by the ship, she wouldn't have noticed another shadow dart from one stable to the next. Then it would have been too late. Devon took a step back into the cover of a low-hanging rooftop. "Beoc," she called. But he didn't hear her over the commotion.

The shadow glided down a slight hill to the borbach's paddock and joined another shadow, that flitted around the crowd (occasionally darting in and out again). Devon's chest seized and her breath rasped against her throat. "Beoc!"

"What?"

Devon put her finger to her lips. "Come here."

A third shadow slinked out of the unsuspecting crowd and joined the other two. The three shadows shifted, and Niko appeared not twenty yards from where they stood.

Devon stopped breathing.

How was he here? And worse, if Niko was here, that meant he got past Kamau and Bree. So, what did that mean for them? Were they hurt? Were they dead? Devon shuddered at the thought. "Pull it together," she muttered under her breath. *Somehow, they were okay. They had to be.*

"What are you looking at?" Beoc said, interrupting her thoughts.

Devon scanned the Repository. They couldn't take the main path. It led straight for Niko. To make things more difficult, if she told Beoc *why* she wanted to avoid the crowd, she'd have to tell him about the crown too.

"What are you looking at —?"

Thinking fast, Devon scanned the slight hill down the path. "Is there any way into the Shipyard that doesn't lead past that paddock?"

Beoc knitted his eyebrows but still not seeing what Devon had, shrugged. "The only entrance into the Shipyard is at the end of the Repository."

"Unless. . . . " Devon's voice trailed off, and she scanned the pasture. There was a clear path straight through the borbach's paddock. "Could we cut through there?" She pointed out the slim path between the rows of giant stables, smack in the middle of the paddock.

"Are you nuts?" Beoc eyed her uncertainly. The borbach was still causing a ruckus, as a dozen magiks tried to lure him into one of the giant stables.

"You said yourself you preferred them. You even said you wanted to ride one."

"Not that one!" Beoc nearly shouted, panic-stricken. "I don't want to be anywhere near *that one!*"

Devon pointed to the back of the stable. "We'll cut through there. We won't be anywhere near the borbach." *Or Niko*, she finished in her head. Before Beoc could come up with another reason to protest,

The Monsters and the Airships

Devon took off for the pasture and hoisted herself over the fence. Niko had chased her all the way here, but he wasn't going to catch her. She was going to slip right past him. She was halfway to the first stable by the time Beoc caught up to her and grabbed one end of the awkward trunk.

"Go faster," he urged.

Devon grinned, pleased. It seemed Beoc had an adventurous side after all. But, spotting them race through the open paddock, the trainers sent a stream of yells and curses that made his eyes wide with fear.

"FASTER," he yelled.

Devon laughed as she picked up speed. The thrill of adrenaline made her feel alive. It had been too long since she had done something this foolish. "For a second, I thought you weren't going to come," she shouted over the pounding of their feet, and the hollers from the stable boys.

"I wasn't," Beoc panted. They reached the first giant stable and turned sharply down the path. "But you saved me on the Fairy Ferry, and . . . we made a deal —"

They reached the end of the stables, but were still too close to Niko, so Devon swerved deeper between another row of vast stables, pulling her trunk and Beoc behind her. The curses and shouts got louder. Heavy thudded footsteps declared the trainers were in pursuit and closing in fast. Devon guessed at least two, by the multiple thuds. Probably more. "What deal did we make?" she huffed, trying not to think about what would happen if the trainers made enough commotion to attract Niko. Just in case, she swerved left again, further in the field of stables. They were nearly there.

Beoc's knees knocked against the trunk as they pushed faster. "You're going to let me take you to Wrottesley. Then she can't be as mad at me for sneaking out. You owe me now —"

"Really? I thought this might make us even after the Fairy Ferry."

Beoc snorted. "Not even close."

The trainers caught up, just as they reached the end of the paddock. There were four of them. That meant two trainers for each of them, which wasn't fair odds. They knocked into Devon and Beoc, shouting obscenities that would have made Ms. Frances faint on the spot. A lanky stable boy grabbed Beoc and threw him towards the fence. "You nutbrained, blithering twits!"

"We're going! We're going!" Devon held up her free hand to show they were yielding.

"Shut up!" he blared, and shoved her backwards —

"Idiots!" Another stable boy shoved Devon again, and she tripped.

"Get out of here!" They clamored at once.

Beoc gripped one side of the valise, and Devon dragged the other. "We're going!" With no fight from Devon or Beoc, the stable boys sauntered off, still lashing obscenities —

Unfortunately, the commotion had caught the attention of the crowd of magiks — just as Devon had feared. Amidst the crowd, Niko glared, spotting them. He pushed through the crowd and then launched into a sprint, straight for her.

"RUN!" Devon dragged Beoc forward, but he dug his heals into the ground. "RUN!"

"I can't run anymore."

"Beoc!" Devon spat desperately. Her head filled with images of Niko trying to kill Beoc, like he tried to kill Leni. Head pounding, she whirled towards the crowd and pointed out three figures, now running towards them. "I think they might arrest us!"

Beoc shook his head. "Only the guard can arrest you." But as the figures raced faster — straight towards them with fierce determination and obvious anger — Beoc's chest heaved. "Run. Run!"

Beoc and Devon sprinted, as fast as they could, with the valise between them. They passed beneath a magnificent stone arch, with Shipyard engraved in it, and slid into a vast crowd of busying magiks.

The Monsters and the Airships

Beyond the arch, they came upon rows and rows of airships — each one slightly different from the next. Magiks in uniform ran past, shouting, laughing, and calling to shipmates. Passengers chased after their children and scrambled to purchase tickets at painted booths, not unlike those at Brume Gate. The bustle had an air of excitement that was contagious.

But wanting to put as much distance between herself and Niko as possible, Devon hurried through the Shipyard. Gigantic airships, all in different shades of earthy browns, mustard yellows, and forest greens, hovered high in the air. The smallest ships spanned a dozen feet with one mast and sail, while the larger ones were over a hundred. The more bizarre ships had sails that jutted out from the hull like wings. Others had giant, blood-red tarps that puffed up like balloons.

"This is the Shipyard," Beoc wheezed unenthusiastically, as she dragged him along.

"It's incredible!" she breathed. Devon weaved through the crowd, not daring to look back in case Niko spotted her and ducked behind a large ship.

Beoc unfolded a crumpled ticket. "I'm on the Ballarat — what about you?"

Devon pulled out her own. "Me too."

"Do you think we lost them?"

"For now, maybe." She scanned the nearby ships and then scanned them again. Niko was nowhere in sight. And if they found their airship quickly, they might slip away. But if they didn't, well she dreaded to think of what would happen then.

A grayish-brown airship, with Sky Snail painted on the side, caught her attention as a balding man led the mistreated Mendaecus inside a large crate. A tinge of regret twisted in her stomach. She nudged Beoc and pointed out the Mendaecus. "Guess someone bought him after all."

"Poor fool," he said of the balding man.

Around them, the airships started to take off.

"Beoc, what time does the Ballarat leave?"

"Five-thirty," he read off the ticket. Worry etched across his face. "It's five thirty-eight."

"No!" Devon grabbed her valise. If they missed their ship, they'd be stuck here. Niko would find them for sure. "We can't miss that ship —"

"BEOC!" a voice called from above them. High in the sky, a nimble boy with strong arms, tan skin, and black hair dangled from a chocolate airship. Behind him, blood-red sails caught the wind like dragon wings. "Over here!" he shouted.

"Look!" Beoc pointed to the hull. Painted on the side was the word *Ballarat*.

"They haven't left!" breathed Devon.

They sprinted for the ship. As they reached it, the boy slid down the rope so speedily he shouldn't have been able to stop. Just before he hit the ground, he wrapped the rope around his leg, and landed lithely in front of them.

"Neat trick," Devon panted. She scanned the shipyard again, edgily. The crowd was thinning and nearly half the ships had taken to the sky.

"Nah. You pick up pretty quick on one of these." With one hand still holding onto the rope, the boy held his other hand out to Devon. "I'm Rhet," he said, shaking her hand.

"Devon." She pointed to the Ballarat. "We need to get on that ship!"

He raised a thick eyebrow at Beoc. "Figured. I'm guessing Wrottesley doesn't know you're off school grounds."

Beoc shifted his feet guiltily.

"Don't look so worried." Rhet laughed. "I'm not going to rat on you. Better come on though. The cap' won't wait any longer."

On cue, a loud horn blew, and the captain called out, "ALL ABOARD!"

The crew hurried about, preparing for takeoff. Two boys slid to the ground beside Devon. "They comin' on board?" One of them started for the valise, offering to take it.

"Yeah," Rhet replied.

They hastily carried her trunk to a lift. And while it was hauled on deck, more crewmates untied the knots that anchored the ship to the ground. Rhet didn't miss a beat. "Come on then!" He ushered them forward as the ship rocked.

Beoc hobbled for one of the dangling ropes.

"No. Beoc, not that way. The ladder! Over there —"

"Right." Beoc raced for the ship with Devon

sprinting beside him. By the time they reached it, her heart was pounding in her chest.

She wholly regretted letting him climb first. All of his earlier clumsiness returned tenfold. As he climbed, he shook so violently, the ladder banged against the hull. Fearing he might fall on top of her, Devon wrapped her arms through the rungs and hung on tightly. They were still climbing when the ship jerked upward — giving her a queasy feeling in the pit of her stomach. Untethered, the ship sprung into the air as she clutched the rattling ladder and tried to breathe. At least, she had escaped Niko once again.

By the time they climbed on deck, the Ballarat was high in the clouds. The crew scrambled across the ship, showing off on ropes and beams like aerial acrobats, and they balanced on the riggings like gymnasts.

Beoc shuddered as he crumbled against the ship.

Devon slumped beside him and hid that she was shaking too.

"All right there, Beoc?" Rhet dropped down beside them. "For a moment, I wasn't sure you'd make it," he teased, but Devon could see a hint of concern in his eyes.

"A 'course." Beoc cleared his throat. To prove he was fine, he abruptly sat up. His knee knocked over Devon's knapsack, spilling the contents. "My bad." Beoc grabbed the bag. "I got it." But as he scooped up Devon's belongings and stuffed them inside, more fell out. The Crown of Guilledon clanked against the wood floor.

Mesmerized by the sparkling jewels, Beoc snatched it up. The moment his fingertips touched it, it transformed. The thick gold melted, thinning and twisting. And it shaped into an imperial crown, domed with an extravagant velvet inlay. The lavish rubies disintegrated. Beads of gold grew into brilliant sapphires and lustrous pearls. Beoc's eyes rounded with hunger. "Woah!"

"PUT IT BACK!" Devon's chest squeezed, terrified. A dozen, disastrous things that could happen raced through her mind.

But, hypnotized by the sudden embodiment of his own, most magnificent, crown, Beoc ignored her. He lifted it to the top of his blond hair (translucent in the beating sun). The domed-crown twittered precariously as the wind blew against it.

"BEOC!" Devon shrieked in horror.

The ship lurched to the side — and the crown blew from his fingers. Devon reached out, but the sudden reel of the ship carried it out of reach. It rolled across the deck, straight for the edge of the ship.

Devon dove. She skidded across the rough wood, scrambled the last couple feet, and grabbed it — just as it teetered in the open sky.

"Whew!" Beoc gasped, realizing what he'd nearly done. "Good thing you got it then."

Devon stuffed the crown (now a thin gold band) back in her knapsack. She swung the bag over her shoulder and glared at Beoc. He hadn't done anything on purpose — but what if his clumsiness caused her to lose it? She couldn't imagine what she would do. She was in the middle of the sky — soaring over hundreds of miles of open air! She cringed at the thought of facing Mr. Mustafa and telling him she lost the infamous Crown of Guilledon.

"Sorry," blundered Beoc.

"It's fine." Devon said through gritted teeth.

Rhet coughed awkwardly. His dark eyes glanced between them.

"How far is Thysia?" Devon forced, stiffly changing the subject.

"It isn't far when you travel by air. See the mountains there?" Rhet pointed to a cluster not far from them. "Those are the Bearded Mountains. Thysia is just south of the tallest one. To the west is Grimwood Forest, and on the east is the Screaming Lake. Airships aren't allowed to dock inside Thysia. So, we'll land on the edge of the Grimwood Forest."

Beoc moaned as the ship lurched again, and despite her anger, Devon felt sorry for him.

"You don't look so good, mate." Rhet crouched over him.

"I don't feel so good." Beoc tugged at the collar of his shirt.

Remembering his sensitive stomach, Devon scooted over.

A great gust of wind rocked the sails. "I think I'm gonna be seasick."

Rhet laughed. "You can't get seasick — we're in the air." He pulled a wad of olive-colored grass (that reeked of fish guts) from his pocket. "Here —"

"Eww." Beoc wrinkled his nose. "No thanks."

"It's Duckweed — it'll make you feel better."

Gingerly, Beoc took it and held it out. "What do I do with it?" He pinched his nose with his other hand.

"Chew it, numbskull." Rhet chortled. " It helps with nausea."

Beoc gave Devon a pitiful plea for help, and it would have worked had she not seen him sick on the Fairy Ferry. She shrugged. As far as she was concerned, he should eat as many of those things as it took, not to barf again.

"Don't be a pansy." Rhet tore off a chunk of Duckweed and chucked it into the side of his mouth. "See . . . it won' hurt ya," he garbled.

Beoc stuffed the rest of the Duckweed in his mouth and gagged.

"Look." Rhet pointed to the beautiful, sky-scraping mountains with peaks surrounded by soft clouds. "We'll be there soon." Already half-way up the ratlines, Rhet chuckled, as he went back to work.

CHAPTER FOURTEEN
The Troll Guard

The crew brought the airship to a landing port on the edge of Grimwood Forest. Thirty feet from the ground, the crew tossed ropes off the side and slid down to secure the ship. Once it was steady, half a dozen passengers lined up to climb down the ladders.

This time, Devon didn't let Beoc go first and was back on solid ground in good time. Beoc however, caused a traffic jam on the way down. He came up panting and sweating, while passengers threw him dirty looks as they passed.

"Yo, Beoc!" Rhet called, dangling from a rope twenty feet above them. "See you at Gordimer. Take it easy, man." As he climbed back up the rope he called to Devon, "Nice to meet you."

The Ballarat soared up in the sky, leaving Devon and Beoc on the steep mountain cliff. Cool air tingled against Devon's skin. Thin yellow grass grew tall and swayed with the wind. Flowers bloomed wildly without design or purpose and a fresh breeze carried the scent of mountain air through the sky. Though it was beautiful, no one lingered with the heart of the city so close.

"Come on," Beoc waved Devon forward.

A bend in the path led them inside the edge of Grimwood Forest. Ornate, iron lampposts lined the pebbled trail. Coal-black oaks, gray walnut trees with leaves the color of blood, deep-blue weeping willows, and other magical plants that would put an ordinary botanist into an excited frenzy grew abundantly. A wicked mountain lay behind the city, concealed by a layer of clouds.

"It's quite a place, isn't it?" said Beoc. "I grew up here, so I forget sometimes how cool it really is. I'll show you around before we get to Gordimer. But we better hurry, Wrottesley hates it when you're late for supper."

Beoc continued his chattering habit as they walked. By the sound of his cheerful voice, he didn't seem to have a worry in the world. If only Devon was so confident. Everything had changed in the last few days. She had lost her friends, her home, and everything she knew. It's not that she would go back to her old life, but it didn't mean that she wasn't nervous about stepping into her new one. Ms. Frances used to say, "If you're going to do something, then do it right." Not that she usually listened to Ms. Frances, but in this Devon agreed completely. From here on, she wanted to do everything right.

The path came to an end, and the line of iron lampposts led them to an enormous sculpture of three warriors in battle. One, whispery like the wind, struck down an invisible opponent. The second, half human-half beast, charged into battle with ferocity, and the last, a beautiful woman, fearlessly shot a powerful blast of magic from her hands. It was a magnificent statue. "That's a shadow walker . . . a shapeshifter . . . and . . . a witch?"

"Yep. They're the founders of Thysia," Beoc explained. "They sacrificed their lives protecting this city."

Before Devon could ask what they were protecting it from, a more immediate concern caught her attention —

Towering beyond the statue, a golden gate with precious gems sparkled against the setting sun. Blocking the gate stood two menacing creatures. Both were easily over eight feet tall. They had spikes down their calves and shoulders and thick, heavy limbs with bare chests and feet and hair that grew like moss. They wore armored loincloths and heavy weapons across their backs.

"Beoc, what are those?"

"Trolls," Beoc replied. "Smarter than most people think . . . but they don't hear too well."

"Trolls?" Devon stilled.

"Yeah. They guard the gate."

Devon examined it more closely. The magnificent golden bars were formidable enough, but there were no walls attached to the gate. "Couldn't someone just go around it?"

"How would they do that?"

"Well, I don't see any walls —"

"You wouldn't, would you?" Beoc said obviously. "The gate was built by borlaugs," he finished, as if that explained it.

Flummoxed, Devon blinked blankly. Elsie had mentioned borlaugs too. Now, she wished she would have asked more about them.

Seeing Devon's confusion, Beoc tried to explain. "Borlaugs are sort of like trolls. At least they're big — bigger even — but they aren't fighters or warriors. They're quite useful though. I couldn't imagine Thysia without them."

"What do they do?"

"Metalsmiths, for starters, and craftsmen, like you've never seen before. They're the inventors of the magik world. If you have an impressive magical object, you can bet a borlaug made it. That gate is indestructible, and the wall is invisible. No one I know has ever seen what it looks like. No one except a borlaug, and they won't tell anybody. The idea is, if you can't see it, you can't figure out its weaknesses. One thing that trolls and borlaugs do have in common . . . is pride."

"I've never heard of trolls having pride before."

"That's cause you've been listening to human stories," he said mater-of-factly. "Come on. They'll start getting suspicious if we hang around."

Devon followed Beoc, and as they got closer, the two trolls were easily distinguished from one another. The taller, a greenish-brown one with a spiked club, leaned against the gate looking rather bored — while the other, a sturdier and tougher-looking troll, sharpened the blunt end of his club to a nasty point.

"Balfour. Gull." Beoc waved awkwardly. "How's it going?"

The two trolls glared with malicious scrutiny, as Devon and Beoc approached. The hairs on Devon's arms tingled. She was getting the feeling that something was wrong, and usually . . . that feeling was right. She slowed her pace. "Beoc, is there another way in?"

Beoc raised an eyebrow. "Of course not . . . well, not officially . . . I mean, not that I know of," he corrected.... "They're fine," he assured her, and then, raised his voice in case the trolls hadn't heard him. "Having a good day?"

"Humpf." The shorter troll grunted, deep and throaty ... and slashed his blade against the club so forcefully that a chunk of wood flew several feet.

The taller, greenish-brown troll grimaced, baring his teeth.

"I don't think they like us." Devon slowed, dragging her feet. "Maybe we should come back?"

"Nonsense." Beoc waved off the thought. "I told you, my father works for the Bureau of Magical

Security and Defense. He oversees the troll guard. They know who I am. That big one is Gull, and the green one is Balfour."

Against Devon's better judgment, Beoc continued for the gate. As they reached it, the trolls didn't move aside to let them pass. Rather, they came forward, leaving only a slight opening (straight through the middle of them).

Beoc dropped his eyes — losing courage.

Damn. Devon slipped past him, taking the lead. *When approaching a guard dog, you never show fear.* Everyone knew that.

Devon passed Gull, making a point to stare back (keeping her face expressionless) despite the putrid, reeking smell of his breath. When she made it past safely, she turned to the second troll — the taller, more intelligent-looking one — Balfour, Beoc had called him.

"Arrgh!" Beoc yelped from behind.

Devon swung around. Gull had grabbed Beoc by the collar and wrenched him up, high in the air.

"What a' you doing — ?" Beoc thrashed, kicking helplessly, his feet dangling above the ground.

In the second Devon's attention turned to Beoc, Balfour swung his club at her legs. The short spikes scraped through her skin, as the force of it knocked her over. She hit the ground hard. Before she could recover, Balfour loomed over — his club against her chest threateningly.

"Ugh." Devon coughed, wheezing for the air knocked out of her . . . Determined not to show weakness, she grouched, "That hurt —"

"Guaf, Guaf. Guaf." Gull laughed, still holding Beoc by the collar.

"Don't mistake us for friends, shifter," Balfour growled at Beoc. "We knows who you are and whos your dad is. . . . We let you pass, but we don' like you none."

"We don' like you none," Gull repeated.

Balfour leaned over Devon and sniffed. It was all Devon could do to not start shaking right there. Then the stupid trolls would really have a laugh. She wouldn't give them that satisfaction. "Get off —"

"I know what you are," Balfour growled, pushing the club harder against her chest. "I cin *smell* it. Jus' like I cin smell the magic in your bag. There ain't none I ever smelled like you before, but I knows it when I smells it. Them other magiks might not know," he nodded to Beoc who was still thrashing and pleading to be put down, "but *trolls*, we know."

Devon shoved at Balfour's leathery, wrinkled face . . . but it didn't budge. "You stink —"

Balfour grabbed Devon's hair by the roots and yanked her up. "You gon owe me a favor. If you don' want no one else to know — when I says to come, yous better come."

Devon stared him down ... and they scowled at each other (his violent eyes, into her wild ones). Devon nodded imperceptibly. "Fine. Now put us down —"

"Let the brat go," Balfour gnarled.

Gull dropped Beoc. He fell to the ground in a heap and griped loudly. "Ow. Ow. Ow."

Balfour jerked his hand free of Devon's hair, pulling a few strands with it. She tried not to stumble as she grabbed Beoc and pulled him through the gate.

CHAPTER FIFTEEN
The Thief

Once they were out of range from being overheard, Beoc huffed. "Stupid trolls. I've been through here a hundred times since they got the front gate promotion. They know exactly who I am. You'd think they'd be a little friendlier." He caught his foot on a gnarled root and stumbled. "Wait till my father hears. I could have their jobs in an instant." Beoc snapped his fingers.

Devon stayed silent. She wouldn't have expected anything different from trolls. Not after the fairytales she heard at St. Frances. Trolls bullied travelers. They looted. They killed. Everybody knew that. Though, those were just fairytales. This was real. And these trolls were guards ... So what did Balfour mean? *I know what you are. . . . I cin smell it.*

A rustle in the trees made Devon jump. She whirled around and squinted into the lining of the great black oaks and twisted trunks. Why didn't she feel relieved? She had made it to Thysia! All the danger over the last couple days had led to *this* moment — she was finally here. So why didn't she feel safe? Instead, every step she took came stilted and rigid, and she couldn't stop fidgeting with the strap of her knapsack. . . . *It was Niko.* He hadn't given up. She was sure of it. Somehow, he had made it past Kamau and Bree and chased her to the Repository — all for the crown. It just didn't *feel* over yet.

"Beoc, how do trolls know who is allowed to pass through the gates?"

"What do you mean?"

"Could a shadow walker, who say . . . was exiled . . . get through? Couldn't he just turn into a shadow and slip by?"

"It's not possible," Beoc shook his head, still grumpy over their treatment. "A troll would smell 'em. Even if you were invisible, a troll would know someone was there. There's no tricking trolls —"

Devon relaxed, her muscles loosening, as she walked.

"Look at that!" Beoc stopped short and pointed to a purple bruise on his arm. "Balfour and Gull know exactly who I am, and they treated me like a . . . a . . . criminal!"

Devon forced a concerned look across her face. "It doesn't look too bad. Besides, don't you heal fast?"

"That's not the point!" Beoc clipped sourly.

The short walk from the gate led to the edge of a hill that overhung the most dazzling and lively city. Crystal streams (large enough for barges and scows) ran sparkling clear water through vibrant streets. Intricate homes and uniquely delightful shops were engineered in all sorts of designs — on the sides of cliffs, the edges of hills, and the tops of trees. More were stacked above others (sometimes crookedly) but always in the most fascinating manner.

"This . . . ," Beoc beamed over the top of the hill, "is Thysia." He brushed the hair from his face and admired the magnificent city. "The heart of Thysia," he pointed to the middle of the city, "is the busiest part. We call it the pith."

Devon peered down at the bewitching city, at a loss for words. "It's . . ."

"It gets better," Beoc promised. "Come on."

As they left the brush and mountains behind, the city came to life. A vast assortment of metals, woods, and neatly tiled stones were cleverly built into homes. Armored trolls patrolled the cobbled streets. Small boats, in the shapes of coracles and gondolas, carried wizards, and elves through the city streams. And on land, bickering dwarves pulled trade carts, stacked with herbs and wild roots, from the Grimwood Forest, into the city.

The Thief

"Ya always be saying that you're the best," lamented a red-bearded dwarf. "Ya got the best haul. Ya went the bes' way. Ya made the mos' Gubbins." The red-bearded dwarf kicked the cart belonging to a black-haired dwarf, with the tip of his shoe.

"And ya always be jealous," taunted the black-haired dwarf, kicking his neighbor's cart in return. "The ladies don' find it attractive, ya know."

Several dwarves chortled, and the red-bearded dwarf flushed as bright as his hair. His voice rose over the clatter of their carts, "Men will settle it like dwarfs — so let us be men!"

All at once, the dwarves dropped their burdens and tasks. They hurried to their carts, and selecting the heaviest barrels, boosted them over their heads as mightily as they could. Laughing, they heckled each other with catcalls and insults.

One at a time, each dwarf gave up — dropping his barrel on the street, breaking the wood, and spilling the contents. Then, the defeated dwarf deposited a portion of his haul into the middle, while the remaining dwarfs pealed a renewed wave of laughter and insults that would only mean anything to a dwarf.

"Come on," said Beoc, pulling Devon's attention away from the dwarves. "They could be there all night."

"Just another minute —"

The dwarves dwindled off, until only three remained. Sweat poured down their faces. Their hairy arms trembled and shook from strain, and their steely expressions unyielded, with determination and pride.

"Give up yet, lad?" mocked the black-haired dwarf.

"I'll carry this barrel to my grave," gnashed the red-haired dwarf.

"I don't want to wait that long," whispered Beoc.

The third dwarf, a bald one with a brown beard down to his chest, collapsed to his knees — the barrel still teetering above him. The cluster of dwarves burst into a clamor of shrieks, catcalls, and bets.

SNAP. The red-haired dwarf's barrel cracked, and the latch popped off. Crops and wares spewed into the street. Staggering under the jolt, and then the sudden shift of weight, he stumbled and tottered. Swaying like a seesaw, he rammed straight into the black-haired dwarf — knocking them both, and their barrels, to the ground.

There was a sudden, wide-eyed silence as every dwarf froze in shock — and then, all at once, they exploded into cheers and jeers. The bald dwarf won! He collapsed — tears of pain, relief, and happiness trickled down his cheeks as he lay sprawled out, across the ground.

"This is your fault!" growled the Black-haired dwarf. "You butterfingered PEABRAIN!"

"Put your beard where your mouth is!" The red-haired dwarf raised his fists.

"My woman fights better than you —"

The red-haired dwarf's eyes bulged. "YOU POMPOUS, BLIMP-HEADED, BOOZE NINNY!"

"AGHHHHH," screamed the black-haired dwarf.

"GRAAAAAHH," bellowed the red-haired dwarf.

And they both charged. They tackled each other to the ground and rolled around, punching and kicking, while the other dwarves tried to pull them apart.

"That's our cue." Beoc reeled backwards, scrambling out of the way.

"Right." Devon hastened after him, and it was a short walk before they came to the first street.

A mechanical sign, that read Forger's Court, adjusted its height as they came near. Along the street, homes and shops were constructed with more ingenious designs — possessing all sorts of gizmos and gadgets, mechanical drones, and strange machinery. Someone who knew very little of mechanisms and apparatuses etcetera, would say they looked like the inner workings of a clock — though it was much more complex than that.

"That's where the borlaugs live," said Beoc. "Most

of 'em anyway — some live in the inner city where their shops are, but most choose to live with other inventors so they can keep their work secret. You could probably guess by all the inventions —"

Beoc pointed the opposite direction — past the wild trees of Goblin Gorge. Vines, shrubs, and moss overran stone huts. Streetlamps stopped at the entrance (so that even with the setting sun emitting a reddish orange glow — darkness already clouded the dirt lane). "That's where the goblins live obviously. Not the hobgoblins though — They live down Rotted Root Knoll, beside the Screaming Lake." As if suddenly remembering that Devon didn't know much about Thysia, Beoc added, "Goblins are bigger and meaner . . . and well . . . you've met the hobgoblins."

"What other kinds of magiks live in Thysia?"

"Well, let's see." Beoc babbled, as they continued into the city. "Shapeshifters and shadow walkers a 'course — elves and dwarves — and then there are the fairies, imps, sprites, and pixies. Oh, and the trolls, borlaugs, mages . . . let's not forget about them. . . . But those are just a few. . . . There are more obviously —"

The deeper they got into the city, the busier it became. In the Pith, as Beoc called it, all sorts of magical dwellings jumbled together in a disorganized fashion that situated perfectly with one another.

Arched doors, pointy rooftops with bargeboards, glimmering sconces, cupulas, colorful shutters, and dormer windows gave the city a fairytale feeling. Glowing lanterns floated along the crystal streams in an eerie but beautiful way. Black trees with plump fruits lined the cobblestone roads, and short, painted signs had names like Dwarf Lane, Evergreen Hedge, Winter Light Walk, and Old Hunting Bend.

"What is that?" Devon pointed to a patchwork, metal shop. Compared to its neighbors it was rather run-down, with a crooked sign, peeling paint, and a rank smell of rot.

"That's Blotches, the Blacksmith," said Beoc pitifully. "My pa says the owner doesn't get much business anymore. It's a miracle he lasted this long. The borlaugs are putting him out of business. These days, no one wants anything that isn't made by a borlaug."

Beoc pointed to a large bay window, lined with rows upon rows of tiny bottles. Inside, an old man applied a thick paste to a dwarf's wounded leg. "Over there is the Apothecary," Beoc said brightly. "If you need to get patched up, that's a good place to go."

The orange sun dipped deeper beneath skyline, strewing a brilliant cast of colors over the horizon. Thysia was as busy at dusk, as you could suppose it would be any other hour of the day. Not like in Hasty, where everything closed at dark. Rather, in Thysia the city came alive at night — rebirthed with spirited and jolly magiks.

Warlocks and mages (with tall, pointed hats that folded at the top) ducked in and out of various shops. Shapeshifters and shadow walkers clung together in tight groups, shifting amongst themselves. Glowing fairies (smaller than the size of a child's hand) buzzed through the sky and transfigured into taller versions of dazzling men and women with sparkling wands and glittering wings. Pixies sang bewitching tunes with the hum of their wings. And nearby, a cluster of rather short, pointy-eared magiks, clothed in a fashion of earthy colors, leather boots, and bows slung across their backs, strode past, deep in conversation of some political matter.

"Beoc, what are those —?"

Busy checking the street names, Beoc barely glanced up. "Elves. Thysia is lucky to have them. They've brilliant minds — every single one — perfect strategists. Everyone wants to hire an elf, and quite a few hold positions in the United Governance of Magiks." Deciding the route, Beoc sprung forward. "This way —"

"Where are we going?"

"I thought we might stop in on a friend — if you don't mind?"

Though she wanted to stay in the heart of the city, Devon couldn't help wondering, "Shouldn't we get to Gordimer?"

"It's on the way," Beoc assured her.

"All right." Devon shrugged. It was probably best to head straight to Gordimer, but here, in the buoyant and sparkling city, worries of Niko felt . . . silly.

Beoc stopped in front of an unusual shop, built of gears and locks, with a vaulted door. He hurried up the stoop and knocked three times. The raps echoed down the street. A long minute hand clicked to the twelve o'clock position. A mechanical phoenix (made of copper, bronze, and gold) swooped out of a life-sized cuckoo clock door. It glided around them (its metal eyes keenly watchful) and soared back up to where it came. The door shut behind it, and they waited in silence.

"Is something supposed to happen?"

"Well, yeah." Beoc knocked again.

A giant pendulum swung. The gears turned, and the vaulted door opened. A humongous beast of a man (larger than both Gull and Balfour, with coarse, olive-green skin, and a mechanical arm constructed of solid gold) blocked the entire doorway. Instead of weapons, tools stuck out of his belt, his apron, a leather strap across his chest, and dozens of pockets.

He bent over (crouching beneath the door frame) so that Devon could see his face. A patch hid one eye, but his other eye was inquisitively alert. "What do I owe the pleasure, son of Windsor Hobbart?"

Beoc's ears turned pink. "It's just Beoc." He shot a quick glance at Devon, hoping she hadn't heard. "I was just checking in on the . . . um . . . order my father placed."

"I'm sorry, Beoc, it's not finished yet. Tell Windsor magic of this level takes time to mature."

"Right. Of course." Beoc leaned around him, stealing a peek inside the shop. Mechanized noises were ticking and clicking, clacking, and snapping all on their own. Being unable to see past Tarik, Beoc straightened again. "Tarik, this is Devon."

"Hello, friend of Beoc."

"Pleased to meet you," said Devon.

"Tarik is the finest magicsmith in Thysia," Beoc boasted. "You wouldn't mind showing her your shop, would you?"

"Of course, young Windsor." Tarik stepped to the side. "Any friend, of the descendant of Hobbart, is most welcome."

"Descendant of Hobbart?" Devon muttered curiously, as they slid through the open doorway.

Beoc flushed deeper and lifted his shoulders in a shrug. "Windsor, my dad . . . he's uh . . . not just in the Bureau of Magical Security and Defense. He's a Hobbart . . . well, I'm a Hobbart, and he . . . I mean us . . . we come from a long line of important magik officials."

"Wow." Devon gawked.

Tarik sat at one of several workbenches, and still, he towered over them. "Every Hobbart before you has come to do something great. I'm eager to see what becomes of you, young Beoc."

"I'll try not to let anyone down." Beoc sauntered over, gloomily.

Eyebrows raised, Devon looked over Beoc, seeing him differently than before. His quick apologies, and clumsiness made sense now. His whole family were prominent magiks, giving him a lot to live up too. At least, he had a family though. He didn't need to pretend they were stuck in a faraway place. He had a family right here — one he could be proud of.

Had it not been for the impressive sight before them, she would have tried to wipe the dejected look from his face. However, she was momentarily awestruck.

Tarik's shop was an enormous room with a domed ceiling. Inventions filled the walls all the way to the top. Some were stationary, but many were automated. Hammers and hatchets, tongs and chisels, and hundreds of handsomely crafted pieh tools were arranged everywhere (even hanging from above). There were several workstations — one specially equipped for blacksmithing, another for goldsmithing, a different one for coppersmithing, one for bladesmithing, and a finer one with delicate tools for jewels. There was even a funny little corner decked with hundreds of clocks — perfect for a horologist.

Neat stacks of raw materials such as differently colored woods, blocks of copper, and bars of gold sat ready for use. Silver, piled in mounds, glowed by a fiery hearth. Three enormous forges with brick chimneys, roaring with heat, were strategically placed around the shop. Rough sculptures, carved from wood and metal, decorated the walls like trinkets and little, motorized robots moved about the shop performing some task or other. Like miniature assistants, they gathered and carried, cleaned, and tinkered, making all sorts of noise as they went.

"I see your drones are getting more advanced," Beoc said, impressed. Already he had forgotten his dampened mood. He moved to examine a drone driving on tracks. It zoomed back and forth, sorting a pile of scrap metal, and ignored Beoc completely.

"I've developed new mechanisms for cognitive

understanding," said Tarik. "I have more advanced drones, but this one's name is Doohickey."

"Doohickey?" Beoc snickered. When Tarik didn't join in, Beoc forced back his laughter and coughed deeply. "What sort of tasks does Doohickey do?"

Spotting some inventions that hadn't been put away, Tarik moved them, using his golden arm and claw. "Doohickey performs menial tasks that an apprentice might do. It fetches tools and scraps, sweeps, and sorts metal. There are a few kinks." Tarik scratched his head. "I can't understand why it gets offended when I ask for oranges."

"Oranges?" Devon blurted.

"What about lemons?" Beoc joked.

"No, those are fine," Tarik shrugged, missing the joke, again. "He gets a bit testy with juice though."

"Why ask for oranges at all?" asked Devon.

"An inquisitive child," Tarik encouraged, impressed. "To break beyond the boundaries of drones. I ask them to perform all sorts of labors. Borlaugs pride themselves in advancing both magic and technology, and I must do my part."

"Can I take a closer look?" Beoc asked, hoping to appear inquisitive as well.

"Of course, young Windsor."

While Beoc examined the various drones, Devon

explored the shop and soon found herself beside an anvil where Tarik forged heavy metals. She ducked down to admire another one of Tarik's self-thinking robots. This one was moving parcels of diamonds (black, white, and sparkling yellow) to a workstation — where they were to be crafted into something spectacular.

Just then, a reflection on a shiny brass mechanism caught her attention. . . . Something scurried behind her, and Devon whipped around.

A stealthy creature with pointed ears, a green hairless body, a long scar across it's bare chest, and nails, sharp as knives, scrambled under the table. It moved so quick and craftily, that Devon nearly missed it.

Fortunately, whatever had its attention, captured all of it. The little creature scuttered past without noticing her (half-concealed behind the anvil). It crept along the shadows, scanning the workshop greedily, looking inside one thing and under another. It paused beside the pile of diamonds, picked one up, and held it to the light, letting it glimmer. Satisfied, the creature snatched a handful of diamonds in its tiny fist (causing a dozen more to tumble down the pile and spill across the floor). Unbothered, it stuffed them into a pouch, tied at its waist.

The Thief

Devon gasped and ducked behind the anvil. *It was stealing.*

Breathing hard, Devon waited — afraid to move in case it heard her.

No sound.

She held her breath, closed her eyes, and counted. After nearly ten horrible seconds, a light scurry, skimmed across the floor. Devon shot around the anvil and glimpsed it at the last moment. The creature stopped at a stone wall and pushed against one stone after another, until a hidden stairway revealed itself. Then it darted down the stairwell, and the wall began to shut.

Devon glanced back at Tarik, engrossed in a conversation with Beoc. "T-Tarik," she spluttered.

"One second." Beoc waved for her to be silent. Whatever Tarik was saying had captivated his attention.

Devon whipped back to the stone stairwell, eyes wide.

Of course she shouldn't follow it. Everything about this was suspicious. Tarik had an intruder. And so far, she had managed to stay out of trouble. Undoubtedly, the best thing for her to do would be to stay out of it, but something about the excitement of a secret passage drew her in. Whatever Tarik was hiding beneath his shop was suddenly and irresistibly tempting. What was down that secret passage? Perhaps more treasures, like the ones he so unmindfully left to the care of robots. Devon glanced back at Tarik and Beoc, still deep in discussion. Wouldn't she be doing Tarik a favor by following the creature? It had stolen his diamonds. Wasn't this her chance to prove herself?

Devon pulled the knapsack from her back and hurried to the stone wall. Just as the door shut, she slipped inside the hidden staircase, pushed aside all rational thoughts, and placed the Crown of Guilledon on her head. The wall closed behind her, and she stood in utter darkness.

Devon cleared her mind. She needed to control the crown and not let it control her. Once her thoughts were empty, she focused on becoming a shadow. The sounds of the room above were loud and distinct — the soft crackling of the fire — the clicking of the robots — the chatter of Tarik and Beoc. *Focus. You can do this.* Devon closed her eyes, blocking out the sounds, and whisked away. Like the wind, she slid down the wall of the stairs, after the intruder.

This was nothing like the weightless way she morphed to conform to the jagged crevice. She was limitless. She became the darkness (the cool chill that stole a child's breath away and gave it fear in return).

The Thief

At the bottom of the stairs, Devon began to lose control. Fatigue overwhelmed her. Unable to grasp the power any longer, the magic slipped away, and Devon tumbled on the floor of a furnished apartment.

Frightened that she had been heard, Devon crouched behind the corner by the stairs. Leaning heavily against the wall, she pulled off the crown and slipped it into her knapsack. Silently, she prayed the creature hadn't heard her. After a moment, she peeked around the hidden passage and into an unexpected room.

It possessed all the things a living quarter would, such as a tidy bed, a washtub, a wardrobe, and a rather neat table already set for supper. A pot of stew steamed from the table, filling the room with a delicious smell of roast and onions. *This must be Tarik's home . . . , and she had interrupted him right before supper.*

Too distracted to hear the thump, the green creature scurried across the room, and back again. It rushed about the apartment, light as a feather, opening drawers and cabinets and such. Within moments, the creature discovered a hidden safe inside Tarik's wardrobe. It leaned its head against the cool metal and began turning the dials.

Devon inched closer. The floor creaked, and the creature stiffened.

Ever so slowly, it turned an ugly, hairless head with yellow eyes that pierced across the dark room.

A tiny gasp escaped Devon's lips.

"Who is nosey?" The creature's eyes flashed, furiously.

Devon stiffened, unsure what to do. She hadn't expected it could talk.

The creature leered and flashed grimy, foul teeth. It took a threatening step closer, and the dim light caught the deep scar across his chest. "Yous are getting into trouble."

"You're the one going through someone else's things!" Devon shot back, a little shakier than she would have liked. What kind of creature was this? And now that she was facing it, what was she going to do . . . ? Could she still catch it? But then, it didn't look like much of a choice. She had trapped it down here, and now that it knew she was here, she doubted it would let her alert Tarik to its burglary. One of them was getting out and one wasn't.

The creature unfolded a handful of claws, clicking them against each other threateningly. Devon cringed. It must have realized the same thing. The creature dropped to the floor, so lightly it didn't make a sound, and crawled closer.

Well, there's no turning back now, she told herself. All she had to do was pin it. *This is just like catching Cook's mice — except bigger — with bigger teeth.*

The creature lunged, and Devon catapulted to the side. She rolled across the floor and stumbled to get up. Barely slipping to the side in time, it flew past again, catching her arm with one of its claws. A sharp, intense pain shot up her arm, followed by a searing burn. Blood soaked her shirt.

The monster slid across the room, it's nails scratching against the stone. SCRREEECH.

When it came to a stop, it catapulted across the room again — straight for Devon's chest.

Devon dropped, headfirst. It flew past, swiping her legs, and shredding her jeans like a hand full of knives.

Devon cried out as pain ripped through her skin. Breathing heavily, she staunched the blood with her hand. *It's going to attack until I do something. I can't keep dodging it. If I don't catch it now, I might get seriously hurt.* Desperate, Devon lurched for the creature. She flew through the air —

The pupils of its yellow eyes widened in surprise.

POP. It disappeared . . . and reappeared on the far side of the apartment.

Devon skidded to avoid crashing into a cabinet and hit a bench instead, knocking it on top of her.

WHISH. The creature shot a whirling ball of black magic.

It hit the cabinet above her — BOOM — blasting it from the wall. The ceiling shook. Splinters of wood sliced across the room, and the impact threw Devon back. The hanging line of pans came crashing down with a racket that rang through the shop.

The sounds above went quiet. Surely, Tarik and Beoc heard the crash. Any moment they would realize someone was downstairs and come bounding after them.

Realizing it was out of time, the green monster shot the safe with another blast of black magic that BOOMED through the apartment. Stones flew from the wall. Tarik's personal belongings soared across the apartment. His dinner table toppled over, shattering the china, and his supper poured out onto the floor.

As the dust settled, Devon blinked, eyes burning. Her ears rang from the explosion. Smoke made it hard to see. Half the wall was torn away, and the safe hung open.

Devon squeezed her hands against her ears to stop the ringing. The green monster scurried across the apartment and wrapped its claws around a leather pouch.

"No!" Devon pushed herself up —

Heavy footsteps thundered above. Tarik bounded down the stairs, and Devon's heart skipped a beat. She wished she had stayed upstairs. Snooping through a borlaug's home was a horrible idea ... and getting caught at it was worse.

The green thief darted up the wall just as Tarik burst in with Beoc on his heels.

Tarik took one look at his destroyed home, the open safe, and the green monster clutching the pouch. "NO!" he boomed and lunged his full weight at the creature. He landed on top of it, crushing it beneath him —

Devon felt a surge of relief. With the creature caught, Tarik couldn't blame her for wrecking his home.

"Hegh. Hegh," the creature chortled. POP. It disappeared ... and reappeared on the ceiling above them.

"THIEF! CATCH THAT GREMLIN!" bellowed Tarik and swiped at the creature with his metal arm.

POP. It disappeared again ... and reappeared by the furnace, closest to Devon.

Devon dove (just as Tarik lunged again). Right before they collided, Devon rolled out of the way — Tarik missed the gremlin and tumbled into his ruined supper. In a flash, the gremlin was up the side of the wall, across the ceiling, and through the passage.

"NO!" Tarik bounded up, chased after it, and they were gone.

A wisp of smoke tinged the air as Devon picked herself up. This was all her fault.

"What are you doing down here?" Beoc exclaimed, flabbergasted. "This is his *home!*"

Devon forced her voice steady. "I saw it sneak down here, and I followed it —"

Beoc blanched. "That was a gremlin — a vexing, ungovernable lot! They cause destruction purely for the pleasure of it!" His baffled expression softened, mixing pity with disbelief. "They also happen to be very talented thieves —"

"Do you think they'll catch it?" Devon asked, heart sinking.

"Maybe . . . if Tarik calls the Troll Guard in time —"

BONG. BONG. BONG. A low-pitched bell vibrated across the city.

"What is that?" Devon's voice faltered. It sounded like an enormous metal bell — except, the sound was everywhere.

Beoc threw up his hand for quiet. He hurried to a window. "Shh."

BONG. BONG. BONG. The bell pealed again, echoing from invisible speakers all over the city.

"I don't believe it!" Beoc's face went pale.

"What is it?" Devon hissed. Suddenly, she had the urge to run.

"It's the city's defense alarm." Beoc gaped oafishly. "It means we're under attack." Beoc ran for the stairs. "Come on!"

They hurried through the secret passage. By the time they were upstairs, Tarik was gone. They scooted around the forges, anvils, and self-moving mechanics, and headed for the heavy metal door. Beoc shot Devon an incredulous look, "I can't believe you chased a gremlin through Tarik's home —"

"I didn't know! I just wanted to help."

Beoc pulled open the heavy metal door and hurried outside.

BONG. BONG. BONG.

"We'll worry about it later. We have bigger problems at the moment. We have to get to Gordimer *fast*."

The street was empty, except for Tarik, who bellowed down the stone walk, "GUARD! GUARD!"

A clash of metal echoed down the street. In unison, a squad of trolls marched for them. Devon avoided Tarik's gaze and hurried down the stone steps. He probably hated her for going through his private rooms.

"*Why* were you in my home?" Tarik loomed over them.

Devon caught his gaze and instantly wished she hadn't. Without a thief, there was no one else to blame but her. "I'm sorry, I . . ah . . . followed the . . . gremlin. I d-didn't know it was going into your home."

"There is no way she could have known Tarik," Beoc promised. "This is her first time in Thysia. If you ask Headmistress Wrottesley, she'll confirm it."

Tarik frowned, a large wrinkle creased through his forehead, and his mouth fell into a sad line. "I will also inform her that her students meddled through my home and enabled a dangerous thief to dispossess me of a priceless artifact."

Beoc's mouth fell open. "But —"

"No doubt," Tarik interrupted, "this diversion . . . " he waved at the pair of them, "made the burglary successful."

Devon slumped. She hadn't thought of that. By not alerting the break-in, Devon helped the gremlin escape. Now, Headmistress Wrottesley (whom she hadn't even met) would hear Tarik's complaint, and think the worst of her. What if Mr. Mustafa found out? She had only just promised him to stay out of trouble yesterday.

"Come on. We have to get out of here." Beoc pulled Devon by the arm. "I, uh, hope you catch the thief, Tarik," Beoc said kindly.

"Me too," Devon added sincerely.

Tarik kept his penetrating glare on the pair of them. "As do I . . . for all our sakes."

A heavy thadump announced the arrival of the squadron of trolls. They stood in a tactical, diamond-like formation, protected at each angle. An emblem in their armor gave uniformity to the mishmash of metals and weapons. Each troll was so terrifically dangerous, that if Devon were to choose one to fight, she would opt for none at all.

"Troll Guard," growled a battle-scarred troll (with a hideous hammer resting on his shoulder).

"A gremlin has stolen a valuable artifact. One entrusted to my care by the president of the United Governance of Magiks — Humphrey Blunderdolt, himself." Tarik's voice deepened, stressing the importance of the matter. "He escaped west through the city. I think he's headed for the Gates of Thysia. If he makes it to Grimwood Forest, we'll never catch him."

BONG. BONG. BONG. The low-pitched bell tolled again, urging the trolls towards the source of distress.

"This is of *utmost importance*," Tarik implored.

"You have scent?" The troll rested his hammer on the ground and glowered.

Tarik held out something sharp. Recognizing it, Devon's stomach twisted in knots. Bile rose up her throat, and she gagged.

"What is it?" Beoc whispered, shaking.

"One of the gremlin's claws —"

Tarik handed it to the troll. Unaffected, the battle-scarred troll sniffed deeply. His face contorted, and he growled to the other trolls in a language Devon didn't understand. "Ek þekkja."

"What did he say?" Devon whispered.

"I don't know," said Beoc. "He's speaking Trollurd — the language of trolls."

"I said, *I know*," the battle-scarred troll growled and handed the claw back to Tarik. "Darrog," he snarled.

A lean troll with wickedly sharp double swords, and curved horns protruding from his jaw stepped forward. The tactic formation adjusted, filling in the empty spot.

"Or-uak is alive!" the battle-scarred troll snarled savagely. "All trolls go to gate. No magik go in. No magik go out. NONE," he bellowed, eyes bulging. The sound vibrated down the street.

Startled, Devon leapt back. Beoc was no better — he whimpered and stumbled.

"Gaag," Darrog grunted and took off down the street. BONG. BONG. BONG.

The leading troll roared out in temper. "Grraaaah! Or-uak is behind this!" he spat (his lips curled with hatred). He grabbed another troll from the formation. "Turn off alarm."

The Thief

"Arg," the troll grunted and took off.

Devon grabbed Beoc's sleeve and pulled, snapping him from his petrified state. "Let's go."

"Good idea."

Devon and Beoc hurried deeper through the heart of the city, where curious magiks lingered in the streets. As word spread that a gremlin was behind Thysia's alarm, Trolls marched for the gate in squadrons, to a formidable beat (steady and unyielding).

As they hurried, something nagged Devon's thoughts. She had this strange feeling that there was more to all of this — it just didn't feel right. They were missing something. The gremlin in Tarik's home was clever. Too clever. It managed to get in and out almost undetected. Loud wasn't its style, and it didn't seem like setting off a resounding, obnoxious alarm all over the city was something it would do — not even for a distraction. It would have wanted to sneak out unnoticed. Not alert the whole city. And if she were the gremlin . . . she wouldn't head for the gate.

"Beoc, something's wrong!" Devon slowed to a stop, slightly out of breath.

"What?" Beoc stopped suddenly and bumped into her. "What's wrong?"

"I don't think the gremlin is behind the —" A scraping sound carried across a windy breeze, and

Devon cut off. Her hair whipped across her face. "What's that?" She strained, listening intently.

"It s-sounds like wind," Beoc said shakily.

"No," Devon stammered. "What's the other sound?"

"I don't hear anything —"

"It sounds like . . . rumbling and crashing, and . . . ," Devon gaped in horror, "screaming."

The sound picked up again, getting louder —

YAAAHHHHHHHH. A shrill scream erupted behind a tall row of magic shops, followed by another, and then the city was filled with screams that spread like fire. Beoc grabbed the handle of her trunk and whipped around, searching for the right way to run.

A vast gray ship came into view, casting a shadow over the city. It soared crookedly, broken in the sky — not high enough to clear the rooftops. It scraped against the tops of trees and shops, shattering the clay like rain. Shards of shingles bounced and exploded against the cobblestone like hail. Magiks screamed and ran for cover as the city came down on them.

Devon grabbed the other end of the trunk, and they sprinted for cover under a low hanging bridge that crossed a narrow canal. "That's the Sky Snail!" Devon gasped.

Beoc didn't turn to look. Instead, his legs pumped faster and steered them under the stone bridge.

"Rhet said airships don't come into the city —" Devon panted, over distant screams.

"They don't. There's no port." Beoc collapsed under the bridge.

"Then why —" she stopped midsentence. *It suddenly all made sense.* Who had been chasing her all the way from Hasty? Who would do anything for the Crown of Guilledon in her knapsack? . . . "The bell wasn't a distraction. It was —"

"It's hijacked!" a magik screamed shrilly.

"RUN!" yelled another.

"AAAAAHHHH!"

All along the block, magiks scattered as the city rippled into chaos. Shapeshifters, witches, elves, and dwarves panicked in an unruly discord as the Sky Snail soared straight for them.

CHAPTER SIXTEEN
The Hijacking

The Sky Snail weaved around. Magiks screamed and scrambled for cover. Wizards brandished their wands, blasting obstacles out of the way. Fairies shrank to the size of walnuts and flew into the trunks of trees. Braver ones fired glittering shields, protecting shops from the destruction of the Sky Snail.

"Quick," Devon yelled over the sudden panic. "We have to get out of the way." Devon ran with her awkward trunk, as fast as she could carry it. They zipped down one street, then hastened down another, but the Sky Snail had no direct route. It soared this way and that, sharply turning and tearing through the city.

"Where are the trolls?" panted Beoc.

"They went to the gate — they're not going to make it here in time."

A cupula crashed, splintering the walk with bits of painted wood and metal. Lingering magiks were sprayed with splintery fragments, and the street filled with shrieks.

The Hijacking

Devon swerved and took a sharp turn, then picked up speed.

"This is terrible," Beoc gasped. He grabbed the other end of the trunk, so Devon could run faster.

Devon grimaced and tried to block out the cries. If the Shadow Reign got the crown, the whole city would suffer like this. The invasion would destroy the city, killing hundreds of magiks.

"Do you think the gremlin is doing this?" Beoc heaved, as sweat dribbled down his shirt.

"No. But I have a bad feeling I know who did — and if I'm right — that airship is chasing us."

"CHASING US?" Beoc belted.

Devon glared up. The airship turned sharply and steered straight for them. "We need to get to Gordimer — quick!"

CRACK. The Sky Snail crashed through a tower. Stone and wood fell from the sky and ricocheted off the ground.

"Come on!" Devon dragged Beoc down an empty street, where taller buildings hid them from view. They stopped at a curious shop with ink-stained windows and a loud da-um, da-um, da-um, snap, coming from inside.

"Who stole the airship!" Beoc demanded.

Devon hesitated. Kamau had told her not to trust

anyone, but his life was in danger too. She had to tell him the truth. It was only fair. "Back at the Repository, we weren't being chased by trainers — those were shadow walker assassins. They tried to kill me in Hasty and followed me here."

"Shadow walker assassins!" Beoc repeated, dumbstruck. "What do they want with you?"

"I promised to keep it a secret."

"Are you kidding me?"

"I promised!" Devon said firmly. She wasn't going break her promise to Hammad. No one was going to hear about the crown — not from her anyway.

Beoc shot her a look of disbelief and ducked around the corner of the shop. His head buzzed around, looking for something he recognized. Anything that would tell him where they were. He pointed out the sign, Enchanted Chronicle. "We're too far off-track. We have to go back."

"Back! Beoc, we can't go back!"

"We're still several miles away." He threw his arms up defeatedly.

"Beoc, the shadow walkers will kill us!"

Beoc slid down the wall. His head fell in his hands, and he ran his fingers through his hair.

Devon crouched beside him. "Listen to me. We have to Gordimer. You can't freak out on me right now."

The Hijacking

"I CAN'T FREAK OUT ON YOU!" Beoc shouted. "AN AIRSHIP IS TEARING APART THYSIA, AND YOU SAY ASSASSINS ARE LOOKING FOR YOU!"

"The airship won't last much longer — it's falling apart! And when the trolls figure out the gremlin isn't at the gate, they'll come back. We just need to get to Gordimer."

"This is my fault, isn't it? We should've just headed straight to Gordimer!"

Devon grabbed Beoc's arm. "If it's anyone's fault, it's mine. Right now, you need to get up. We have to —"

"What?" Beoc's eyes rounded.

"Shhh."

"What is it?" Beoc stood up, breaking his petrified state.

"It's a . . . neigh."

Devon's head shot up as the Sky Snail soared over the city, missing one roof but crashing into the next. On the side of the hull, a muddy and half-starved Mendaecus frantically tried to get free.

"It's stuck!" Devon jumped up, horrified, as the terrified creature was hammered through another rooftop.

Beoc trembled beside her. "He's done for —"

"We have to save it!" exclaimed Devon.

"We can't possibly help —"

"He'll die," Devon clipped wildly. Her blood simmered. It was bad enough the unwanted creature was mistreated, but now he was caged up in a hijacked ship while it was rammed into rooftops! Was a Mendaecus's life worth so little? Kamau and Bree might not approve of the reckless plan forming in her head, but she wasn't going to let that Mendaecus die. "I won't leave him," Devon said stubbornly. "We'll wait until it's closer and then make a run for it."

"No. No. I'm not doing this again!" insisted Beoc. "NO!"

"Fine. Hide." Devon shoved her trunk into his chest.

They locked eyes, both afraid this was the last time they would see each other. Clamping her jaw, Devon took off.

The CRASH of the Sky Snail masked Devon's footsteps as she raced down the street. Her mind protested with each step. Niko had hijacked that Sky Snail — she just knew it. Which made this reckless and stupid. The absolute opposite of what she should be doing — but she wasn't going to let that Mendaecus die.

Once Beoc was out of sight, Devon pulled out the Crown of Guilledon and dumped the knapsack, along with all her belongings, on the cobble walk.

She doubted she would ever see it again. But that was something she would worry about later. After making sure she was alone, Devon placed the crown on her head, and raced for the Sky Snail. *Okay, focus.*

The sounds around her disappeared. Tiny hairs tingled along her palms, prickling her skin. Her senses heightened. Every sound became pronounced — the beat of her heart — the pounding of feet, as magiks raced through the city — even the ragged breath scraping through her lungs. *You can do this.* Devon leapt into the air and burst into a shadow. She flew up, higher and higher, until she soared over the roof. Midair, her body ripped into billions of weightless molecules, and she hovered, ghost-like, in the sky.

Fire had spread across the ship, engulfing the deck in flames. Thick plumes of smoke made it hard to breathe. There was no sign of anyone onboard. Still, she kept to the shadows and flew around the hull. Spotting the cage, Devon propelled forward.

The Sky Snail zig-zagged for another street of shops with fresh roofs, and tall, pointed steeples. And Devon knew, in its tattered state, it couldn't take much more damage.

The Mendaecus brayed and bucked with a renewed vigor, as Devon reached the cage. Metamorphosing, she appeared from her shadow and reached through the bars. "Shh. It's okay."

Nostrils flaring, the Mendaecus reared up and bucked again.

"It's me." Devon reached further.

Recognizing her scent, the Mendaecus settled, and breathing heavy, he snorted and whined, shaking his muddy mane.

"I'm going to get you out of here" Devon whispered. She tugged on the front of the cage, but the latch was jammed — dented in from some blunt force it took. She tried not to panic. *You can do this*, she thought. *Just break the lock.*

Devon thought of Niko. He hand had turned sharp like a sword. And with the crown, she should be able to do it, too. She concentrated harder. Slowly, her hand stiffened — the bones fused — a searing pain flashed — and before she could scream, it stopped. From her arm hung a heavy blade.

"Here goes nothing." Devon coiled her arm — and brought it down with as much force as she could muster. Her arm trembled — the metal lock collapsed — and the door creaked open.

"I did it!" Panting, Devon ducked inside. "I can't believe I did it!"

The Mendaecus reared up and came down hard.

The Hijacking

The cage tremored under them. And the ship steered for a tall-standing roof.

"Woah. Steady." Devon backed up, with her hands up. "We need to get out of here, or we're going to die."

The Mendaecus brayed.

And Devon inched closer, letting the beast catch her scent again. Then in one swift move, she pulled herself on its back. She dug her hand into the muddy mane, readying herself. "I've never ridden a horse before — or one of you — so, I'm counting on you not to kill me."

They reached the first rooftop (a tall, steepled tower), and the Sky Snail scraped against it, shaking terribly. The ship's hull tore into the neighboring shop, shattering the windows and tearing the walls off the building. Below them, wizards and fairies shot colorful spells that ricocheted off the ship and exploded around them like shooting stars.

The Mendaecus pawed anxiously, and Devon pulled back on his mane. "Not yet —"

They breached the next roof (a sturdier one with a flatter rooftop), and the force of it threw Devon back.

Devon grabbed the mane again, tapped her heels into the Mendaecus's belly, and yelled, "Yah!" The Mendaecus leapt from the cage.

The jump was smooth, for the Mendaecus. It wasn't

smooth for Devon. She didn't know where to secure her legs. Was it in-front or behind the tiny wings? And before she could choose, the funny creature was in the air. Unable to secure herself, Devon nearly fell off the back, during the leap and over its lumpy head, on the landing.

Desperate to be free, the Mendaecus broke into a gallop across the roof. Seeing there was no more roof to run, he reared back and tossed Devon into the air.

Devon tumbled down the side, catching herself just before she fell. "Blasted animal," she rasped.

The Mendaecus leapt from the roof to a lower, neighboring rooftop and galloped through the city at an impressive speed for such a wide creature.

"You're welcome!" she screamed.

The Sky Snail groaned terribly and finally stopped on Blotches, the blacksmith. The ship creaked. . . .

"No," gasped Devon.

And it toppled over, destroying what remained beneath it.

BOOOOOM!

The explosion vibrated across the city. The ground shook like an earthquake. The strength of it knocked Devon back. She hit the tile hard, knocking her head against the scratchy surface. The thin band of gold snapped down the middle. Both halves of the infamous crown, fell from her head and rolled off the rooftop. Hanging precariously over the edge, she reached out, only able to save one.

For a moment, Devon lay against the cool clay, trembling. Blood trickled down her skin, and she wiped it back, smearing it across her hands, making them wet and slippery. "I'm okay," she breathed. "I'm okay." Finally, after what seemed like ages, she stood up, wobbly, and looked out across the city.

The entire block crumpled. The shops closest to the explosion suffered the worst, parts being entirely missing, while others were pulverized by the explosion. The Sky Snail itself was no more. A mound of disintegrated bits lay where it had once been.

Darkness spread across the street.

Four shadows darted from the wreckage and spread out. Even from her rooftop, Devon recognized the thin, gaunt face from the Repository — Braxuis Baumbach the Assassin. Behind him, the handsome boy from Hasty flew up and stared down at the burning city. Every muscle in Devon's body froze. Niko Throntropt's eyes landed on her — trapped on the roof. It was too late to run.

"*Finally.*" Niko swooped from the sky, floating amidst his shadow. He landed on the rooftop. Pulling the darkness inwards, he turned human. "There isn't anyone to save you this time," he taunted. "So hand it over."

Devon's hand twitched, and she balled it in a fist. "I'll give you nothing!" she screamed. Not that it mattered. The crown was broken. It was good Beoc had hidden. She couldn't outrun Niko anymore, and there was no need for Beoc to die too. She clenched her jaw and faced Niko, hoping she didn't seem afraid.

Niko flared, hate simmering in his eyes. "Where is it?"

"It's broken."

Niko slashed his blade threateningly. "YOU'RE LYING!"

"I'm not!" Devon held up the broken piece she'd saved. For the first time, the crown remained in it's true form, with thick gold and gaudy gemstones. Only now, it was a broken piece of metal, caked with age and rust. The emeralds and rubies were dull under centuries of dirt. The magic was gone. "It's over."

"LIAR!" Niko rushed forward, grabbed her, and threw her off the roof. She tumbled down the last length of tile. As the air blew past and the momentum picked up, she had time for one thought: *This is it. This is how I die.* She closed her eyes as she fell, wishing she had learned how to shapeshift. If only she had the crown —

The Hijacking

Devon's arms tingled.

The rushing wind stopped.

She became the darkness. It poured out from within her, blackening the remaining bits of light, and she took flight, soaring the rest of the way down. At the ground, she floated midair before turning back into herself and landing softly on her feet.

Did the crown still have magic? Devon glanced down at the rusted metal. It didn't look like it — but she had thought of flying, and it happened? How else could the crown have saved her?

Niko flew off the roof and landed beside her. He sneered and glanced over her, distrustfully.

Devon tucked the broken piece inside her jacket.

"How did you do that?" he accused.

Devon stayed silent, unsure if he'd seen the broken piece of crown. Maybe she had used the last bit of magic inside. *Yes, that was it,* she thought.

"You're not a shadow walker!" He eyed her suspiciously. "You lied! You used the crown's magic just now!" His eyes raked over her head, searching for the crown.

Devon found her voice and said steadily. "The crown broke during the blast — you broke it!"

"No. You used its magic," he accused. He stepped to the side, cutting off her best angle of escape. "I saw you use the properties of nephrite in Hasty! A true shadow walker can only become the essence of another, but a skin thief *steals* the properties of others! Which means, you've learned to control the magic of the crown," Niko spat venomously. "Impressive. Now, where are you hiding it?" He glanced over her. "GIVE IT TO ME!"

"No."

"Give it to me, or I'll kill your friend, hiding down the block. What a coward. I'll make sure he doesn't live, like Leni."

"NO!" Devon launched for Niko. She shapeshifted as each memory became will. Ferocity drove her attack, and Devon morphed from one thing to next, forcing Niko to retreat. She snapped with the head of Bree's cougar — stabbed with the horn he used to hurt Leni — and swung Balfour's spiked club. The edge scraped against his chest.

"ENOUGH!" Niko dodged the next swing and shoved her back.

Devon shifted again — a heavy sword of nephrite and a shield of black diamond grew from her arms. "AHHH!" She attacked head on, anger driving her forward. But Niko was experienced. And he dodged each slash of the sword. One after another, with ease that wavered her confidence.

Niko ducked under the next wild swing — and hit her square in the chest.

Devon flew back and hit a lamppost — banging her head against the metal and knocking the air from her lungs. Numb, she crumpled to the ground. The sword and shield disappeared, and she lay there, ears ringing, as she fought a strong desire to close her eyes.

"It's over." Niko loomed over her. "Give me the crown."

WHACK. The Mendaecus came out of nowhere, braying and snorting — and rammed Niko in the back, horn first. He reared up, driving the horn through Niko's chest —

"AHHHHHHHHHHH!" Niko screamed. Agony and disbelief twisted across his face.

The Mendaecus dumped Niko on the cobblestone walk.

Blood seeped from a hole in Niko's chest. Shocked, he covered the seeping blood.

Devon grabbed the Mendaecus and pulled the braying creature away.

Braxuis Baumbach appeared from the shadows and Devon dragged the Mendaecus further back. He stood over Niko, cold and heartless. His eyes filled with hatred. He tossed the other half of the crown at Niko. "Mission's over."

"Help —" Niko reached up to Braxuis.

Braxuis crouched beside Niko, careful not to touch him. "It looks to me like you're dying."

Niko groaned. "Please —"

"I don't think I will," Braxuis rasped, in his deep voice. "With you gone, I can take your place in the council."

Niko pushed himself up. "You scum. You're the first one I'll kill. "

Braxuis slashed Niko across the chest, hard and deep.

Eyes wide, Niko sucked in one last, ragged breath, and then exploded into shadowy flakes, dead.

A soft breeze blew where Niko had been. Devon blinked. And two shadows converged from the darkness. They transformed beside Braxuis.

"The Mendaecus killed Niko," Braxuis rasped. "Kill it!"

"NO!" shouted Devon.

Vroooooom! A vivid red and green trolley whipped down the cobblestone. It weaved this way and that way, racing around the debris, causing a ruckus that echoed through the street. Behind it, a patchwork motorbike rumbled, puffing purple clouds of smoke.

Suddenly, the street was alive. Strange animals and loud rumbling motors transformed into an odd

The Hijacking

assortment of stately dressed changers, elves, fairies, and dwarves. The motorcycle squealed. It reared to a stop and shapeshifted into a gray-haired man with a hooked nose, toned muscles, and a walking stick. Behind him, the vibrant trolley transformed into a fierce, dark-skinned woman, with braided hair, pulled back into a mohawk.

"Spread out," the gray-haired man directed.

A dozen angry magiks surrounded the block.

The steady beat of a distant march returned. Thadump. Thadump. Thadump. The trolls were finally returning from the gates.

"Looks like I'm out of time," Braxuis spat.

"But . . . !" protested one of the shadow walkers.

Braxuis shoved him back. "We need to get out of here!"

"You're not going anywhere," exclaimed the fierce woman. "Come out with your hands up, and you'll be taken peacefully. You don't want the alternative —"

Braxuis raised his hands in surrender. "I suppose I have no choice."

Two stately dressed magiks clumped over.

A wicked grin spread across Braxuis's face.

Devon's eyes widened. Behind Braxuis, a third arm formed from his shadow, grasping a hooked dagger.

"WAIT!" screamed Devon.

The Hijacking

Braxuis swung — cutting a path through the unsuspecting magiks. They dropped, as he slashed through the odd assortment of officials, leaving a trail of bodies. Within seconds, Braxuis broke through the perimeter and was free.

The old man shifted back into the smoking motorcycle and crashed into Braxuis. They wrestled, shifting and fighting so fast it was hard for Devon to keep up, and then the old man pinned Braxuis on the stone walk. A second later, he clicked heavy shackles into place.

"ARRAHHH," Braxuis bellowed. But the more he struggled, the brighter the manacles at his hands and feet tightened. "You'll never keep me locked up! NEVER. There isn't a prison in the world that can hold BRAXUIS BAUMBACH THE —"

The old man swooped down — and stuffed a balled-up sock in Braxuis's mouth, cutting him off.

"Tha's better." The old man wiggled his sockless toes. "Hush up . . . or I'll stuff your mouth with the other one."

Braxuis gagged. And the scattered streets were quiet, except for the distant screams of magiks, filling the streets, as they faced the wreckage left behind from the Sky Snail.

Devon sunk to the ground, her legs crumpling

The Hijacking

under her. It was over. Niko Throntropt was dead. The Crown of Guilledon was broken. But at least the Shadow Reign would never get it. Exhausted, she leaned back against the Mendaecus, and he bumped his head against hers, checking that she was alright. Devon let out a long sigh. "I'm okay."

CHAPTER SEVENTEEN
The Vanquisher . . . No? . . . Well, We'll See.

Trolls marched from all over the city. They surrounded the demolished block, coming in perfect unison. The wind whipped the sails of the disintegrated ship. And the steady THADUMP finally stopped.

Movement caught Devon's eye in the alley. And Beoc peeked out from behind a corner. He hurried over with her valise. "Sorry I didn't h-help," he blathered. "I thought you'd come to your senses. Then I saw that shadow walker throw you from the roof, and I didn't know what to do! I thought you were d-done for." Overwhelmed, he dropped down beside her.

"It's all right." Devon nudged him. None of this was his fault. It was best he stayed out of the way. Niko would have killed him.

Kamau and Bree left the eccentric crowd of magik officials and strode over. Bree eyed Braxuis (still chained up beside the gray-haired man), Beoc's untarnished clothing, and then whirled to Devon.

The Vanquisher... No?... Well, We'll See.

"We're barely in the city five minutes before the alarm starts tolling! And here you are, in the thick of it!"

"Careful. Someone might think you care." A grin crept up the corner of Devon's mouth.

Bree rolled her eyes, offered her hand to Devon, and pulled her up. "I went to a lot of trouble to keep you safe. I don't want to see it wasted."

Kamau beamed down at the pair of them, in a fresh maroon and black cloak (that swooped behind him) and a crisp, dashiki suit. "You made it to Thysia."

"I said I would."

"Yes. And it couldn't have been easy — but you did it." Kamau nodded to the gray-haired man. "Dodge. You got your culprit, I see — as usual."

Dodge grunted. "Course."

"I'm glad you're okay," spilled Devon. "When I saw Niko in the Shipyard, I was worried you didn't make it."

"Niko?" Bree blanched. "He's here?" She whirled, eyes raking the block. "We only saw Braxuis. We need to alert the others!"

"Which way did he go?" Kamau's staff glowed bronze, and he floated up. His cloak rippled with the magic wind swirling around him.

Devon grabbed Kamau. "Wait! Niko's dead."

"What do you mean, dead?" Bree gawped, incredulously.

The Vanquisher . . . No? . . . Well, We'll See.

Devon took a deep breath, and it all came out at once. "I saw Niko and Braxuis in the Repository. I lied to Beoc — I told him they were trainers — that were mad because we jumped the field — and I convinced him to run." Beoc pressed his lips together but didn't interrupt. "We lost Niko in the Shipyard, and I thought we were safe once we got to Thysia, so we explored the city. We were in Tarik's shop *during* the burglary. We would have already been at Gordimer, but then Niko hijacked the Sky Snail." Devon brushed the mane of the funny-looking Mendaecus. "This Mendaecus was trapped on the airship. I couldn't leave it to die. I went to save it, and Niko found me."

Above them, a swarm of bats swooped across the dark sky, and Bree glared icily. "You mean you risked your life to save a Mendaecus!"

"The Mendaecus saved me back," Devon defended. "He stabbed Niko with his horn. Niko is dead!"

Intrigued, Kamau floated over to the Mendaecus, who was trying and failing to pull up teeny bits of moss with his large teeth. "Not many Mendaeci have horns." He scratched the creature's ears. Abandoning the moss, the Mendaecus sniffed Kamau.

"So the Mendaecus killed Niko," Bree repeated — still unable to believe it.

The Vanquisher... No?... Well, We'll See.

"Actually, Braxuis killed Niko." At this, everyone turned a surprised look at Braxuis. "He said he could take Niko's place in the Shadow Reign."

Kamau's face filled with disgust.

"Exactly why we don't trust the Shadow Reign," mocked Bree. "Look at this city!" She threw her hands up to the smoking shops, scattered fires, and ravished remains of what was once a lively, and beautiful street. Noticing the crown was missing, Bree leaned close and whispered, "I ... ah ... don't see your headband."

Devon's shoulders slumped. There was no point hiding it. She pulled out the broken piece of gold and retrieved the other half from the cobblestone. "It broke when I was trying to save the Mendaecus."

Kamau took the dull, lusterless crown. "The magic is gone."

"Are you sure *all* the magic is gone?" Devon asked. When she fell, she was still able to turn into a shadow. She couldn't do that without the crown. "There must be some left."

Kamau shook his head and said kindly, "I'm sorry. I know you've been through a lot these last few days, and tonight especially, but there is no more magic in the Crown of Guilledon." He handed Devon the broken pieces.

"Good riddance." Bree crossed her arms.

The Vanquisher . . . No? . . . Well, We'll See.

Beoc's eyes popped open. "That was the Crown of Guilledon!" he blurted, aghast.

Dodge pushed himself up, using his cane to hold his weight, and limped over. Blood trickled down his shoulder. "The Crown of Guilledon, huh? So that's what Braxuis was after." He quirked an eyebrow at Kamau. "This will have to be in the report. No way around that. Magiks will want to know why shadow walkers stole an airship and ran amuck through the city."

Kamau inclined his head. "Of course. As it's broken, I see no reason to hide that it's been found. On the contrary, we should spread the word, so that the Shadow Reign doesn't send more assassins after it." Turning to Devon and Beoc, Kamau added, "What's important is that you two are okay."

"But I still broke it," protested Devon.

Dodge looked her over. "By the sound of it, you managed not only to keep the Crown of Guilledon safe, but you also took on a Shadow Reign assassin *by yourself*. Not bad if you ask me."

A swell of relief filled Devon's chest. "So you're not angry with me?"

"Hah," snorted Bree. "Like I said, good riddance!"

Dodge glanced over his hooked nose. "What's your name, kid?"

The Vanquisher ... No? ... Well, We'll See.

Devon lifted her chin. "Devon Connor."

"Dodge Badfus," he held out a sturdy hand, approvingly, and shook Devon's with a firm grasp. "Pleasure to meet you."

"Nice to meet you too."

"I'm Beoc," Beoc interjected, holding out his hand.

Dodge squinted, so that his wrinkles drooped over his eyes. "I know who you are, Beoc. I saw you hiding in the alley. Don't blame you though," he said gruffly. "You know your pa wouldn't like you out here." He pointed the knob of his cane at Beoc's chest. "Next time the bong tolls, get out of the danger zone," he scolded.

"Yes, sir," said Beoc.

The swarm of bats splayed above, blacking out the sky. Then, they swooped down in a ribbon, that funneled around like a tornado. Converging at the ground, they became one, and Hammad Mustafa stood in the middle of the street. He folded his arms across a midnight-blue jacquard sherwani, speckled with silver moons and stars. As the wind dissipated, his silver-dusted shawl settled.

All of Devon's courage vanished. It was only yesterday, he asked her to stay out of trouble, and here she was, her first day in Thysia, at the scene of a hijacked airship and just blocks away from a burglary.

The Vanquisher ... No? ... Well, We'll See.

Not to mention, the crown he trusted her with was destroyed. From the way his eyes twinkled darkly, Devon understood he was angry. She opened her mouth to explain, but nothing came out. This was the exact thing he had requested she not do — anything that might embarrass him. At least Amy Gray wasn't here to say *I told you so.*

"I thought that was you flying around up there, old friend," Kamau greeted. "Did you survey the area?"

"Yes. ... And I heard everything," he said with a

The Vanquisher . . . No? . . . Well, We'll See.

quick glance at Devon. "So, I'm already caught up," he added, business-like. He held up his finger, warning her not to break her promise and reveal that they had already met.

"May I?" Mr. Mustafa took the broken pieces from Devon, and even in his hands, the tarnished hunks of gold remained lusterless and dead. The Mughal crown did not return. Holding them together, he pursed his lips.

"I'm sorry," Devon said in a rush. "I'm so sorry. I-I know it was important."

Mr. Mustafa tore his eyes from the broken crown. "You chose the life of one of the *least* loved creatures above one of history's most infamous treasures." He handed the pieces back to Devon. "And I'm *proud* of you. No treasure is worth more than life. Life is the greatest treasure of all."

Behind him, Kamau puffed proudly.

"Perhaps," Hammad Mustafa sighed deeply, "Kamau is right, and this is all for the best. These assassins were willing to go to great lengths to steal this crown. I believe you're wise, Kamau, to spread the word that the Crown of Guilledon is no more."

Kamau nodded in agreement. "It would deter the Shadow Reign from any more attacks, for now at least.

"What should we do with the Mendaecus?" asked Dodge.

The Vanquisher ... No? ... Well, We'll See.

"It belongs to the owner of the Sky Snail," Beoc offered, still hoping to be of help. "We saw him leading it onto the ship."

Dodge shook his head sadly. "Dead. Got the report as soon as the assassins stole the airship. No family neither."

"So, the Mendaecus is a warden of the city now." Mr. Mustafa rubbed his eyes tiredly.

"I suspect no one will want him." Dodge looked the Mendaecus over and made a dissatisfied click with his tongue. "There's a meat factory in Bulwark. Poor thing will end up chopped liver —"

"No! I want him," Devon blurted.

Dodge, Beoc and even Leni whirled around, open-mouthed. "You can't be serious?" said Dodge.

"He'll cost a ton to keep," added Beoc.

"I don't care. He doesn't deserve to be treated like this." Devon scratched her fingers across his underfed belly, up his muddy coat, and through his knotted mane. "Wings or not."

"I suppose it's all right," Hammad said, mulling it over. "There are stables at Gordimer." He tugged his beard. "You'd have to buy him from the city. . . . I suppose, for a Mendaecus without his wings ... and considering that you're doing the city a favor by taking him ... I believe fifteen Gubbins is fair."

The Vanquisher . . . No? . . . Well, We'll See.

"Fifteen Gubbins!" Beoc's mouth dropped open. "The merchant wanted four hundred!"

Hammad chuckled. "You don't have to go far to find a crook willing to swindle you, and there are plenty of them in the Repository."

"That's for sure," snorted Dodge.

"Do you have that much?" Hammad winked, pretending not to know, though he had supplied her and knew the exact amount she had.

"Yeah." Devon pulled the pouch of Gubbins from her valise and held up a fist full of coins.

"Let me see." Hammad counted out the coins and held up fifteen Gubbins. "It's all settled then." He pocketed the coins. "I'll have my assistant take care of the official paperwork when I get back to the office." He pointed to the Mendaecus. "He'll need a leash of some sort."

"I believe I can help with that." Kamau pushed back his sleeves. "It won't be permanent . . . unless. . . ." Kamau's eyes landed on the broken pieces of the crown. "May I use these?" he asked Devon. "To make the enchantment permanent?"

"Um . . . ," Devon faltered, surprised they were leaving it up to her.

Ever so slightly, Hammad inclined his head, and then said loudly, "I believe there is no other use for it."

The Vanquisher ... No? ... Well, We'll See.

Dodge shrugged. "Looks like garbage to me."

"Wonderful." Kamau waved his staff. The broken pieces soared up over the Mendaecus. The gold began to glow. The luster returned, and the crown molded into a finely crafted bridal. Beautiful rubies, emeralds, and sapphires appeared along the molten gold.

"A gift," said Kamau. "For the brave Mendaecus and kind-hearted magik."

The Mendaecus neighed and snorted, trying to free himself of the enchantment.

"Woah!" sputtered Beoc.

"It's the most beautiful gift ever." Devon ran her fingers along the bridal. To think, just a few days ago, she was digging a broken watch out of the garbage. "Thank you." She blinked back the burning in her eyes and turned away before anyone could see it.

"Dodge." The fierce woman with a wild mohawk came over. Sweat dripped down her toned arms, and her dark hair clung to her back. Behind her, a guard of trolls carried two unconscious men, cuffed at the hands and feet, with thick shackles that glowed brightly with magic. "We got both of 'em."

"Better than that," Dodge grumbled. "That one," he pointed to the gaunt-faced shadow walker bound and gagged on the ground beside them, "is Braxuis Baumbach the Assassin!"

The Vanquisher ... No? ... Well, We'll See.

The woman whipped around. "Braxuis! We've been after him for *months!*"

"*And*," added Dodge, "this kid and her pet Mendaecus took down Niko Throntropt."

Devon's face flushed. Beside her, Beoc's did too.

The fierce woman stared back, open-mouthed. "Impossible!"

"Ryker will be disappointed he didn't capture Braxuis himself." Dodge chortled. "But it's enough we got him." He frowned at the destroyed block. "How many injured?"

The woman's face softened. After a brief hesitation, she said steadily, "Three. ... Xander was taken the Magik Emergency Ward. ..." Her voice carried off, holding something back.

Dodge braced himself. "Tell me, Tiggy."

Tears filled her eyes, but her jaw hardened. "Wiley is dead."

Dodge threw his cane on the ground and launched himself at the unconscious shadow walkers.

Tiggy grabbed him and held him back. "Not like this, Dodge. Not like this."

"AHHHH!" he screamed and kicked his cane. It flew several feet, before clapping on the stone walk and rolling a bit further.

Tiggy retrieved it and held it out to him.

The Vanquisher . . . No? . . . Well, We'll See.

Reluctantly, Dodge took the cane back. He waved for the trolls to take the prisoners and leave. "Get them out of my sight."

The trolls turned and marched, thadump . . . thadump, in perfect unison, taking the shadow walkers with them. More trolls surrounded Braxuis.

"Not that one," grunted Dodge. "I'll take him in myself."

"Bree and I will join you," Kamau offered in a soothing tone.

"So will I," added Tiggy.

"I suppose I should be off as well." Hammad sighed. "This attack on the city will set the office back for days. I doubt I'll sleep tonight."

"Thank you," Devon mumbled.

Hammad nodded, almost imperceptibly, then inclined his head, in a polite farewell, and swooped up into a swarm of bats that ascended into the sky and flew away.

"We'll see you soon," Kamau promised Devon.

"Hopefully not too soon." Bree smirked, her eyes twinkling.

Kamau waved his staff.

Braxuis Baumbach rose off the ground and floated between Kamau, Bree, Dodge and Tiggy. As they escorted the prisoner away, another guard of

The Vanquisher ... No? ... Well, We'll See.

trolls marched behind — eliminating any chance of escape.

Beoc nudged Devon. "We should get going. I'd rather not be seen here if my pa turns up." He shrugged, apologetically. "I'm really not supposed to get mixed up in things like this."

"Things like what?" Devon grabbed her valise and steered the Mendaecus, so they kept pace beside Beoc. "A siege on the city?"

"Or anything that will make him look bad. He's an important man you know."

"We had some fun though, didn't we?"

Beoc snorted.

As they walked, Devon thought about all the adventures over the last few days — and all the mistakes she'd made. She had reached Thysia, her new home. But she'd also led Shadow Reign assassins into the city, broken the Crown of Guilledon, and gotten mixed up in a burglary. Somehow, she'd prove she was worth the trouble everyone went through to get her here safely. She'd learn everything she could about this world. And one day, she'd be an amazing magik. Who knew, maybe she'd learn about her parents along the way and even get to see Leni again. But for now, Leni was safe. Niko Throntropt was dead, and instead of facing another terrible day at St. Frances Institute for Heirs and Orphans, she was going to find out who she was meant to be.

"Come on, Mendaecus," Devon tugged on the gem-encrusted bridle.

"What are you going to name him?" Beoc asked, his cheerful banter returning. "You can't call him Mendaecus."

"I don't know — I haven't thought about it."

There was a cheerful prance in the Mendaecus's stride that wasn't there before. He seemed to know he wasn't unwanted anymore.

"He's got to have a cool name," Beoc said happily.

"He did charge down a shadow walker assassin," agreed Devon.

Beoc circled the Mendaecus. "How about Mendaecus the Mighty!"

Devon laughed.

"Nightmare Guardian?" Beoc rambled off.

"Um, let's keep thinking —"

Beoc jumped in the middle of the road. "Okay . . . okay. I got it." He threw his hands up. "The Vanquisher!"

The Mendaecus nipped at Beoc as they passed, and Devon snickered. "I don't think he likes it —"

Beoc hurried to catch up. "How about . . .

The Vanquisher . . . No? . . . Well, We'll See.

Deathblow. . . . No. . . . Wait . . . wait . . . I got it! . . . *Doom Horn*," Beoc said in his deepest voice.

Devon held back a fit of laughter. "Those are all great names. I mean . . . Doom Horn . . . that's . . . wow . . . that's really great. . . ."

"But — ?" Beoc said, questioningly.

"But I was thinking of when he attacked the shadow walker," Devon patted the knotted mane, "he came out of nowhere, like a ghost. So, how about . . . Ghost?"

"Ghost?" Beoc tapped his finger to his nose. A wide grin spread across his face. "I like it.

THE END

ABOUT THE AUTHOR
Janet Loup Maupin Gajigianis

Since childhood, Loup wanted to be many things — a jockey, a sailor, a fencer, a treasure hunter, an artist, and even an amateur mixed martial artist. While she wrote short stories as a child, she never imagined that she would write this story today. Like all things she does, Magiks and the Crown of Guilledon came from the heart.

Check out her website at enchantedchronicle.com where you can get more details on the world of magiks, news, updates, and upcoming releases.

Made in the USA
Middletown, DE
31 January 2023